BROTHERHOOD

Mason & Sterling Thrillers
Book One

David Beckler

SAPERE
BOOKS

BROTHERHOOD

To Jamie

happy reading

David Bell

Published by Sapere Books.

11 Bank Chambers, Hornsey, London, N8 7NN,
United Kingdom

saperebooks.com

ISBN: 978-1-912786-43-5

PROLOGUE

A six-foot-high steel spike fence topped off with coils of razor wire guarded the scrapyard. A gap in the fence made room for a pair of gates fashioned from a frame of scaffolding poles bolted into rough rectangles. Random pieces of sheet steel welded together in a patchwork of rust filled the spaces between the poles. The gates stood open, a heavy chain and padlock hanging from the centre of one of them. Piles of crushed and rusting vehicles occupied the yard, its patched concrete surface covered in a thin layer of mud infused with old motor oil.

The Range Rover rolled forward through the gap. A chorus of barking and snarling broke out. Behind the fence, two large, unkempt Alsatians leapt to their feet. Separated from the rest of the yard by a wire barrier, they threw themselves against it, showing their canines in greeting.

Summoned by the barking, a grey-haired figure strode out of the opening at one end of the container. He advanced, wearing a scowl. The men in the car waited until he came closer, then, at a signal from their leader, all four threw their doors open and leapt out.

The grey-haired man hesitated for an instant before he recognised them and ran to the container, shouting a warning.

In response to his shout, two younger men emerged from the container. Each carried a scarred baseball bat with thick tape covering the business end. Although outnumbered, they didn't appear cowed. One of the men from the car produced a sawn-off shotgun. The two parties faced each other across the filthy concrete.

The dogs became more frenzied until the larger of the two leapt the fence. The gunman swung the barrel of the shotgun towards the snarling animal.

The discharge ruptured the morning air and the dog, hit in mid-leap, yelped before bouncing off concrete and landing in a heap in the muck. Shot in the chest, it lay twitching in a spreading pool of blood. The boom of the shot echoed off the surrounding buildings.

The leader of the invaders cursed and checked the street, then led his men back to the car. He paused at the car and shouted, "This isn't over."

The car reversed and shot out of the yard before spinning its wheels and, tyres screeching, raced away.

One of the younger men threw his baseball bat at the car; it fell short, clattering on the road. The other helped his father to his feet. The older man shook off the helping hand and went to his dog, cradling its head as its eyes filmed over. He glared at the receding car, muttering, "I'll fucking make you pay."

CHAPTER 1

Philip Mason hunched his shoulders into his jacket and peered through the steady drizzle. He glanced behind him but the car seemed to have disappeared. He must have imagined it. Ahead, in the darkness, loomed the disused mill where the others waited. The closeness of its abandoned hulk increased his unease and his steps faltered as he approached the arched entrance into the courtyard. Liam, following a pace behind, barged into him and his head bounced off Philip's solid shoulder.

"What you stopped for?" Liam examined his crushed cigarette before flicking it away. It hit the glistening cobbles, releasing a shower of sparks.

A feeling of dread weighed Philip down and, seized by an overwhelming urge to turn back, he studied the darkened building. The broken windows and boarded-up openings showed as darker shadows in the monolithic bulk. Philip tried not to imagine empty eye-sockets in a skull.

"Come on, Phil. I'm getting soaked."

Dismissing a sense of foreboding, Philip shook himself and clambered over the low gate, before leading the way across the courtyard towards the entrance to the basement. The door resisted before opening with a creak, and an earthy odour enveloped them. Philip hesitated; the dark cavern absorbed the faint moonlight. Sensing Liam's impatience, Philip made his way down the stone staircase. The darkness intensified with each step and at the bottom he paused, inhaling the stench of decay. A rustle, and a small, quick animal scuttled away from them.

"Whooo, spooky," Liam said, and shuffled forward.

Despite his apprehension, Philip recognised his friend's false bravado. The desire to turn and run gripped him, but it was much too late to back out now.

"Where the fuck are the others?" Liam demanded. "I've got better things to do on a Sunday night."

A bright light clicked on, blinding Philip. Loud voices shouted incoherent instructions. Even though he expected this reception, Philip's heart jumped. Four shadowy shapes rushed Liam, and Philip watched, disconnected, as the figures forced his friend into a chair.

"Take his arm." Mugisa's order jerked Philip into action.

He grabbed Liam's right arm. On the other side, Asif fought to hold him. After a few seconds, Liam's struggles subsided and, once he'd stopped shouting, Anthony recited the charge.

"Liam McLaughlin, you are charged with stealing from the brotherhood." Anthony's voice shook.

"How do you plead?" Mugisa demanded.

"Fuck off," Liam said. Spots of spittle sprayed Philip's cheek and the stink of stale cigarette smoke filled his nostrils.

Mugisa paused before responding, "The prisoner pleads guilty. We will consider the sentence." He stepped into the shadows and held a muttered conversation with the other two.

Liam's breathing reminded Philip of a cornered animal, but he couldn't let his sympathy for his friend weaken him. Liam didn't deny his crime. He'd even boasted about how much he got for the video's he'd stolen from them. The discussion finished and Mugisa came closer.

"The punishment for betrayal is death," Mugisa intoned with utter conviction.

Liam tried to jerk free and Philip hunched over to get a better grip of his wrist. In the ensuing silence, Ryan giggled.

Even in the gloom, Philip sensed the cold glare from Mugisa, and the laughter faded.

Liam turned to Philip. "Phil, let me go," he whispered. "Please."

Philip stared into the darkness. A machete had materialised in Mugisa's right hand, glinting in the torch-light as he advanced. Liam stopped struggling, mesmerised by the blade. Philip had always dismissed Mugisa's claims of his violent past as bravado, but not any longer.

"You're fucking cracked, the lot of you." Liam's struggles resumed and his wrists jerked, sweat making the skin slippery. "You've had your laugh. Now let me go." His voice rose. "I'll give you the money." Mugisa continued implacably and in desperation, Liam said, "I won't say anything to Ritchie."

Mugisa towered over him, machete raised high.

Liam moaned and slumped in the chair. Philip relaxed his hold and, as if seized by an electric current, Liam jerked. Philip managed to hold on but Liam ripped his left arm free of Asif's grip, swinging the fist at Philip. With a wet smack it hit his eye. The shock and pain made Philip cry out and reel away.

Liam ripped his other arm free and lurched to his feet. A blow on the side of his head made him stagger and his hand flew to his neck. Blood welled up between his fingers. Philip stared, numb, and for what seemed like minutes, nothing moved in the room.

Liam grimaced in pain. "You fucking bastard. You're dead." Still clutching his neck, he staggered towards the exit, pausing at the bottom of the stairs. "Ritchie will have the lot of you!"

Mugisa reacted first and pointing the machete, yelled, "Stop him!"

Liam shot up the stairs. The fear which helped him break free spurred him on. At the top of the stairs, he crashed through the doors and out into the open air. Philip blinked to clear his vision and tried to control his breathing, unable to believe what had happened. The faces of the others reflected the shock gripping him. When nobody responded Mugisa lowered the machete.

"We have to stop him getting away."

Philip said, "What you going to do?"

"Stop him causing trouble." Mugisa strode towards Philip, his voice rising.

Philip stayed put, his pulse racing and he clenched his fists. They stood toe to toe in the gloom. Although well matched in size, Philip had never dared challenge Mugisa. "What? Say, 'Sorry I cut you Liam, keep quiet about it?'"

"It was an accident. If you hadn't let him go, he wouldn't have been hurt."

The rebuke stung and Philip's retort died on his lips. He groped for something to say as Mugisa's glare bored into him.

Then Asif said, "If he tells his uncle, we're all fucked."

This broke the spell and Mugisa led the way. The four of them collected their bikes and set off up the stairs. Philip hesitated for a few seconds before following. Liam needed his help.

Liam ran through darkened streets lined with boarded-up terraced houses. His heart pounded and fear blocked his thoughts. The wound sent shards of pain through his neck and jaw. Blood dripped onto his shoulder. How bad was the cut? He didn't dare stop to check. His steps faltered and he studied the houses. None showed signs of habitation. He must have turned the wrong way. He had to get away before the others arrived.

Liam charged into an alleyway, past piles of stinking rubbish. His breath came in short gasps, scouring his airway. Why the fuck hadn't he listened to Philip nagging him about giving up smoking? A stitch spread from his side, almost making him forget the pain from his cut.

He paused and listened but could only hear his ragged panting and the pounding of the pulse in his ears. More blood dripped, coating his shoulder. A wave of nausea and light-headedness made him stagger and he placed a hand on cold damp brickwork. He made a decision and went left, searching for signs of life in the rows of empty houses.

A light flickered from an upper window. Energised, he started towards it, but a mountain of rubbish blocked his path. Frantic to find another way in, he retraced his steps and dashed into the street, revived by the prospect of refuge.

The light wasn't visible from the front and he hesitated, trying to work out which house it came from. A distant shout alarmed him, but his strength seemed to be draining away and a mass of hot pain radiated from his neck. Resisting the urge to rest he hurtled back the way he'd come. He plunged down the dark alley, crashing into obstacles as his legs betrayed him.

At the end of the alleyway he paused, resting against the brickwork and listening. His vision swam and his strength ebbed until he didn't think he could go on. A whisper came from behind him and a shadowy figure moved. Energy jolted through Liam and he ran on Bambi legs. After three steps his left foot slipped sideways, and wind-milling his arms, he fell. He crashed into the nearby wall. Shockwaves jarred his skull and flashing light filled his vison. He bounced off, slamming head first onto the cobbled street and into merciful blackness.

Mugisa dismounted and propped his bike against the wall. He unclipped his light and shone it at the mound in the alleyway. Liam lay on his back, his clothes filthy and dishevelled and a grimace frozen on his face. Blood pooled at the side of his head. Mugisa hadn't thought the wound fatal, but he'd seen enough bodies to not need to check. Lights flickered and the others arrived together, halting a few yards away, shock and disgust distorting their features.

What had they expected? They had to share the responsibility. Mugisa passed the machete to the nearest one. "Cut him."

Anthony's eyes widened with fear and he pulled his hand away, letting the blade clatter onto the cobbles.

"Pick it up," Mugisa hissed, "and hit him with it."

Anthony hesitated but then obeyed and edged towards the prone body as if approaching a deadly mamba. He took a breath before swinging the blade. Mugisa snorted his contempt — the blow wouldn't have sliced a strand of elephant grass. Anthony gave him a fearful glance before landing a second blow to Liam's torso. The other two took their turns. Asif went last, then dropped the weapon. Mugisa retrieved it, filled with disappointment at their weakness. At least Philip wouldn't let him down.

Footsteps pounded the cobbles and Philip rounded the corner, slowing when he got closer. He opened his mouth to speak but stopped, staring at the body at their feet with horror. Mugisa stepped forward and thrust the handle of the machete at him. Philip knocked it away then ran.

Mugisa hefted the machete and returned to the body. He wiped the blade on Liam's coat and returned it to the scabbard under his jacket. His disappointment at Philip's behaviour turned to anger.

Philip's long strides devoured the ground, but he knew the others would soon catch him on their bikes. The horror of what he'd seen threatened to overwhelm him but he mustn't panic. He should have stopped to help Liam. But he *must* be dead, with all that blood round him. Mugisa's pitiless expression made his legs weaken, but he tried not to think, just concentrate on running.

After some minutes, lights appeared ahead. He'd reached one of the main roads that led, like the spokes of a wheel, from the city centre. Even at this time of night there would be traffic. His shoes, not made for running, chafed, and anticipating reaching safety he slowed, limping towards the street lamps.

A faint sound from behind made him spin round. A figure on a bike was almost on him. The image of Liam's bloody body gave him a jolt of energy. He ran. The skin on his neck tightened in the expectation of a blow.

In a few strides, he arrived at the refuge of the well-lit road and faced his pursuer. The cyclist halted, waiting at the edge of the ribbon of light. In his panic Philip couldn't identify him. Instead, he peered into the distance, hoping for signs of a vehicle and safety. Headlights approached, and he ran into the middle of the road, waving his arms.

The driver slowed and hope made Philip giddy. Then the car swerved, passing him with horn blaring. His pulse thrashed in his ears and he looked back. Four figures waited in the shadows.

CHAPTER 2

The pupils rose as the teacher gathered her books and scooped them into her satchel. Shafts of bright sunlight shone through gaps in the thatching. She checked the time; it was past twelve and she had under an hour to get to the next school. The children chattered at the prospect of escaping the confines of the classroom.

She focussed her stern gaze on them and they fell silent.

"Now children, remember, we have a test tomorrow. You won't forget to do your homework?"

"No, Miss Kitumba," they responded, The Boy leading the chant.

"Do you all have your books?"

"Yes, Miss Kitumba." Twenty-two small hands shot up, each holding a thin bundle of grubby papers.

"Good." She paused and looked over their eager faces, unable to resist The Boy's infectious grin. Of all the children she taught he showed the greatest promise. "Okay, then you may go."

They made for the door and she smiled as they shot out of the hut like a flock of startled guinea fowl. Some made straight for home but others stayed near the schoolhouse and The Boy organised them into two teams.

In a homestead four hundred metres away, The Boy's mother studied her daughter preparing the cornmeal and smiled. At twelve years old, Sanyu was almost a woman and her mother knew it wouldn't be long before she had to marry.

The girl noticed the scrutiny and faced her mother, a question in her eyes.

"Your little brother will be home soon. You'd better get his lunch ready."

Byron Mason listened to the hubbub of fellow drinkers enjoying their Sunday evening before the start of the working week. Dark walls and subtle lighting combined with a cheery log fire to create a welcoming atmosphere. Despite being in London, the pub could have been in any remote English country village. Tenderness filled him as he studied Louisa, their unborn child not yet showing. She caught him staring and winked. As if at an unseen signal, the conversation at the table paused and the other four people stared at him. His cheeks grew warm and they burst into laughter. The women gathered their handbags and rose to their feet.

"I'll have the same again." Louisa stroked his nose as she passed him, her shoulder-length blond hair brushing against him.

After giving him their orders, the other women followed her. Byron regarded his wife with a mixture of pride and affection. Tall, and with a good figure, she excited attention from the other men in the room.

"I'll get these, Byron. You're celebrating." Glen sprang to his feet.

"Nonsense, it must be my round by now. I haven't bought a drink all night." Byron gathered the glasses and stood up, his eyes smarting as he entered the smoke layer. They'd had a smoking ban in California for three years, and he couldn't wait for them to introduce it here.

"I'll give you a hand."

With Byron leading, the two men shouldered their way through the crowded room. He smiled, listening to the conversation and laughter. Half a head taller than most of the other men and with the build of a heavyweight boxer, he received his share of admiring looks.

While they waited to get served, Glen said, "That was out of the blue, Byron. Lilly's only just one. Are you ready for two rug-rats?"

"I'm not getting any younger. I want to have a few kids and still enjoy life after they've left home."

"A few. Have you discussed this with Louisa?"

Byron's laugh rumbled across the bar. "It was her idea to have another one now." He grinned at the thought of their second child. "Both Louisa and I come from big families and we don't want Lilly to grow up without brothers and sisters."

"Doesn't always work out though." Glen studied him in the mirror behind the bar.

Thoughts of his siblings made Byron pause. "It's up to us to make sure it does."

"So you reckon it's your mum and dad's fault? This thing with Samuel—"

"You know nothing about it."

"What I *do* know is my dad regretted not talking to his brother until it was too late. Like I told you, you should get in touch. You'll only—"

"Leave it, mate." Byron's good mood evaporated.

"It's not just you now. Lilly's got cousins, she has a right—"

"I said, leave it."

People each side of them edged away.

"Okay, okay." Glen took a step back and held up his hands. "Let's not fall out."

Byron's reflection in the mirror behind the bar returned his frown. "Sorry, mate, we're supposed to be celebrating. Let's get these back or the girls will wonder where we are." Maybe he could try to build bridges with Samuel next year before the millennium ended. Although whether his brother, or his wife, would be open to an overture was another matter.

They left the bar, clutching their drinks, and Byron spoke over his shoulder. "How about you two? You'd make a great dad and neither of you are getting any younger."

"I'll tell Imogen you've noticed her wrinkles."

Byron nudged him in the ribs and they both laughed.

"What's so funny?" Imogen demanded, smiling and taking her drink.

Byron grew hot. "Nothing. Just messing around."

The loud click from the speaker above the hatch into the kitchen announced another fire-call and Firefighter Adam Sterling groaned with frustration. He wanted to be busy, but this was the fourteenth shout of the night and he still hadn't finished the evening meal he'd started six hours earlier. He wolfed down another mouthful of chilli, now a congealed mess following several trips to the hotplate and rushed to the engine house as the piercing notes of the siren faded away. The others waited on the first pump.

"Come on, slowcoach," Station Officer Reid said.

"Sorry, Boss. I had to have food, I'm bloody starving."

"Gannet," Mal observed, to laughter.

The pump lurched out of the engine house and Adam stepped into his boots before pulling up his leggings. The vehicle raced round the first corner and Adam braced himself, glancing across at Mal, his partner for the night. With over twenty years' service, Mal was 'senior man' and the team leader. Adam noticed he'd already dressed and was struggling into the straps of his breathing apparatus set.

"You'd better hurry, Adam. It's just around the corner."

A rush of adrenaline energised Adam and, thrusting his arms into the sleeves of his tunic, he fastened the zip. The two pumps made their way through deserted streets, and blue lights reflected from windows as they glided past. The brakes hissed and the pump came to a stop. Eager to see what awaited, Adam slid across the bench seat and followed Mal out onto the pavement, the heavy cylinder on his back making him clumsy. Just behind them, thick black smoke poured out of an opening above the front door of a terraced house. A mixture of excitement and apprehension made Adam's pulse race.

"Okay, lads. Go under air. Mike, check round the back. Pete, get the sledgehammer," Station Officer Reid said, his voice calm.

Adam started up his set and the comforting flow of cool air passed over his cheeks. He pulled the head-straps tight and took a deep breath before putting on his helmet and following Mal along the line of hose which had sprouted across the pavement. Mal reached the end and picked up the branch plugged into it, releasing a blast of water into the gutter. Adam seized the tail of hose and concentrated on trailing Mal. The voices and sounds of the pumps merged into the background. The splintered remains of the door lay beside the front steps and Mal crouched in the doorway.

Behind Adam, Reed hovered, trying to see past his men. "Check for missing floorboards, Adam, and look out for needles. These houses are popular with junkies. Find the electrics and knock them off."

Adam listened to these instructions, his mind on what awaited them, and he ran through what he'd learned in the last three years and countless hours of training. Mal blasted the ceiling ahead of them and a shower of debris fell. When this stopped, he led Adam into the house. Thick, viscous smoke engulfed them when they stepped through the front door, absorbing the beams of their lamps. Adam kept low, but within seconds heat infiltrated his flash-hood, forcing him lower.

Dragging the hose he followed Mal into the smoke. Mal blasted the fire and the hose jerked in Adam's hands, like a serpent coughing. The water hit the flames, generating clouds of steam which enveloped the two men. Intense heat penetrated Adam's clothing and sweat poured off him. He panted, using up precious air.

Adam went even lower, trying to burrow into the floor, searching for the cooler atmosphere. He ignored the lumps of debris jabbing him through his leggings and crawled into the house. The sounds of another team came from behind, and their shuffling steps on wooden treads told him they were going upstairs. He found it hot enough downstairs. It would be worse for them, fighting their way through the layers of heat.

Mal grabbed his shoulder. "The main fire's in the back room. Do you want to take it?" he said, his voice muffled by the facemask.

He thrust the branch into Adam's hands and moved aside to let him pass. Adam tucked the hose under his arm and Mal dropped in behind him, keeping a hand on his shoulder. Flame showed under the smoke and leaning forward, Adam fired off a blast of water. More steam enveloped him and he could see nothing. Then it cleared and the flames returned, smaller and less bright.

He advanced and sprayed them again. Mal disappeared, giving Adam a moment's anxiety until sounds of his colleague searching the adjacent room reassured him. He crouched in the doorway and blasted the ceiling of the room beyond until bits of it stopped falling.

Mal returned. "Let's go in."

Adam moved into the room attacking the flames each side of the doorway. They died as he hit them and the heat reduced. Centimetres at a time, they advanced, knocking down the fire.

"Hole in the floor on our left, Adam."

Prompted by the call, he checked each step but soon reached the far wall. A scan of the room confirmed he'd extinguished the fire.

"Give me a hand here?" Mal's voice came from his left and leaving the hose, Adam shuffled across to join him. "Window's got a security grille." Mal gripped Adam's sleeve and directed his hand to a smooth piece of metal. "This end feels loose at the top. You're taller, can you knock it out?"

He hit it with the heel of his hands until the end popped out, creating an opening at the edge of the board. Adam pushed the panel, widening the gap. Smoke and steam rushed out of the top of the opening and cool clean air replaced it. After more pushing, another anchor point gave way and working together, they removed the metal plate, leaving a wide hole. The air cleared and Adam's torch illuminated the back room. Broken kitchen cabinets lined two walls and, in the gap for a cooker, stood a wheelie bin.

"We'll use the bin to put the crap in," Mal said, then the radio on his set crackled.

"Station Officer, come in." The sub officer's urgent tone made Adam pause.

"Go ahead, Mike."

"Geoff, we have persons reported."

The news sent a jolt through Adam. Although he knew they should treat every building as if it might contain casualties, he hadn't seriously thought they'd find someone in here.

"Say again, Mike?"

"Persons reported, Geoff. There's two casualties next door. First floor, back room."

"Roger, Mike. Two persons involved. Do you need help getting them out?"

"We're leaving them in situ," Mike said.

Adam paused for a moment, knowing what that meant, and said a quick prayer.

"Roger, I'll let the coppers know," Reed said. "Mal, how are you doing?"

"The fire's out on the ground floor." Mal picked up the hose and blasted a pile of smouldering debris with water.

Thin wisps of steam and smoke floated in the air. Adam shone his torch at the smoke-blackened wheelie bin. Heat had disfigured the top half. He grabbed the half-melted handle, but the bin resisted, its soft wheels stuck to the lino. He got a better grip and jerked, but it fell forward, disgorging its contents onto the floor.

Adam studied the dark pile for a few moments before prodding what appeared to be a bag of rubbish with the toe of his boot. He froze when he realised what he'd disturbed. Scenes from a village in Kuwait flashed into his mind.

He straightened. "Mal, come over here."

Mal strode over and saw the dead body illuminated by Adam's lamp. "You all right, Adam?"

Adam nodded and Mal reached for his radio.

Detective Chief Inspector Siobhan Quinn finished the can of Red Bull and wrinkled her nose. She'd have much preferred a coffee, but even if she'd found the espresso machine amongst the boxes in her new flat, it would have taken too long. She shivered, coveting the warmth of her bed as the wind hurled rain at her kitchen window. The smell of fresh paint from the work she'd done last night mingled with the pungent odour of the drink.

She read the address again and located it in her new street atlas. She'd spent her first few days driving around Manchester getting to know her new patch and had a rough idea of the way. Satisfied she could find it, she put the empty can in the bin and strode into the hallway. At the cheap mirror hanging behind the front door, she checked her reflection and, satisfied she'd pass muster, set off.

Twenty minutes later she drove down yet another narrow terraced street. She'd already pulled over once to get her bearings but could see nobody around to ask. A blue light flickered in the gloom and giving thanks, she accelerated towards it. Two fire engines took up half the street and beyond them several police vehicles and a car she recognised as Eddy Arkwright's from the three child seats crammed into the rear. She'd only met him twice, but the sergeant seemed competent.

She parked past his car, grateful the rain had eased, and put on her 'incident kit': disposable overalls, waterproof boots and nitrile gloves. The firefighters moved around their fire engines, stowing their gear, and a couple paused to study her. A constable with a clipboard guarded a house with smoke-stained brickwork above the openings.

"DCI Quinn," she said, flashing her ID card and stepped in through the gaping doorframe. A wave of humid heat hit her. Metal plates on the floor denoted the path, keeping feet out of the charred slurry and preserving evidence. A string of lights illuminated the corridor.

Siobhan paused in the doorway leading to the fire-blackened room. The smell reminded her of the peat fires at her grandmother's. Overlaying this, the sweet acrid stench of burnt plastic and something else she didn't want to think about. Powerful floodlights filled the centre of the space with harsh light, leaving the sides in shadow. Wisps of steam rose from the charred floor timbers.

The lighting focussed on the bin and the body spilling out of it. Besides anger that someone had done this to a fellow human, she felt the stirrings of the excitement she always experienced at the start of a big case.

A detailed video and many photos would preserve images of the scene, but she wanted to see the victim in situ. A figure on the other side of the room, like her dressed in disposable coveralls, switched off his torch and straightened. She recognised the distinctive outline of her sergeant.

"Morning, ma'am." His voice, gruff and low, matched his appearance.

"Morning, Eddy, and as I told you on Friday, I'm not the Queen." She smiled at him. "Boss or Guv will do."

"Yes, Boss."

Both wore coveralls but the similarities ended there. At six foot three, Eddy Arkwright towered over her. His build attested to his former pastime as a rugby league prop forward. She'd heard how a serious knee injury had ended his playing days and almost cost him his police career. At thirty-two, he'd filled out, and the coverall strained to contain him. A broken nose and cropped brown hair gave him an intimidating air.

In contrast, she stood at five foot four and a bit, and doubted she weighed half what he did. The coverall she wore bulged with excess material. Eddy switched his torch back on and she leant forward to examine the body. Even though she expected it, the sight made her throat burn. He looked the same age Declan would have been. *Come on Siobhan, this is not your brother.* To catch the perpetrator, she needed to stay detached. She must see the ruined flesh as evidence, a means of trapping the killer, not the remains of a young man.

She swallowed before asking, "Do we know what happened?"

"Fire brigade found him; I think it's a him, unless it's a very ugly woman." Eddy's grin died under the withering look she gave him and his cheeks reddened as he continued. "They got the call at 04.17 from a taxi driver. One of the lads is getting his statement. They got here at 04.21 and broke in through the front door."

"What about the back?"

"That had a security grille on it." He flashed the torch beam at it. "The firemen ripped it off afterwards, to let the smoke out."

"Has anyone taken prints off it?"

"No, Boss."

"Get it done please, both sides," she said.

"They found the body at 04.43 and—"

"How come they took twenty minutes to find him? It's not a big house."

"I'm not sure, Boss." She signalled for him to continue. "Like I said, they found the body and let our guys know. A patrol car was already here. The station officer assures me, apart from moving the bin when they discovered the body, everything else is as they found it."

She looked around the walls, noting many black scuff marks at floor level, and sooty glove-prints higher up.

"I'm sure," she murmured.

He ignored her comment and continued, "They found the two upstairs earlier, at 04.41."

She straightened and flexed her knees.

"They can take him away once SOCO are happy. I'll speak to the fire officer."

She left Eddy to carry out her instructions and returned to the front door, her mind racing through the steps needed to get the investigation up to speed. This was her first working day in a new force, and she knew she would have to rely on Eddy's local knowledge in the early stages. She dismissed the churning in her stomach. One of her reasons for transferring was to work cases like this.

CHAPTER 3

The Big Man in military fatigues filled the front passenger seat of the battered Toyota Land Cruiser. Behind him, six others, far younger, sat in silence as they contemplated the action to come. Each of the following vehicles carried a full complement of passengers.

When the mismatched convoy set off, just before dawn, excitement had gripped the occupants. Young and fit, they were eager to put their training to use. Four hours travelling in the dusty heat, and the realisation some of them may not return had dampened their enthusiasm.

The Big Man checked the time. They should be there within the hour. He studied his fellow passengers who became aware of his scrutiny and squared their shoulders, putting on determined expressions. A veteran of many such expeditions, he knew they would be ready when the time came.

The night air infiltrated Adam's tunic and the cooling sweat saturating his t-shirt made him shiver. They had finished stowing equipment on their vehicles and he wanted to return to the station to have a shower, or at least change into clean dry clothes. He sipped from the mug of sweet tea their driver had somehow rustled up.

"These your first fatalities, Simon?" Reed asked the probationer, detached in for the night from one of the quieter stations in the division.

Even newer than Adam, he still had his red spot, meaning he couldn't wear breathing apparatus into fires. Already shell-shocked by how busy they'd been, he'd become even more subdued on discovering the bodies of two drug addicts overcome by smoke in the neighbouring house.

Simon nodded.

"What about you, Adam?"

Adam had seen more dead bodies than he cared to remember. "We had those two in the RTA just after Easter, Boss."

"But yours was a nasty one. Are you okay?" Concern infused Reed's voice.

"I'm fine, Boss."

"I bet you've seen much worse," Mal said.

Yes, but a few years ago, and in what Adam regarded as a different life. The sight of the carnage in so unexpected a setting, a house much like his own, had shaken him. He saw movement in the doorway to the house and a figure dressed in protective coveralls came out. Either a copper or one of their technicians.

Her gaze lingered on him for a second. Slim and petite, with big green eyes and strawberry-blond hair, she looked delicate. She unrolled her purple rubber gloves, shivered and strode up to the station officer. Up close Adam noticed the small scar above her right cheek.

"Station Officer?" she said.

He held out his hand. "Station Officer Reed. Geoff."

"Detective Chief Inspector Quinn. Siobhan." A Yorkshire burr overlaid a soft Irish accent.

Adam elbowed Mal out of the way and picked up a mug from the tray in the pump bay. "Do you want a brew?" He held out a steaming mug of tea.

"Thank you." She returned his smile.

Adam's stomach fluttered. "They've all got sugar I'm afraid."

"That's okay, thanks … er …?"

"Adam."

"Thank you, Adam." She saluted him with the mug, took a sip and spoke to Reid. "I know you've already spoken to one of my colleagues, so please bear with me."

"Ask away."

"You had to break in, I understand?"

"Yes, the door was secure when we arrived. Pete smashed the lock."

"What about the back?"

"My sub officer checked it." Reid gestured towards the other pump. "But I'm fairly sure he couldn't get in."

Her expression grew serious. "You took twenty minutes to find the body. How come?"

Adam wanted to protest but kept quiet.

"We weren't expecting occupants," Reid sounded defensive. "The place was derelict."

"I'm not making accusations, Geoff." She held her free hand up. "I'm just trying to build a picture of what happened. Who found the body?"

"Adam." Reid jerked a thumb at him.

"Can you talk me through what happened, Adam?" Siobhan's eyes grew darker as she studied him. The amusement of earlier gone.

A surge of irritation flared. *What do you know about firefighting?* "By the time we arrived we encountered a developed fire and a ceiling temperature of almost a thousand degrees—"

"That's about gas mark twenty, love." Jed, the driver of the second pump had joined them.

Siobhan stiffened, irritation, then disappointment, flickering across her features. "I presume you didn't waltz in at ceiling height."

Adam's neck grew hot. *Thanks Jed, you arsehole.* He continued, giving Siobhan an account of the firefighting and search, and she nodded in encouragement. "We'd checked all the rooms and cupboards. I moved the bin to see if we could use it to take out the crap but it fell over. You saw what came out."

"That explains why it took twenty minutes." She returned her mug. "Thanks for the tea," she said and addressed Reid. "What's your sub called?"

"Mike Holt. They're all on the pump." He waved towards the other vehicle. "They've been hammered, so he'll probably be dozing."

"Thanks, Geoff. Please make sure you all provide written statements before you go off duty."

She walked over to the second pump without giving Adam a second glance.

"Philip, get up now or you'll be late," his father called for the third time. "Don't make me come up there."

Philip burrowed into the pillow. He couldn't handle going to college today. The knot in his gut felt like a large ball of rubber bands.

His mother's voice carried. "Leave him to me. He came home late last night."

"That's no excuse; he needs to learn about responsibility. He *is* seventeen."

"Get going, Samuel, otherwise *you'll* be late."

His father called his goodbyes and after a few moments the front door slammed. Philip studied the ceiling, the events of last night racing in his thoughts. The relief he'd experienced when he saw the night bus had soon passed, replaced by the fear Mugisa and the others would be waiting for him at home.

He could still see the savage determination on their faces. Guilt over his role in getting Liam to the mill compounded the horror of what had happened to his friend. Why had the others killed him? When Philip discussed it with them, they'd agreed to scare him and rough him up. Had they all planned it or did Mugisa pull their strings as he so often did? Unable to dismiss the images, Philip squeezed his eyes shut and as he remembered his friend, tears soaked into his pillow.

A loud knocking on his bedroom door jolted him and he sat up, pulse racing, until he heard his mother's voice.

"Philip?"

"Hold on, Mum, I'm coming," he croaked.

He wiped his tears, struggled out of bed and pulled on a pair of tracksuit bottoms. Rebecca stood outside the door, concern in her eyes.

"Are you okay, Philip?" She studied him.

He managed to stop himself shifting his feet. "I'm fine, Mum."

"You don't look fine. What time did you get in last night?"

He shrugged.

"The shower came on at half two. Why did you stay out so late?"

He shrugged again but her frown told him he needed to give an explanation. "I went to Mugisa's to work. We had a project to finish." Philip sniffed. "Mum, is it okay if I don't go in today? I'm not feeling great."

She examined him and he shifted his feet, chewing on the inside of his cheek, certain she could read his thoughts. She placed her hand against his forehead and he relaxed, comforted by the familiar gesture.

"Mmm, you *do* feel hot. I'll get you a couple of aspirins. Now get back to bed."

Philip crept under the covers and switched on the bedside lamp. She returned a few minutes later with the tablets, a glass of water and a cordless phone.

"Take two of these. I'll leave you the phone; ring me if you feel worse. I'll pop in at lunchtime. Do you want me to bring you breakfast before I go?"

"No thanks, Mum."

"You must be *really* ill." She smiled and after kissing his forehead, she left him.

Philip lay in bed and listened to the sounds of his family preparing for a new day. The usual noises seemed somehow alien as if what he'd done and witnessed just a few hours ago had changed his world. Panic gripped him as he contemplated the fallout from last night.

Mugisa sat in the kitchen of the house he still couldn't think of as home. The memory of Philip's behaviour infuriated him. He took a bite from a piece of toast as Joseph Walcott entered the room.

"Good morning, Matthew. How are you today?" Joseph said.

Mugisa had learned to respond to this name, but it didn't belong to him. He nodded, finished chewing and swallowed.

"I'm very well, sir. And how are you?"

"You don't have to call me sir." Joseph smiled and took a seat. "Call me Dad, like I told you."

Unwelcome memories of his last meeting with his father assaulted Mugisa.

"Good morning. Good morning." Miriam's cheery voice broke through the silence. "Breakfast?" she asked.

"This will be fine, thank you." Mugisa waved his last piece of toast.

Miriam tutted. "It's not enough for a growing body."

"Let the boy be, dear. You know he doesn't eat much in the morning."

"Breakfast is the most important meal of the day—"

"You'd better get on and make mine then." He smiled to rob his words of offence and winked at Mugisa. "You came home late last night, Matthew."

Mugisa kept his voice even and held Joseph's gaze. "I went to Philip's. We had to finish a project."

"If you want to stay out late, that's fine." Joseph glanced at his wife but she'd found something of interest on the floor. "It's just we worry if we don't know where you are."

"Sorry, sir, I'll tell you next time." Mugisa bobbed his head, concerned at the unexpected interrogation. "Can I go now?"

"Of course, son."

Mugisa said his goodbyes and left the kitchen. One thing he'd liked about living here was that they both went to bed early, so they never knew when he got home. And before today, they'd never questioned him. If that changed, he might have to do something about it. He pulled on his jacket, his mind already on how to deal with Philip.

The silence in the kitchen thickened as they waited for the front door to slam. Joseph studied his wife, wondering what she was thinking.

She spoke first. "Are you happy with him staying out so late?"

"Why not? Philip's a nice boy and I've met his parents. They're a decent family. It's good for him to mix with people like them."

Miriam frowned. "He's out late a lot and I don't like it. You know what they said about him. He needs stability, routines."

"Yes, but he also needs to find his own feet. The counsellor thinks he's doing fine, 'remarkably well-adjusted' she said last time."

"Mmm … you know my opinion of her: book wise, life foolish."

"I'll talk to him tonight and suggest he spends more time studying at home. I might even get him a computer. A friend at work said he can get them cheap." Joseph thought his wife was worrying about nothing. Despite the dreadful start in life the boy had endured, they'd done a good job since he'd come to live with them.

Siobhan studied the papers on the desk in the unfamiliar office. Although Harrogate was the more historic city, the irony that her last station was a modern concrete edifice and she now worked in an old building wasn't lost on her. She checked the time: five minutes before she had to go. She summoned Eddy, mulling over the details of the incident as she waited for him. Undertakers had removed the bodies and forensic examinations continued at the crime scenes. The drug addicts found upstairs had seemed asleep; the reddening of their features and soot marks round their nostrils the only clues to how they'd died. In contrast, the body in the wheelie bin looked anything but peaceful.

"Boss?" Eddy stepped into the open doorway.

"Eddy, we need to identify our victims as a matter of priority." She saw his expression. "Sorry, I don't mean to…" She offered a smile. "Can you check the incident room is ready for me? I'm off to see the Chief Super but make sure everyone's in there for my briefing in half an hour."

Eddy left and Siobhan set off for her rendezvous, a slight fluttering in her stomach. The chief superintendent's secretary led her into his office without delay. A young high-flier, he had a reputation as a running fanatic, maybe one reason she'd got the job. He looked up from the papers on his desk and smiled.

"Good morning, Chief Inspector. Welcome to GMP. We've landed a particularly nasty murder on you on your first day."

"Yes, sir."

"In at the deep end. Well, I won't keep you. Please take a seat and give me a quick outline." He gestured to a chair in front of his desk.

Siobhan sat down and started, eager to return to her investigation. "There are three victims." She described their injuries. "It looks like the boy in the bin was the target and the two upstairs died because they were in the wrong place, so I want to treat this as one incident. I'll obviously not rule out the possibility someone set the fire to kill them and *accidentally* involved the dead boy, however unlikely that seems."

"Good idea: avoids duplication and we don't want to run up unnecessary overtime bills. The investigation into Shipman is eating resources."

"We think the victim in the bin died outside and the killers hid him in the house afterwards. We found a big patch of blood in the alley."

"Killers?" His brow furrowed.

"It would have taken at least two to carry the bin into the house."

"How did they get in? The council should have secured those houses."

"It looks like they'd removed the grille securing the back door but reattached it when they'd finished."

"Hmmm." He frowned. "Do we know who he is?"

"Not at the moment. We found a student ID on him but couldn't read it, soaked in blood. Forensics are trying to get something from it but, until they do, we've got nothing."

"Would you say whoever killed him knew what they were doing?"

She nodded, remembering the youth's injuries. "Despite the damage to his neck and upper body, his face remained untouched apart from a graze and a bruise on his forehead. It's possible his attackers deliberately avoided damaging it, maybe to make sure identification wasn't delayed, as a message..."

He pondered this for a few moments. "You're aware we've had more than our share of gang killings in the past." He grimaced. "An ambitious journalist made sure the *whole country* heard about these, and some of those victims were young lads." He fixed her with a penetrating gaze. "I'm dammed if I'll allow it to start again on my watch. We need to catch whoever's behind this ASAP."

"I understand, sir."

"I hope you do, Chief Inspector. You have the chance to make your mark. How you handle this will determine how you're viewed in this force."

"Yes, sir."

"I'll expect you to keep me updated on *all* developments, however minor."

Siobhan's insides shrank. "Of course, sir, but I assume you won't want me to hold up the investigation in order to appraise you."

"Of course not."

Siobhan held his gaze.

"You'd better get to it then." He picked up his pen and returned his attention to the pad on his desk. "Your superiors in North Yorkshire had a high opinion of you, but you'll discover it takes more to impress me."

I bet it does, you pompous arse.

CHAPTER 4

The teacher left in a battered white Fiat. A cloud of black smoke pursued her as she made her way to the next village school where another class of pupils awaited her arrival.

The Boy looked around at the group who remained and organised two teams from amongst them, making sure they shared out the weaker boys evenly.

Four small piles of schoolbooks provided the goalposts and a bundle of rags, tied together into a small solid sphere, acted as a ball. The well-matched teams played a closely contested game. One side claimed a disputed goal and the boys stood arguing in high voices.

A shrill scream rent the air, silencing them. Bewildered, they looked at each other, in search of guidance. The Boy reacted first, concern for his mother and sister propelling him homeward. The others followed and soon all the boys picked up their bundles and ran homeward.

Siobhan checked her reflection in the mirror above the sink. She attempted to still the butterflies fluttering in her stomach. Not only did she have to make sure she did her best for the victims; she also had to win over the whole team. Apart from Eddy, she didn't know anyone else. She'd met a few of them fleetingly, following her final interview, but knew she wouldn't remember any names. Taking a deep breath, she squared her shoulders. "Come on Siobhan, you can do this," she muttered to herself, knowing once she started she'd be fine.

She walked into the briefing room at half past eight. A low murmur of conversation and the smell of damp clothes greeted her. Officers in uniform and detectives sat in most of the chairs facing the front of the room where Eddy had set up an incident board. Beside it stood a lectern with a glass of water on it. She walked to the front of the room. The other officers fell silent and focussed on her. Her cheeks grew warm and she hoped she hadn't gone bright red.

"Good morning," she began.

"Good morning, Boss." Eddy led the chorus of response.

She gave him a grateful smile and continued. "For those who haven't met me before, and that's most of you," she said, scanning the room, "I'm Chief Inspector Quinn."

A few nods greeted this. Everyone stared at her.

"We are here to investigate the deaths of these three people." She indicated the board. "As you can see, Eddy's divided the board into three columns and added a brief description of each victim, details of when and where they were found, along with short accounts of their injuries. We can add photos and names later, along with accurate information from the post-mortem report." Without referring to notes she gave an outline of the incident, including a summary of the information gleaned from the fire crew.

"The first job is to identify the victims, in particular the young lad in the wheelie bin. One interesting thing about him is that, despite his terrible injuries, his killers hadn't damaged his face, apart from a graze on his forehead and a bruise here." She stroked her left temple.

A hand shot up. "Yes, Detective…?"

"DC Youssef Khan, Boss," he said in a broad Birmingham accent. "I think I know the girl: she's a junkie called Ingrid. She has a tattoo of a red rose on her right hand, like it says up there." He pointed at the board. "But she's got red hair, not blonde…"

"Do you have any background on her? A surname?"

"Sorry, Boss. I just know she squats in the area and begs outside the local shopping centre. She's sometimes with a bloke called Dave, and his description fits the other guy." He pointed to the last column on the board.

"Boss, there's a clinic behind the shopping precinct with a needle exchange. They might know her," Eddy volunteered.

"Thank you. Can you find out, DC Khan? Check if the photos of both victims are ready and take them with you."

Khan nodded and made a note.

"Boss?" Another hand raised and Siobhan signalled for the detective to speak. "DC Stefan Dabrowski. You say the other victim's a student. Should we check the universities and colleges, to see if anyone fitting his description is missing?"

"I'd hate to think how many students bunk off on a Monday morning." A ripple of laughter greeted this. "Not a bad idea, but let's explore other avenues first. Thank you DC Dabrowski." She addressed the room. "Until we have more information about the victims and how they died, I want the rest of you to concentrate on finding witnesses. That means house to house. Is there much CCTV in the area, Eddy?"

"Not street cameras. There might be traffic cameras on the main road but that's a fair distance away."

Siobhan tried to hide her disappointment. "Please get someone to check those?" Eddy nodded, and she saw another hand raised.

"What about the businesses in the area? There's not many but some will have CCTV to protect their premises," a uniformed constable said.

"Good idea, Constable...?"

"Matthews. Debbie Matthews."

"Take charge of that please, Constable Matthews." Siobhan checked the time. "Let's reconvene here at 14.00 by which time we should have more information about the victims. Thank you everyone." The team dispersed and she took a sip from her glass. *That wasn't so bad.*

Even from his bedroom, the banging on the front door sounded as if the visitor was trying to smash through it. His heart pounding, Philip jumped out of bed. He pulled on his tracksuit bottoms before struggling into a sweatshirt and hurrying through his parents' room. As usual, it looked like a show home, in contrast to his untidy den. Keeping behind the curtain, he looked down but couldn't see the face of the man peering through the letterbox. He could however see the large silver SUV parked across the drive and recognised it with a jolt of apprehension. Liam had pointed it out. It belonged to his uncle Ritchie. What the hell did he want? He couldn't already have discovered his part in Liam's death.

Ritchie McLaughlin hammered on the door again. Philip's legs trembled and his mind emptied. He decided to just stay behind the curtain and hope the visitor left. McLaughlin moved away from the door, stepping into Philip's line of sight, and looked up at the house. His gaze passed across the front windows until he looked straight at Philip. McLaughlin looked like an advert for a menswear shop, except for his shaved head and foreboding expression. Philip froze. After what felt like an age, he saw movement on the drive and his mother appeared in her nurse's uniform. He gulped in a lungful of air, realising he'd stopped breathing.

Rebecca Mason walked towards the visitor. "Can I help you?" she asked.

McLaughlin faced her and she studied his expensive clothes and shoes before her eyes locked on his. Philip almost felt sorry for him.

"Hello, I'm Ritchie," he said, extending his hand and wearing an insincere smile.

Rebecca stared at him until his smile faded and he withdrew his hand. "Well Ritchie, what do you want?"

McLaughlin looked at her and then back at the house, staring straight at Philip.

"Are you going to answer me?"

The man still didn't answer but moved closer and loomed over her. His mother looked tiny and Philip's muscles tensed. If McLaughlin touched her, he would go straight down there and batter him, regardless of who he was. Before he could act, his mother surprised him by laughing at McLaughlin.

"Ritchie," she said, "my father was a bully and he was bigger than you. Now, either tell me what you want, or leave."

McLaughlin stepped away, his complexion reddening. "I wanted to speak to Philip." He studied the window, making Philip cringe. "I'd say 'your son', but you're not old enough—"

"Don't bother, Ritchie. Flattery doesn't work on me." She glanced up at the window. "Philip's not available now. Why do you want to speak to him?"

McLaughlin looked at the window again and Philip attempted to melt into the room without moving. "I just wanted to know if he'd spoken to my nephew, Liam; his mother's worried about him."

"Tell her I'll give Philip your message and he'll ring her if he's got anything to say."

While she spoke to McLaughlin, Rebecca had manoeuvred him round and she now stood between him and the door. McLaughlin scowled when he noticed and he spun on his heel before walking stiffly to his car.

Philip's high opinion of his mother increased, but the glow of pride faded as he realised he now had to face her. The front door closed and, from the hall below, his mother called his name.

By the time she got upstairs, Philip had returned to bed. Her footsteps sounded in the hall outside and she rapped on the door, opening it before he could reply.

"Philip?"

"Yes." He tried to make his voice sound sleepy.

The light switch snapped on and he screwed up his eyes at the harsh overhead light. "Don't try to make out you slept through that racket. I could hear that thug banging on the door from the corner. Why did he come here?"

Philip sat up and blinked, trying to come up with an explanation, but unable to do so, he shrugged.

"Don't shrug at me, young man. He said he's Liam's uncle. Why did he think you know where Liam's gone?"

Starting to shrug again, he thought better of it. "I don't know, Mum. He's a bit of a nutter."

"Yes, I could see what kind of man he is and I don't want him coming to our house." She looked at her watch. "Thanks to our visitor, I haven't time to make your lunch. You'll have to get your own."

"Yeah okay, Mum. I'll be fine." His limbs trembled but he caught himself before he sighed.

"I don't doubt it." She kissed his forehead and killed the light. "This isn't over, young man. I want an explanation from you when I get home tonight."

Philip lay on his back and listened to the sounds of his mother leaving the house. The front door slammed and, as the echoes died, his thoughts returned to his predicament.

Mugisa and the others wouldn't rest until they'd silenced him. Liam's uncle would also return and, despite his mother's courage, he realised she wouldn't stand a chance if McLaughlin attacked her. Worse still, next time it might be one of his sisters. What he knew of McLaughlin made him shiver.

How had he got himself mixed up in this? And, of more concern now, how could he escape? He needed someone he could go to for help. Not the police: his part in getting Liam to the mill made him an accessory to his friend's killing.

A sound from the front door cut through his thoughts and he lay frozen, straining to hear above the surge of his pulse pounding in his ears. He roused himself from the temporary paralysis and, taking the telephone with him, shuffled to the front window.

He couldn't see anyone on the drive and he studied the street. Through the hedge, he caught a glint of silver paint. A large car sat at the kerb. His heart missed a beat.

Backing away from the widow, he left his parents' room and sat at the top of the stairs, sweat pouring off him. When his breathing slowed, he switched on the handset and dialled the number. His parents wouldn't be happy, but he couldn't think of anyone else.

Siobhan sat in her office preparing for the afternoon meeting when her phone rang.

"Boss, I've got a Mrs McLaughlin here who says her son Liam's missing. She's got a photo and I'm pretty sure it's our lad."

The knowledge she'd have to inform the woman of her son's death tempered her excitement. "Good work, Eddy. I'll come straight down." She checked the time: past one thirty.

After closing the file, she stepped out into the main office. "Please tell everyone the meeting's postponed until 16.00, Youssef."

"Right, Boss."

Impatient to identify their young victim, she rushed to the interview room. Siobhan opened the door and a woman of about forty started. She was attractive in an obvious way — Siobhan's mother would have described her as 'brassy' — with too much make up and heady perfume which made Siobhan's eyes water. Eddy had his head down, going through the standard missing person's form.

"Good afternoon, Mrs McLaughlin, my name's Siobhan Quinn."

"Maria." The woman offered a damp hand.

Siobhan sat down and Eddy passed her the form with a photo of a smiling lad in school uniform on top of it. The contrast with the image of the butchered youth in the burnt-out house shocked her but she didn't think the mother noticed her reaction. She read through the notes and gave the victim's mother a sympathetic smile.

"Sorry to keep you waiting, Maria. Can I call you Maria?"

Liam's mother nodded.

"Can you tell me when you last saw Liam?"

Maria looked thoughtful. "Just after breakfast yesterday. He'd got up late; he'd been out drinking..." She smiled apologetically. "I know he's only seventeen..."

"I understand, Maria. We've all done it."

"Like I say, he ate breakfast about eleven. I did him a fry-up. He loves a fry-up but we don't have time most days; couldn't afford it, anyway."

"Did he say where he was going?"

"Oh yes, he was meeting friends at the pub. They were going to watch the match. We don't have Sky at home." She mentioned a pub Siobhan remembered passing on her way into work.

"Popular with students," Eddy said. "I reckon Liam wouldn't have been the only one under eighteen."

"What time?" Siobhan asked.

"About one. The match started at three."

"What about once the match finished?"

"He rang me from the pub to say he was going to a friend's to do some work. They get loads of homework."

"Do you have the friend's name?"

"Philip Mason."

"Have you got his address?" Eddy said, not hiding his eagerness.

Maria produced a scruffy notebook. "He keeps all his friends' numbers in here. I rang them all from work this morning."

"Can I have a look?" Eddy held out his hand and Maria gave it to him. He found the address.

Siobhan took over, not wanting Eddy to get ahead of himself. "So you've spoken to Philip?"

"I rang, but he put the phone down and he hasn't answered since."

"Are you sure it was him? You didn't get a wrong number?"

"That's what Ritchie said, my brother-in-law," she explained. "But I'm sure. I recognised his voice. Ritchie's going round to speak to—"

"Ritchie McLaughlin?" Eddy leant forward, his face tense.

Maria nodded. "Yes, do you know him?"

"I've heard the name." He glanced at Siobhan before continuing, "You say he's gone round to this lad's house?"

"He said he'd go later on, after he'd seen somebody else."

Siobhan gave Eddy a quizzical look, but he shook his head and she returned her attention to Maria.

"Can we keep this?" Siobhan asked, holding up the notebook. "We need to make a copy, but we'll let you have it back." Maria nodded and Siobhan alerted Eddy to her intentions. "Maria, I'm afraid we may have bad news about Liam. We found the body of a young man last night—"

"Liam? What happened? I knew something had happened to him. Was it a car accident?" Her voice became shrill.

"We're not even sure it is Liam at this point, Maria, but you should prepare yourself."

Maria looked bewildered but, with a visible effort, controlled her emotions. She nodded and took a deep breath. "Do you want me to look at the body?"

"Yes, please. If you wait here, I'll get the car and we'll take you." Siobhan stood up and gestured to Eddy to wait with the woman as she fetched her car. She always hated this part of the job and suspected this one would be worse than usual.

CHAPTER 5

More screams and shouting came from the huts, along with the sharp crack of small-arms fire. The boys rounded the little outcrop which lay between their homes and the school. Ahead, the familiar collection of huts they called home lay under siege.

Several vehicles, some with engines still running, had parked in a haphazard jumble amongst the homes. Men and youths had spilled out of them and now moved between the dwellings. All gripped weapons, a few of the older ones with firearms, but most carried Chinese-made machetes or traditional spears.

The invaders rounded up the occupants of the huts, smashing through their flimsy doors and dragging out those who tried to take refuge in their homes. Bodies lay in the spaces between the huts, wounds leaking blood into the black earth. Screams of pain and terror mixed with the excited yells of the attackers.

The following afternoon, Byron Mason sat at his desk, focussed on memorising the cash-flow forecasts before his meeting with the bank. He shouldn't have gone out last night but getting a babysitter wasn't easy. The phone on his untidy desk buzzed. Alison, his PA. He frowned in irritation but she wouldn't disturb him unless she thought it important.

"Byron, I've got a young man on the phone. A Philip Mason. He claims he's your nephew and he sounds upset."

What on earth does he want? Despite not wanting to disturb his train of thought Byron decided to take the call. "Thanks, Alison. Put him through."

"Hi, Uncle Byron. It's Philip." The boy's voice sounded small and distant.

"Hi, Philip. What did you want?" Byron, his mind still on his forthcoming meeting, responded brusquely.

"Err, I wondered…" The boy hesitated.

Byron realised he'd spoken abruptly. "Is everything all right, Philip?" When had he last spoken to the lad? It must have been the Christmas before last, at Dad's.

"Fine, thanks." Philip hesitated again and cleared his throat. "Uncle Byron, I'm in trouble and I need your help."

A surge of adrenaline made Byron sit up, his attention now on the call. "You know I'll do anything I can."

"You mustn't tell anybody, especially my parents."

"I can't promise that." Byron thought for a moment. "I tell you what I'll do. If I think you need to tell your parents, you can tell them."

After a lengthy pause, Philip replied, "Okay. But you must promise not to tell the police."

Byron's scalp prickled. What the hell had the lad got involved in? Had he started dabbling in drugs? Not sure he could make that promise, he didn't reply.

Philip hesitated for a few seconds, then the words tumbled out. Byron listened with growing alarm. When Philip finished speaking, Byron thought for a few seconds before he made a decision.

"Okay, Philip. It does sound as if you need help. I'll book myself on to a train this evening. You're at home now?"

"Yeah."

"Is anyone else there?"

"Not at the moment."

"Don't answer the door to anyone. Keep the phone with you and make a note of this number." He dictated his mobile number. "If anyone you don't recognise comes round, ring 999 and set off the panic button on the burglar alarm. Where are you now?"

"In my room. There's a button in Mum and Dad's room."

"Good. I don't want you to worry, Philip. It probably won't be necessary, but there's no point in taking chances. Ring me on my mobile any time you want to talk, okay?"

"Yeah sure. Thank you, Uncle Byron."

"No problem. I'll see you in a few hours and Philip … don't worry."

Byron ended the call and let out a heartfelt exclamation. If what Philip said was true, he had plenty to worry about. He didn't want Ritchie McLaughlin anywhere near his family. The fact he wouldn't arrive until late bothered Byron, especially if the thug was still hanging around outside the house…

Byron dialled Adam's number, listening to the ringtone in frustration until he concluded his friend wasn't going to answer. Why the hell didn't he get a mobile, or at least an answering machine like everyone else in the twentieth century?

Mugisa pulled up on his bike and paused at the kerb, looking towards Philip's house. He wasn't sure he should give him a second chance just because of a sentimental memory of a boyhood friend. It might make him appear weak to the others. He dismissed his concern and wheeled his bike up to the door.

As he approached, he could hear excited chatter from behind it. Still uneasy, he laid the bike on its side and rang the doorbell. The door flew open and Philip's youngest sister stood in the opening. Despite his trepidation, his spirits lifted.

"Hello, Mugisa."

He returned her smile. "Hello Lucy. Can I speak to Philip?"

"I don't know if he's home. I've only just got back."

She bellowed her brother's name. Behind her, Mugisa saw her sister, who waved hello. Philip had obviously said nothing to them. Lucy shouted her brother's name again and stepped back to let Mugisa into the hall. Mugisa entered the doorway. Philip appeared at the top of the stairs and faltered when he saw Mugisa. A look of panic crossed his face.

"Hello, Philip. I came to see how you are."

Philip rushed down the stairs and shoved Mugisa out of the door. Caught by surprise, Mugisa offered little resistance. He caught the wrought iron handrail and stopped himself falling. The door slammed behind him.

Through the door he heard Lucy. "Philip, what are you playing at?"

"Don't let him in. Ever," Philip shouted, sounding strained.

Mugisa hesitated for a few seconds. The embarrassment Philip's behaviour had caused him changed to anger with every step. He would have to do whatever it took to destroy Philip.

With Eddy giving directions, Siobhan drove to the mortuary. Eddy signed them in and an orderly showed them down a gloomy corridor infused with a musty medical smell. Their footsteps echoed and Siobhan studied Maria, who wore a determined expression. The orderly led them to a wide, dark wooden door bisected horizontally by a scuffed metal plate. He put his hand on the door and paused.

"Are you ready, Maria?" Siobhan asked.

Maria blinked and nodded. Siobhan wanted to leave her to it, but signalling Eddy to wait, she led the way into the room. The smell of disinfectant and bleach intensified. Maria flinched when she saw Liam and, in an almost inaudible voice, confirmed he was her son. She asked if she could spend a few minutes alone with him.

Siobhan re-joined Eddy and seeing the question in his eyes, she nodded.

"Poor woman." He checked the time. "Most of his friends will be at college. I'm not sure when they finish but should we get over there and question them?"

"Good idea, Eddy. How far is it?"

"Less than a mile. I can walk over and meet the others there if you want."

Siobhan considered this for a few moments. "I'll go, if you give me directions. You can make sure Maria gets home and come over afterwards." She handed him her keys.

Not hiding his disappointment, he told her how to get to the college.

"Do you know who did it?" Maria stood in the open doorway.

"Not yet, Maria." Siobhan couldn't help feeling defensive. "We need to speak to the people he saw last night."

"I already told you, he was with Philip Mason," she spat. "He must have something to do with it. I never trusted the black bastard."

The shock must have shown on Siobhan's face.

"What's the matter? Not politically correct enough for you?"

"I don't think the colour of a person's skin is relevant." Heat spread across Siobhan's torso.

"Is that what they teach you to say when you join the police?" Maria gave a grim smile. "I suppose you'll treat him with kid gloves, in case he sues you."

"Mrs McLaughlin, I know you're upset and I'm sorry for your loss but I assure you, we will investigate the death of your son thoroughly. Nobody will get special treatment, for whatever reason. My colleague will give you a lift." Siobhan left before she said anything she'd regret.

As Byron forced his way through the traffic, he realised he was driving too fast and took his foot off the accelerator. With six points on his licence, he couldn't risk getting any more. An unaccustomed feeling of anxiety had gripped him since he'd spoken to Philip, reviving unwelcome memories of his youth.

"...on Thursday, Tony Blair will become the first British Prime Minister to address the Irish Parliament..." the presenter announced over the radio.

"Good for him," Byron muttered and switched it off. Despite Louisa's conviction, he still didn't trust the too-smooth politician. He put a CD in the slot. The mournful voice of Nina Simone filled the car and the tension across his shoulders eased.

The taxi he'd ordered sat outside his house in Chiswick. He signalled the driver to wait, ran to the front door, and let himself in. He walked into the kitchen, and a delighted yell greeted him.

"Daddy!"

He scooped up the small figure in his arms. "How's my big girl today? You been taking care of Mummy?"

She nodded, wearing a big grin.

He lifted her up and swung her round, her squeals of excitement, music to his ears.

Behind their daughter, Louisa mouthed, "Do you want a coffee?"

He shook his head and kissed his wife before lowering Lilly.

"The overnight bag's packed and I've made sandwiches for the journey. Do you know when you'll be back?"

"A few days, maybe." He saw the concern in her eyes and tried to lighten things. "Let's see it as an opportunity to get to know our daughter's cousins." He patted Lilly's hair before stroking Louisa's stomach, barely showing the new life growing in her. "And his, or hers."

"Did Philip say what the problem was?"

"Not really." He looked away and put Lilly on the floor. Louisa wasn't fooled, he could never lie to her. "He's having trouble with some other lads at college."

"Why can't the college deal with it?"

"It's the kind of problem a quiet word would sort out."

"Surely his dad—" Louisa blushed. "Sorry Byron, I didn't mean..."

Relieved to get off the hook, he hugged them both and rushed out to the waiting taxi. As the car wove through the evening traffic, he took out his mobile and rang Adam again. As the phone rang out, his anxiety grew and, although he tried to tell himself he was worrying unnecessarily, the nagging fear wouldn't go away.

By the time Siobhan returned to the station, she'd become reconciled to her disappointment. The walk to Liam's college had ended in frustration; the pupils had already left for the day, scuppering any hopes of saving time by interviewing them all in one place. Still considering her next steps, she made her way into the incident room. Everyone fell silent and regarded her expectantly. Eddy's wasn't there, but she decided to start without him.

"As you might have heard, we've identified the young man whose body we found in the wheelie bin. He's Liam McLaughlin, a seventeen-year-old student." She scanned the officers before her. "I don't have to tell you that none of this information leaves this room."

Eddy's voice drifted into the room filling her with a sense of relief. He made a gesture of apology and closed the door behind him.

"Eddy, any problems with Mrs McLaughlin?" She couldn't read his expression but he shook his head. A hand rose. "Yes, Debbie?"

"I heard the lad's Ritchie McLaughlin's nephew. Do we intend to look at him? There's a good chance he might know something about it."

A few muttered "too rights" confirmed this wasn't an isolated opinion. Not for the first time, Siobhan rued her lack of local knowledge.

"We'll follow the evidence. I gather Ritchie McLaughlin has a reputation, but the evidence we have is that Liam spent Sunday with friends. I want to identify and speak to those friends. Eddy, can you go through Liam's address book and assign the interviews?"

"Boss."

"Debbie, any joy with CCTV?"

Constable Matthews reddened. "There's a few hours of tape to review and I need to go back to a few places tomorrow morning."

"Good. Make sure we check the footage we've got immediately."

DC Khan raised his hand.

"Yes, Youssef?"

"Boss, just to let you know we've got hold of the next of kin of the two junkies."

"Good work." She studied the board where the names of the couple who'd succumbed to carbon monoxide poisoning headed columns two and three. "When can they identify them?"

"Tomorrow. One family are from Hull and the other's from Bristol."

"Okay. Make sure you find out what time they're getting here and pick them up if they need a lift."

He looked like he'd object but just nodded.

Eddy had written out Liam's friends' details on sheets of paper. "Right everyone; before you interview anybody, check their birthdays," he announced. "Anyone born after December '81 is a minor and needs to have an appropriate adult with them. Boss, which officers do you want me to send to interview Philip Mason?"

"You and I will take him." Siobhan had a feeling he'd be key to this case.

CHAPTER 6

The Boy got closer and saw many of the invaders were themselves children, some not much older than the boys he'd played football with. One of these had noticed the arrival of the footballers and let out a cry of warning. Others joined him and they advanced in a line, each holding a weapon by his side. The boys again looked to their leader.

'Run!' he cried and, following a shocked pause; they all did.

The invaders set off in pursuit, brandishing their weapons. They caught the smallest of the boys first, and his pursuer lifted his machete in the air before smashing it down onto his skinny torso. The small boy crashed to the ground and lay still, surprised to be alive. He fought for breath, realising the flat of the blade had hit him. His captor seized his arm and dragged him to his feet.

Similar scenes continued around him and The Boy identified the smallest of their pursuers before running at him. As he closed on his adversary, The Boy recognised surprise and fear in the other's eyes. Before his opponent could react, The Boy's head crunched into the other's torso, and The Boy realised his adversary was a girl. She collapsed with a surprised gasp as the impact emptied her lungs.

Fighting for air, she stayed down, and The Boy leapt to his feet. Her weapon lay on the ground and, without thinking; he grabbed it, and ran on to his home, where his mother and sister would need his help.

Eddy drove and Siobhan sat in thoughtful silence, running through what to expect. Her actions would determine the success of the investigation and she'd seen cases falter because of mistakes made in the early stages. Outside, the cityscape changed. They drove along a road lined with exotic shops and eateries; the air infused with the aroma of curry. A few shops displayed Christmas decorations, but these weren't as prevalent as in the city centre. Twenty minutes later they entered a more affluent area, the houses lining the street were bigger and in better condition.

Eddy slowed and entered a side road, lined with the skeletons of trees. The street lighting left dark shadows on each side of the road but each house occupied a large plot. Eddy pulled over to the kerb and switched off the engine. Siobhan got out, her foot slipping on the slimy layer of fallen leaves covering the pavement.

"It's this one, Boss." He pointed to the house to their left. "How do you want to play it?"

"At the moment, he's a potential witness, that's all. And we just want to find out when he last saw Liam. If I believe he's involved, I'll put pressure on him. Let's find out the family's attitude first." Anticipation made her tingle.

She marched up the drive, studying the imposing house. Lights showed upstairs and in three of the lower floor windows. She rang the bell and, following a short wait, a pretty teenage girl answered the door.

"Yes? Can I help you?" The girl looked apprehensive.

"Hello, are your parents home?" Siobhan said.

The girl shouted into the house, "Dad, somebody for you." She returned her attention to Siobhan, but she noticed Eddy and her smile faded. "My father's coming."

"Thank you." They waited in awkward silence, but at least there wasn't any hostility. *Yet. Let's see how her dad reacts.*

"Come on Lucy, let me see our visitors," a sonorous voice said.

The girl stepped back, pulling the door open to reveal a man of about forty. His huge arms and well-developed shoulders dwarfed the wheelchair beneath him. Siobhan hid her surprise, smiled and produced her warrant card.

"Good evening, sir. I'm Detective Chief Inspector Quinn, GMP Major Crimes Unit and this is Sergeant Arkwright."

"Samuel Mason." He shook hands with both visitors. "And my daughter, Lucy."

A trace of the local accent inflected Samuel's rumbling voice. After checking their identification he smiled and said, "What major crimes have you come to discuss?"

"We need to speak to your son, Philip. Can we come in please, sir?"

Samuel raised his eyebrows and rolled back to let the two detectives into the house. The young girl, eyes wide, closed the door and loitered behind the visitors, hoping to escape notice. Siobhan studied her surroundings. The huge hall would accommodate half the ground floor of her parents' house. The tasteful décor suggested the influence of someone with a flair for interior design and she recognised the wallpaper, a pattern she'd rejected as too expensive.

"Lucy, please fetch your brother," Samuel said. "What do you want with my son, Chief Inspector?"

"We're investigating a serious crime involving one of his friends from college." How would her parents have reacted to a visit from the police when she'd been a teenager? Like this. Polite curiosity, but no concern their child might be involved in any crime.

The sound of Lucy calling her brother carried down the stairs. A door opened, and she held a muttered conversation, then a big youth appeared at the top of the stairs. Halfway down he stopped and his eyes darted. A flutter of excitement made Siobhan's hands tingle and Eddy tensed, ready to respond.

The young man gathered himself and continued down the stairs. Siobhan noted he was about the same height as Eddy and, although still to fill out, he wasn't much slimmer than the sergeant. He looked more than capable of inflicting the injuries she'd seen on Liam's body.

"Philip, Chief Inspector Quinn here would like a word. Shall we go into my study?" Samuel rolled his chair towards a door to the left of the stairs. Philip lingered, waiting for them to follow his father.

"After you, Philip." Siobhan gestured.

Philip hesitated, before trudging in ahead of her. Before following him, she exchanged a glance with Eddy, both of them certain the boy knew something significant. Lucy hovered behind them.

"Lucy, go and help your mother," Samuel announced over his shoulder.

The girl sighed theatrically before stomping away. They entered a large, well-lit room. A partner's desk occupied one corner and, opposite, stood a lift. Dark wooden bookshelves, full of text books, filled one wall. A large sofa and several easy chairs clustered round a circular coffee table in front of a cast iron fireplace.

Samuel invited them to sit and they took seats at right angles to each other, both facing Philip. They declined an offer of refreshments, and Eddy produced a notepad.

Siobhan studied Philip. "We're investigating the murder of Liam McLaughlin."

Samuel gasped, looking stunned by this news. Philip slumped in his chair and covered his face.

Samuel recovered first. "Liam? What happened?" He sat open-mouthed.

Siobhan fixed her attention on Philip, who looked devastated. Whether due to shock or guilt, she couldn't yet tell. "Philip, we're trying to track Liam's last movements and his mother told us he planned to meet you last night. Did you see him at all yesterday?"

After a few moments during which Siobhan wondered if he'd heard her, Philip made a silent appeal to his father.

"Is my son a suspect?"

Siobhan didn't respond.

"Philip visited one of his other friends yesterday evening, so unless Liam went there, he wouldn't have seen him."

She frowned at Samuel, returning her attention to Philip. "Can you tell me whose house you visited?"

Samuel answered for him, "Mugisa's."

"Can you let your son answer, sir?"

Samuel held her gaze before nodding.

"Philip, is Mugisa one of your friends from college?" She couldn't remember the name from the list of Liam's friends.

"He's known as Matthew Walcott at college. Mugisa's his African name," Philip explained in a small voice.

She remembered the name Matthew Walcott. "Was Liam with you?"

He nodded but avoided her gaze.

"Can you tell me who else was there?"

He mumbled a name which she couldn't make out. A glower from his father made Philip sit up and give them three names in a strong voice.

"What time did you leave the Walcott house?"

"We didn't go to his house." His voice returned to a whisper.

From Samuel's reaction, this was news to him. "Can you tell me where you went?" she said.

He shrugged and received another glower from his father. "Different places. We just hung out."

Siobhan tried to keep the exasperation from her voice. "Please try to remember. Were you inside or did you stay outside?"

"Outside, mostly."

"You must be pretty tough. It didn't stop raining last night."

He shrugged.

She wanted to shake him. "What time did you leave the others?"

"About eight," he mumbled.

"And where did you go then?"

"What do you mean?"

"Did you come home or did you go somewhere else?"

"Surely that's none of your business, Chief Inspector," Samuel interrupted. "If he left Liam at eight, then that's when he last saw him. What he did afterwards has nothing to do with your investigation."

She ignored Samuel. "Did you leave Liam with the others?" She glanced at her notes and read out the four names he'd given her.

"Yes." He looked her in the eye for the first time.

"Okay, Philip. We'll now talk to your friends and find out if they agree with your version of what happened. If they don't, we'll be back." A shadow crossed his features. "I have to remind you we're investigating the murder of one of your friends. If you're withholding information which could help our investigation, not only might it delay us finding your friend's killers, but it's a serious offence, for which you can go to prison."

He looked down at his lap, holding back tears.

Her words had a sobering effect on Samuel. But he must know what time his son came home? She witnessed the struggle taking place in his mind. If she said nothing, he'd fill the silence and she willed Eddy to keep quiet. Samuel cleared his throat then glanced at the door.

An attractive, petite woman stood in the open doorway, her skin darker than Samuel's and Philip's. "Did I hear you threaten my son with prison, Chief Inspector?"

"Good evening, Mrs Mason. You heard me explaining to your son and husband the penalties for withholding evidence or giving a false statement."

The two women stared at each other for several seconds. The hardness in Mrs Mason's expression made Siobhan realise she wouldn't get much more here. Not unless they found inconsistencies between the other boys' statements or evidence of Philip's involvement.

Mrs Mason spoke first. "My son doesn't lie."

Philip seemed to offer a prayer.

Don't celebrate yet, young man, I haven't finished with you. "I hope you're right, Mrs Mason. But I suspect he's hiding something. Can either of you confirm what time your son came home last night?"

Samuel exchanged a look with his wife. "Why is that relevant, Chief Inspector? You already know he left Liam at eight." His objection sounded less assured.

His wife's aggressiveness lessened and Siobhan suspected she didn't want to lie, but obviously had a strong urge to protect her son.

"I went to Jenna's." Philip broke the silence and the tension in the room dropped several notches.

Siobhan's lips compressed as she hid her disappointment. "Can you tell me what time you got to Jenna's?"

"Eight thirty."

"Until what time?"

"Late." He looked at his mother. "About two."

"So you stayed there almost six hours?" Siobhan detected a silent communication passing between the boy and his mother as he nodded. "Did you see Liam in that time?"

Philip shook his head.

"Okay, Philip. I'll need Jenna's full name and address. We'll have to speak to her." She glanced at his mother. "To make sure her recollection agrees with yours." Siobhan changed tack. Philip was lying to them about all or part of the evening and he'd obviously lied to his parents. "Did you wear those clothes last night?"

Philip smoothed his top. "No."

"Can we have a look at what you wore?"

Philip appealed to his father.

"Why, Chief Inspector?" Samuel said. "Philip can't be a suspect."

Siobhan thought she sensed fear behind his indignation. "Your son said he was with Liam until eight. I'm sure they would have made some physical contact during their time together. Even if they brushed against each other, fibres from their clothes would transfer. It will help us if we can eliminate those traces."

"Do you have a warrant?" Philip's mother crossed her arms.

"No, Mrs Mason. But I will get one if necessary."

"Then I suggest you do so, Chief Inspector."

"I hoped we could clear this up without having to resort to warrants. We just want to eliminate your son from our enquiries. If we have to spend unnecessary time and resources doing it, it will harm our chances of catching the killers. I'm sure you don't want that."

Siobhan thought she detected a softening in the father's stance but Mrs Mason's resolve remained unchanged.

"I'm sorry, Chief Inspector, but how you allocate your resources isn't my problem. Nobody's taking any of my son's clothing without a warrant." Her tone left no room for argument. "If you want to speak to my son again, you will only do so with our solicitor present."

Siobhan thanked them and rose from the sofa. She could tell Eddy felt as she did. They'd identified their first suspect. A surge of excitement lifted her mood.

Byron checked the time. The train hadn't moved for twenty minutes and the last announcement, a quarter of an hour earlier, had consisted of an apology for the delay but no explanation. A commotion at the entrance to the carriage presaged the arrival of the guard as he attempted to placate the passengers surrounding him.

"What the hell's going on?" a middle-aged woman in a tweed suit demanded.

"There's a problem on the line. The train ahead of us hit a lorry on a level crossing—"

"When will you clear it? I'm visiting my grandchildren and it's their bed time soon."

"They've removed the lorry but need to check the track before we can run on it. That could take an hour or more."

A groan passed through the carriage.

"Anyone hurt?" Byron asked.

"Lorry driver killed and our guy is badly injured." The guard glared at the woman in tweeds who had the grace to look embarrassed.

With a feeling everything was going against him, Byron tried ringing Adam again and getting no answer got hold of the number for his station.

An out of breath Adam came to the phone. "Byron, what's the panic?"

"You okay?"

"Sure, it's PT. This better be important, I was just serving for the game."

"I need a favour. Philip, Samuel's son, is in trouble. A guy called Ritchie McLaughlin thinks he's killed his nephew."

"Shit!"

"You know him?" A chair scraped across a tiled floor and Byron pictured Adam sitting down.

"Of him. You remember Sarah?"

"Uhuh." Byron and Louisa had both cheered when Sarah had finished with Adam, and he seemed to have finally got over her.

"Her dad, Big Mick, was a mean bastard, but even he was scared of McLaughlin."

"Yeah, well he sounds like a sensible man."

A siren sounded then, as it faded, a voice over a speaker. "First! UMIST Sackville Street."

"Do you have to go?" Byron said.

"Nah, I'm on the second tonight. So, you want me to ride shotgun?"

"I'm on my way up but the train's delayed. Can you go over to my brother's place and make sure he's okay?"

"I'll see what I can do. We're riding minimum, so I'll get someone to come in for me, unless the boss agrees to drop to fours. He's only gone to the university, probably a student burnt their dinner, so shouldn't be long."

"I'd really appreciate it, Adam. If McLaughlin finds out Philip's my nephew…"

"You got history then?"

"I was at school with him." The memory of running the gauntlet of Ritchie and his twin Gerry as he travelled to school, still made the skin on Byron's scalp crinkle. The brothers were third formers when he arrived and every kid in the first three years was their prey. They even picked on older kids. By the time he reached thirteen, Byron began a growth spurt which would take him to his six-foot-five frame. As his strength increased, he resisted and stood up for the younger kids, earning the McLaughlin brothers' enmity until it came to a head.

The school day had finished and Byron had forgotten his art folder. He explained what he'd done to the member of staff on the gate, a young supply-teacher everyone recognised as NTM — Not Teacher Material — and rushed back inside. He'd seen Ritchie hanging about by the bus stop, throwing his weight about. At fifteen, both he and his brother towered over many of the teachers. Byron collected his folder and rushed back to the exit.

As he passed the janitors stores, the door flew open. Ritchie leapt out and punched him on the cheek. Unwilling to drop his work, he covered up, something he'd learned at the boxing club. Ritchie rained blows on Byron, but he caught most on his arms. The force of the punches pushed him backwards, towards the door. Byron glanced down the corridor but couldn't see anyone to save him. Ritchie grabbed the folder and threw it to the floor, scattering Byron's work.

Another punch on his nose made his eyes water. Ritchie seized his shoulder and pushed him into the stores. Byron stumbled over a mop just inside the room but stopped himself falling. Ritchie shoved him into the wall, Byron's head bounced off and stars danced across his vision. His tormentor shut the door and advanced, a nasty grin on his face.

"I'm going to teach you a lesson you won't forget, sambo."

Rage overcame Byron's fear and as Ritchie neared, he head-butted his tormentor and grabbed the mop. He swung the handle round Ritchie's neck and pulled. Ritchie, bigger and stronger, resisted, but Byron knew he mustn't weaken. Now he'd fought back he had to win, otherwise the boy would kill him. His arm muscles strained as he struggled to keep the stick against his opponent's throat.

Ritchie tried every trick, clawing at his eyes and hair, stamping on his shin, slamming him back into the wall, then he went limp. Byron took it for another trick but then the acrid smell of urine filled the small room. A dark patch appeared at Ritchie's crotch. Gasping for breath, with arms and shoulders aching, Byron released one side of the mop handle and Ritchie slid to the floor. Had he killed him?

Then a blow slammed into his back. He lurched across the tiled floor but kept hold of the handle. Gerry, Ritchie's twin, stood between Byron and the door, a rounders bat in his right hand. His brother choked and spluttered on the floor, blood flowing from his nose. Byron should have known Gerry wouldn't be far, they went nowhere alone. He threw the mop at Gerry and ran past his flailing arm. He raced along the corridor, Gerry on his heels, and burst out of the school. The ashen faced teacher avoided his gaze. Byron ran towards the road and seeing a gap in the traffic, darted across it. A flash of red came from his left. The van missed him, it's wash tugging at his clothes, but Gerry wasn't so lucky. Gore from his smashed skull sprayed Byron, making him gag.

Adam didn't speak for a few moments. "Bloody hell, mate. That's a sickener. I'll make sure I get off."

The siren sounded again.

"Shit! We've got a bell."

"Car fire." The voice over the speaker announced.

"I must go. I'll get there as soon—"

Two tone-horns wailed.

"Sorry, those are for me."

Byron placed the phone on his table and picked up his cup. His hand shook, and he sipped the cold coffee.

CHAPTER 7

Busy with their own tasks, none of the invaders paid The Boy any heed. His fierce countenance and weapon enabled him to pass, at a cursory inspection, for one of them. Weaving through the scenes of carnage, he ignored the cries and screams of the victims, his friends and neighbours. The door to his home lay on its side. The invaders had slashed the leather strips forming its hinges and they now flapped from the doorpost.

He ran into the gloomy interior and paused, letting his vision become accustomed to the darkness. A shape lay on the floor and, as his vision adjusted, it resolved into two bodies. In the gloom, he could make out his twelve-year-old sister's features, disfigured by a terrible wound across her cheek.

The man who knelt between her thighs looked up in surprise as he fastened his fly. Eyes already accustomed to the darkness, he saw a boy he didn't recognise. The shout of alarm died in his throat as The Boy buried the tip of the stolen weapon in his neck. With a wet gurgle the man fell and The Boy dropped to his knees to cradle Sanyu's head.

"You okay, Adam?" Mal said.

"Sure, why?" Adam braced himself against the side of the cab as the vehicle negotiated a bend. The two-tone horns blasted a warning.

"You're usually first on the pump. Girlfriend trouble?"

"I wish." Adam laughed. "That was Byron, a mate from the marines. His nephew's upset McLaughlin."

"Ritchie?"

Adam nodded. He needed speak to the station officer on the first pump if he was to get the night off.

"Poor lad. What's he—"

"It's a goer," the driver said.

Adam twisted out of his backward facing seat and glanced through the windscreen at an orange glow, then focussed on fastening his tunic and putting his gloves on.

Mention of Sarah and her father brought back unwelcome memories. He'd convinced himself he'd got over her, but…

"Okay, just a reel and watch out for the suspension," the sub officer instructed as the pump slewed to a stop.

Forty metres away, a car, recognisable as a Citroën saloon, sat in the car park of what looked like a disused factory. Flame exploded out of the car's window openings and licked out from under the bonnet, illuminating the car park and building behind it. Thick smoke from the tyres and upholstery flowed out into a plume, darkening the night sky. The stench of burning rubber filled Adam's nostrils and clung to the back of his throat.

Gravel crunched under his boots and he opened the hose-reel locker. The pump note changed as the power take off engaged and, pulling off a length of reel, he operated the gun to test the jet.

"Off you go, mate, remember what the sub said." Mal pulled a bight of hose off the reel and Adam dragged it towards the burning car.

He recalled the first time he'd heard McLaughlin's name. How worried Sarah had been when her dad came up against him when they'd both bid for the same club. She'd convinced herself Big Mick would get killed, but confounding expectations, he'd backed down.

The heat from the flames boiling out of the broken windows made the skin on Adam's cheeks stretch. He blasted water into the car, generating a cloud of steam and drastically reducing the light available, then he started on the tyres. The sub circled the vehicle at a distance, shining his torch at the building a few metres away. Scorch marks disfigured the roller shutter covering an opening and the adjacent brickwork.

Adam worked his way round to the back of the car, pouring water through the rear windscreen, keen to put the fire out and return to station so he could get off duty. The humiliating memory of Big Mick and two of his men breaking into Adam's house and dragging him out of bed returned. The heat reduced as the flames died and he advanced. A shout from Mal made him jump. Then with a low 'thunk' the hydro-gas suspension exploded. A lump of metal shot past him, missing him by less than a metre. Adam leapt to one side and spots of hot wet ash splattered his skin.

"Bloody hell, mate. You okay?"

"Yeah, sure." Shaken, he focussed on the task in hand, hoping the sub hadn't seen his near miss.

The sound of water dripping replaced the noise of burning. A torch beam from behind him shone on what remained of the number plate.

"Hang fire, young Adam," the sub said and Adam turned the jet off.

Mal walked past and popped the boot with a crowbar, releasing damp smoke. Adam advanced and sprayed the inside.

"You almost done, Adam? I'm on a quarter," the driver said.

"See if you can get the key-holder." The sub shone his torch at the scorched shutter. A stencilled sign warned intruders to keep away and gave the name and number of a security company. "I want to make sure it's not spread inside."

Adam's insides shrunk, that's all he needed. They could be here an hour or more. "Can't we break in, Sub?"

The sub examined the front of the building. "If you can find another way in. I'm not breaking through a roller shutter."

Mal fetched torches and a radio and the two of them set off round the side of the building. They'd passed three openings, each as well protected as the front, when Mal said, "You know what this place was?"

Adam shook his head, wondering who he could get to come in for him if the station officer wouldn't agree to drop a crew member.

"A rope factory. This is the rope walk." He shone his torch at the building. "It's over two hundred metres long."

Adam's steps faltered, they'd covered less than a quarter of the distance. Resigned to having to wait, he said, "Okay, let's go back."

They returned to the front and headlights appeared. A large, dark SUV crunched across the car park before stopping in a shower of gravel. Two bulky figures got out and approached the sub who waited at the entrance to the factory.

"Evening gentlemen. We need to see inside to check the fire's not spread." The sub shone his torch at the scorched metalwork.

"Wait here," a sharp-faced man with an overdeveloped upper body and high-pitched voice said.

"We need to have a look."

"You're not coming in. Don't worry, I can recognise a fire." He showed yellowing teeth. A stink of stale sweat wafted off him and his hooded top displayed damp patches under his armpits.

The shutter over the front door rattled, and he disappeared inside, leaving his sidekick guarding the opening. Lights flickered on behind him and Adam recognised a figure from the doors of a club in town.

The sweaty man returned. "It's all clear."

"Can I have your name?" The sub wrote it down, and they remounted the pump.

Adam checked the time. Eight o'clock. They'd been there fifty minutes. He'd be back in the station in twenty. Was Byron still stuck? He put his head into the gap between the rear and front cab. "Sub, I need the night off. Family problems."

"Sure, we'll sort it—"

"FT, Echo five two one." The radio burst into life.

"Go ahead."

"Proceed to chemical incident…"

Adam cursed and sat down, hoping Byron was mistaken about the danger his nephew faced.

Siobhan shivered as she waited outside Jenna Young's house, determined to test Philip's alibi. She shouldn't let personal feelings intrude but the boy's mother had got right up her nose. The light came on and a figure moved behind the stained glass in the top half of the door. A short plump man with curly brown hair, a high forehead and a welcoming smile opened the door.

The dog collar made Siobhan hesitate. "Mr Young?"

"Hello, please call me Geoff," he said in a strong well-modulated voice, and she had no trouble picturing him in a pulpit. "Come in out of the cold."

He ushered them into a tiled hallway with a wooden staircase on the right side, the bright red runner in the centre clashing with the burgundy walls. The aroma of mushroom soup pervaded the air.

"I'm Chief Inspector Quinn, Mr Young." She introduced Eddy, and both showed their IDs. "Can we speak to Jenna?"

"Jenna?" His eyebrows shot up. "She's not in trouble?" He laughed at the idea.

"There's nothing to worry about, Mr Young. We just need to speak to her about one of her friends from college."

He looked relieved. "I'll just fetch her. She was on the phone. Do you want to take a seat in there?" He pointed to a door on their left. "Can I offer you tea or coffee?"

Both declined and entered through the doorway. Siobhan fumbled for a switch and clicked on the overhead light. A large reproduction Chippendale dining table with matching chairs stood on a carpet of yet another shade of red. A glass-fronted dresser stood against the wall facing the window. They took two seats facing the door. Siobhan couldn't account for a vague sense of unease.

The door opened and a tall, good-looking girl, with waist-length blond hair entered. Siobhan remembered, as an awkward teenager, craving the approval of girls like her.

"Chief Inspector, my daughter, Jenna," Geoff announced.

Jenna smiled at both of them, seeming unfazed by a visit from two detectives.

"Hello, Jenna. I'm Chief Inspector Quinn and this is Sergeant Arkwright. Can you both please sit?" She indicated the two chairs opposite her.

Siobhan explained the reason for their visit. She studied Jenna as she told them about Liam's death. Their shock at the news seemed genuine. Siobhan began the questioning by establishing Jenna's identity and confirming she knew Philip. Jenna answered her questions in a pleasant voice, at ease with authority figures.

"What time did Philip arrive at your house?" Siobhan asked.

Jenna hesitated for a moment and sucked the tip of her left thumb before replying, "About eight thirty."

"And what time did he leave?"

For the first time she became uneasy. "About one." She blushed and looked towards her father. "Actually, it was nearer two."

"Are you sure?" If Philip left Jenna's at one, he couldn't account for an hour. She smiled at the girl who nodded uncertainly.

"You realise lying to the police is a serious matter." Eddy spoke for the first time. "This is a murder investigation. If you're not sure what time he left, say so."

The girl's eyelids fluttered and her confident air slipped. "You can't believe Philip had anything to do with it."

Neither of them responded.

"I'm sure it *was* two o'clock." She appealed to her father, licking her lips.

"Chief Inspector, my daughter wouldn't lie to you."

Yet another parent convinced their little angels never lied. Siobhan sensed a hardening in the girl's attitude and realised she would stick to her story. She ended the interview and with a warning they might want to speak to Jenna again, they left.

As they drove away, Eddy spoke first. "I wouldn't mind betting that phone call was from lover boy, telling her what to say to us."

Siobhan agreed, considering her next move. "I want to break Philip's alibi tonight. If we can get just one of them to contradict him, the others will fold."

"Okay, Boss. Who do you want to see next?"

Siobhan didn't need to consider. "Matthew Walcott."

Eddy knew the address. The Walcott house, in contrast to the two they'd just visited, occupied a less affluent part of the city. They drove into a narrow street lined with red brick semis, small front gardens separating them from the road. The owners had concreted over most to make parking spaces for their cars. Eddy pulled up halfway along, outside one of the few houses retaining a garden.

As they waited for someone to answer the door, Siobhan checked her surroundings. A profusion of evergreen shrubs enclosed a tiny patch of manicured lawn. A light came on and a chain rattled. The door opened six inches and Siobhan took out her wallet to let the occupant read her ID.

"Hello. Mrs Walcott?"

"Uh huh." The woman peered at the picture as Siobhan introduced herself then closed the door and removed the chain. The door opened to reveal a large middle-aged woman wearing a floral housecoat and a pair of colourful, plastic-framed reading glasses resting on her head.

"Sorry, Chief Inspector, but you can't be too careful."

Siobhan agreed and introduced Eddy, adding, "We'd like a word with Matthew."

"Oh, I'm sorry but he's not in. What's this about?"

Siobhan tried to hide her disappointment. "We need to speak to him about one of his friends from college."

Mrs Walcott smiled. "He's with a friend from college now; Philip Mason."

Siobhan pulse quickened. "When did he go there?"

"He went straight from college; I think he's having his tea there."

They left and returned to the car.

"Do you want us to return to the Mason's house, Boss? See if he *is* there?" Eddy didn't sound convinced.

"I think these lads make a point of lying to their parents about where they are. I'd love to find out where they really go."

"Do you want to call it a night?" Eddy checked the time.

Although frustrated at missing Matthew, Siobhan fizzed with energy and wanted to press on. "Let's see if Ryan Collins is home. Who questioned him?"

Eddy checked his list. "Stefan and Debbie. I'll give them a bell. Find out if they got anything out of him."

Ten minutes later, they pulled up outside the home of Ryan Collins, a terraced house with a blue door. A large red-faced man snatched it open. He wore a lumberjack shirt with the sleeves rolled up to the elbows and a pair of creased brown trousers. No security precautions for Mr Collins, Siobhan noted and, looking at his ham-like forearms, she wasn't surprised. It would take a brave intruder to try to get past him.

"Have you forgotten something?" he demanded in a pronounced Connemara accent.

The voice transported Siobhan to her childhood. "Mr Collins?" she asked, finding her accent growing more pronounced.

He dismissed her open wallet. "No need, I can tell what you are." His breath carried the hint of alcohol.

"Can I have a word with Ryan?"

His smile faded. "The other two spoke to him. Now, why do you want to speak to the lad again?"

"I need to ask him about yesterday evening."

"That's what they asked." He crossed his arms.

"I appreciate that, Mr Collins."

Eddy moved closer, reacting to the man's increasing hostility.

"Look, the lad's done nothing wrong. I won't have him harassed. You lot think all youngsters are up to no good."

"I can assure you that's not the case, Mr Collins." Siobhan kept her voice level. "We need five minutes with your son to clarify something."

She watched the play of emotions across his face as he came to a decision. "Sorry officers. The lad's had a nasty shock, what with his friend being killed."

The door slammed shut before Siobhan realised what was happening and the click of a mortice lock confirmed Mr Collins' decision. She wanted to kick the door.

Philip took the last of the plates off the drainer and wiped it with the damp tea towel. His parents had maintained the semblance of normality during the meal, parrying his sisters' inquisitive questions about the police. The murder of one of their brother's friends had excited them and even the normally placid Cecily grew animated. His disdain for their childishness faded as he realised he'd have felt the same if this happened to one of them before yesterday.

The doorbell rang, making him jump. Had the police returned with a warrant? Then he realised it must be Uncle Byron, here at last.

Rebecca put down the wine glass she'd just rinsed and dried her hands but Samuel, already by the kitchen door, said, "I'll get it. It's probably Jehovah's witnesses."

"It's all right, Dad," Cecily called from the hall. "I've got it."

The door opened and Cecily screamed. Philip froze. Angry voices shouted. Rebecca gave a cry and grabbing a knife from the block by the cooker, rushed into the hall.

By the time Philip roused himself the door had slammed behind her. Something told him to be careful, and he eased it open, peering through the gap. A large figure had forced his way into the hall, two more stood behind him in the doorway. Philip's insides constricted. Samuel faced them in his chair, grim determination etched on his features. Beside him Rebecca held the ten-inch butcher's knife, pointing it at the men.

Cecily sat on the floor, shocked but thankfully unhurt. He studied the intruders. All three wore masks. He'd wait to see what happened, then pile in, catch them by surprise. He needed a weapon and remembered his mum's wooden rolling pin. One man waved a stick at Samuel and Philip recognised the shotgun with a start. His stomach did a somersault.

"Nobody move." A rough voice with a Salford accent ordered.

The biggest of the three invaders looked at the knife and laughed. The shotgun moved away from Samuel and pointed at Rebecca. Silence reigned as the two sides stared at each other.

"Where's the boy?" the voice demanded.

Philip looked at the back door. Could he get out without the men hearing him? But if he escaped, they'd hurt his family.

CHAPTER 8

Although his sister's eyes remained open, she would see no more. Beautiful, loving and gentle, she was the star around which their lives revolved. Big, hot tears fell and splashed onto her cooling body. Numbed by grief, The Boy didn't at first hear the sounds from the next room.

Guttural grunts overlaid the low moans coming through the open doorway. Unable to think, instinct told him to investigate. He struggled to his feet and, wiping away his tears, he staggered to the doorway. His eyes, now accustomed to the gloom, could make out the scene, almost a replica of the one in the outer room. This time his mother was the victim, and she was still alive.

As she became aware of his presence, she arched her neck to look at him. Her eyes met his with an expression he'd never seen in them. Soft brown irises, which had daily looked into his with love and kindness, reflected her pain and shame. Transfixed, he didn't notice his assailant until a muscular arm snaked round his neck and dragged him out. It was the last he ever saw of his mother.

The taxi dropped Byron on the main road and, already late, he hurried down the uneven pavement, almost tripping over a bulge created by an errant root. The most expensive houses in the city and he had to stumble along in the dark to reach them. He recognised the gateway to his brother's house and beyond it a scruffy car with someone sitting in the driver's seat. Not only did the car look out of place, but from what he remembered, the houses had plenty of off-road parking round here. He checked for a taxi plate but didn't see one.

He considered investigating it, but the imminent reunion with Samuel, and Rebecca, concerned him far more. They'd met up at Dad's, the Christmas before last, and Rebecca didn't even speak to him, barely acknowledging Louisa. Even Philip and his sisters had looked embarrassed. He paused at the entrance to their drive. Despite the cold they'd left the front door open and people stood in the opening. With a growing sense of unease he strode towards the house. A horn blast sounded and without thinking, he understood what was happening. He dropped his bag and ran, hoping the horn would cover up the sound of his footsteps. Two men filled the doorway, with a third further in the house. Byron would have to do this right; otherwise it could end in disaster. Three feet from his target one of the men reacted. But far too late.

Byron's shoulder caught him under the ribs and slammed the man, face first, into the doorframe. The impact made the frame shudder and deflected Byron into the second man. The man's skull hit the edge of the door and he fell. Byron's momentum took him on to his target, the third man inside the house.

Byron smashed into him, his head making first contact. The impact propelled the man forward towards a smaller figure beyond him. They landed in a heap. Byron fell to his knees, stunned by the impact. He shook his head and surveyed the room.

A girl sat on the floor beside the door. She stared at the man he'd hit in the kidney and screamed. A ribbon of blood emerged from under him, seeming to come from whoever he'd hit. A woman, it must be Rebecca. The girl's screams took on a hysterical edge.

Byron scrambled to his feet. He must make sure the three intruders no longer presented a threat. He checked the two men in the doorway: both unconscious.

Samuel had wheeled himself to the woman's side and struggled to disentangle her from the third man. Byron stepped across and dragged the groaning figure off her. Blood saturated her right hand and forearm; Samuel examined her and Byron could tell from his reaction she wasn't hurt.

The girl, who he now realised must be one of his nieces, had gone to her mother and knelt over her, sobbing. Byron rolled the figure over and saw at once the source of the blood. The knife Rebecca held had removed most of the man's left ear and blood saturated his torn ski mask. Samuel stared at Byron, not appearing to recognise him. Byron realised his brother was going into shock.

"Samuel," Byron said. "Can you see to this?" He pointed at the man's ruined ear.

Once he noticed the wounded man, Samuel gathered himself and examined the injury. "Philip," he called.

The kitchen door opened, and a dazed Philip stood there. The young man had grown since Byron last saw him and now stood almost the same height as his uncle.

"Go to my study and get my bag."

Philip didn't react for a few moments then disappeared into Samuel's study.

"Cecily." The girl didn't respond. "Cecily," Samuel repeated louder, but she just looked at him blankly.

"Come on darling." Rebecca stroked her daughter with her clean hand. "I'm fine. Now let me up. The man needs our help."

Rebecca struggled to her feet, and Byron offered his hand but she ignored him and rushed into the kitchen. Cecily, seeing him for the first time, gave a tentative smile. He held out an arm and she clutched it. She sobbed, making her thin body tremble, and he made soothing noises.

He checked the two men by the door, but they hadn't regained consciousness. Philip returned with a bag which he handed to his father. Samuel took out a pair of scissors, leant over the side of his chair, and cut off the rest of the mask to expose the wound. Byron recognised Ritchie McLaughlin straight away. Conflicting emotions passed through him as he recalled the fear McLaughlin had prompted during so much of his school life.

Rebecca returned with a large first aid kit and examined McLaughlin, appearing to recognise him. How would she know a lowlife like him? She shook herself and with practised efficiency, tended to the man's wounds. McLaughlin groaned and began to struggle but Samuel restrained him.

"Calm down," he said. "We're trying to help you. You've got a nasty cut and you need to keep still."

The doctor's reassuring tone calmed the injured man and McLaughlin subsided. A sound by the door reminded Byron he hadn't checked the other two for weapons. One of them groaned.

Byron took two paces towards him then stopped. The barrels of a sawn-off shotgun appeared in the open doorway. Two small, perfect circles pointing at him. Only from this distance they didn't look so small. Behind them, a masked newcomer stared at him from the doorstep. He should have remembered the driver and Byron cursed himself for his carelessness: *I'm too rusty for this.*

Siobhan locked her car and retrieved the keys to her flat. The frustration of the encounter with Mr Collins had made her more determined to press on until Eddy persuaded her to call it a day. He looked exhausted, and she realised it had been over eighteen hours since she'd met him in the fire-blackened house. She recognised her propensity to push too hard. Not everyone shared her stamina.

She reached her flat and let herself in. She'd gone beyond hunger; maybe she'd just have a bath and go to bed. Tomorrow promised to be another long day. She entered the bathroom and a damp cold seeped into her. As she fetched the heater from her bedroom, her phone rang, making her jump. Few people had her number, and work would use her mobile. It must be her mother, wishing her goodnight.

"Hi, Mammy."

"Hello, Siobhan."

Her heart shrank, and she didn't speak for a few seconds. "Hello, Niall," she said through gritted teeth. "Who gave you this number?"

"That's not a very friendly greeting."

"You haven't answered my question." *I bet Mammy gave it to him, she's still hoping we get back together.*

"I didn't realise I was being interrogated."

She could picture his petulant expression. "What do you want?"

"I just wanted to say welcome to Manchester. How's the new place?"

She had no wish to chat to her ex. "Well, now you've said it." His words sank in. "And what do you mean welcome to Manchester?"

"Just what I said. I thought we could meet for a drink."

Her jaw muscles clenched. "That will not happen, Niall."

"Siobhan, I'm sure we can work things out. Why don't we just—"

"No, Niall." She lowered her voice. "We both agreed when we split up, to give each other space, and following me to Manchester isn't—"

"No. *We* didn't agree. *You* decided when you dumped me." He paused, and she heard him crying.

"Niall." She took a deep breath. "It's late and I've work tomorrow..."

"Yeah sure, work," he snorted. "When did you become a hard-hearted bitch Siobhan?"

"Don't swear at me, Niall, and don't ring me again."

She slammed down the handset and stared at the phone for several seconds. Thoughts of a relaxing sleep vanished under a surge of anger. Why the hell couldn't he accept it was over? She unplugged the phone, changed into her tracksuit and, within ten minutes, she set off running on a route she'd picked out on the day she moved in. With every step she took, the worries and stresses of the day melted away.

Siobhan ran fast, her pulse over 180 but her breathing steady. Her leg muscles tightened as her feet flew over the pavement but she'd almost reached home. She passed her car and froze at the sight of a figure fumbling with the lock of her front door. Eddy had warned her of the area's reputation for crime.

Adam wore a bright yellow chemical suit and breathing apparatus. The thought of letting Byron down made him tense. He and Mal reported to the BA control point set up outside the entrance to the building containing the research lab. A line of black hose-reel and a fatter red hose disappeared through the open door. Half an hour of running about, setting into the water supplies and preparing the decontamination unit had made both of them hot. They now formed one of two relief crews. The other team stood by a low wall, a big bulky figure and beside him a petite companion.

"Uh, oh, look who's here," Mal said, grinning at him.

Adam stifled a curse, he'd not spoken to Julie since their intense year-long relationship ended at the start of the summer.

He reported to the BA control officer while Mal joined the other team.

"How are they doing?" Adam gestured at the board which contained six tags, three teams of two.

"The first lot should be out in ten." The officer gestured at Julie. "They're due to relieve them and you two will take over as emergency team." His radio crackled, and he responded, leaving Adam with no option but to join the others.

"Hi Adam," Julie's bright greeting surprised him.

Wayne, her companion, stood and clasped his hand. "Hey, Adam, good to see you, mate."

The contrast to their first meeting, when Wayne tried to bully, then humiliate him, made Adam smile. They'd never be friends but shared a mutual respect after saving each other's lives. With a sense of relief he relaxed and joined in the conversation, enjoying chatting to Julie. In a subconscious gesture, she reached for Wayne's hand and entwined their fingers.

A jolt passed through Adam's insides. But she'd always hated Wayne, making fun of his macho posturing. What the hell was she doing with a bozo like him? Although he'd instigated the break-up he recognised the signs of jealousy.

A summon from the control officer broke into his thoughts. The four of them rushed to the entry point.

"We've got a problem, go under air and I'll brief you," he said.

Adam's pulse jerked, and he hooked the facemask harness over his head. Whistles shrilled and regulators hissed as four BA sets started up.

"Team one's gone missing," the control officer continued, naming the crewmembers. "Last seen firefighting on the first floor of block B2." He tapped the plans of the site; a copy of which Adam had studied on their way. "The hose-reel should lead straight to it. Be careful, the lab's full of nasties, and if possible, avoid this cabinet." He held up a picture of a metal cupboard with a chemical hazard sign on it. "That's where the hydrofluoric acid is kept. Don't get anywhere near it, as it will pass through your suit *and* fire kit."

And straight through your skin to attack the bone, Adam added silently.

The crews finished dressing, checking each other to make sure no part of their skin or fire kit remained exposed. The distress units twittered as they removed their tags and handed them to the officer. More crews arrived.

Adam and Mal followed Julie's team to the entrance. Wayne picked up the black hose-reel and paid it through his hand as they entered the building. At least visibility remained good inside, with harsh strip lights illuminating the institutional corridor. The two lines of hose followed a parallel path but after fifty paces, the black hose-reel led them up a flight of stairs. Mal kept the entry control officer informed of their progress over his radio.

A thin haze floated at ceiling height, getting thicker as they advanced. The noise from four regulators and four pairs of boots, echoed off the walls. Then a faint dirge sounded, and Adam's blood quickened. A pair of doors split the corridor, the two halves kept apart by the hose. Julie reached them first and pushed.

The noise increased. Unmistakeable. A distress unit. Apart from training exercises, he'd only used one once, and the incident still haunted him. Julie hadn't been BA that night, but all four of them hadn't forgotten the ordeal.

Wayne moved ahead of Julie, a protective gesture she seemed to allow, then they advanced, moving fast. The smoke grew denser, making progress more hazardous. The strip lighting ceased working, and the temperature rose. Adam ducked down below the haze. The colour warned him this wasn't just smoke.

Ahead, a torch beam shone upwards, lighting up the ceiling. The lamp attached to the chest of a yellow clad figure on the floor.

"Seen him," Wayne replied to Adam's warning.

As they got closer Adam noticed the second figure, slumped against the base of the wall. Debris covered the corridor and pieces of ceiling tile hung down on wires. The sitting figure attempted to rise when he saw them but didn't have the strength.

His companion lay on his side, his chemical suit blackened and ripped. An explosion had destroyed the doorway to their left, leaving a jagged hole. Flames flickered in the opening, but the hose-reel lay under rubble.

Working quickly, Wayne and Adam, the two biggest, picked up the prone figure and the other two helped his team mate. The temperature increased as the flames got hold. By the time they reached the stairs, reinforcements with water arrived and the parties exchanged information as they passed each other.

Outside, ambulances waited and after decontamination, the two injured firefighters travelled to hospital. Adam checked the time. Nine thirty. Byron must have arrived by now.

Byron raised his hands to waist height, palms downwards, and retreated. The gunman advanced into the house, waving the shotgun like a baton.

"Get away from him," he shouted and pointed the shotgun towards Samuel and Rebecca.

"They're helping your friend," Byron said.

The gunman swung the gun towards him and gave a start. His panting betrayed his agitation and Byron tensed, concerned he'd pull the trigger by mistake.

"Did I ask you to speak?" The gunman's voice wavered, and he stared at Byron.

Byron looked away, not wanting to antagonise someone so close to the edge.

"Step back. Now!" he demanded.

Byron moved away from him and the gunman blinked before scanning the room. One of the men in the doorway groaned. The gunman kicked both of them and stepped into the room. He gestured with the shotgun and Byron retreated. The man's forefinger rested on the trigger guard, but Byron couldn't risk tackling him. In this space, a sawn-off would do untold damage. Philip and Cecily also retreated and Byron gestured towards Samuel's study. Philip took the hint.

Samuel broke the silence. "Your friend's lost a lot of blood; he needs to go to hospital. The bleeding's stopped but he'll need stitches and medication."

The gunman hesitated and studied McLaughlin. A large blood-soaked bandage covered his left ear, and the exposed skin round it looked pale as a fish's belly. The gunman hesitated and Samuel took this as permission to continue his treatment.

Philip had edged towards the door to his father's study. Byron needed to distract the gunman without getting shot. A guy this on-edge would either freeze or shoot anything that moved. The two fallen men in the doorway stirred and, without prompting, the gunman checked on them. Byron allowed himself to relax. The gunman jerked the barrel at him, holding it in trembling hands, and took a deep breath. The first of the two men at the door regained his feet and leant against the frame before extending a hand to the other.

Rebecca said, "We've done what we can, but it's only temporary." She pointed to the bandage. "As my husband said, he will need stitches."

The gunman nodded. McLaughlin looked to have recovered and he sat up. Philip had slipped half way through the door into Samuel's study so Byron stepped towards McLaughlin and extended a hand.

"Get back!" The gunman waved his shotgun and Byron obeyed.

One of the men from the door helped McLaughlin to his feet. Once upright he scanned the room. "Where's the boy?" His voice shook.

"Forget him, Ritch—" the gunman said.

McLaughlin glared at him, then addressed the two men he'd arrived with. "The fucker can't be far, find him."

"We'd better get going."

"Your friend's right," Byron said, resisting the temptation to use Ritchie's name.

McLaughlin faced him, seeing him for the first time and recognition bloomed. "You. I should have fucking—"

"Let's go!" the gunman said, his voice rising.

A siren sounded on the main road and McLaughlin led the way out, giving Byron a look to chill his insides. Byron had hoped to have a few days up here before McLaughlin found out he'd returned.

Philip saw Byron gesture towards his father's study and checking the gunman's attention was elsewhere, he shuffled backwards towards the door. With his heart thumping he willed the man to keep looking away. His father spoke and

Philip edged closer to the door, perspiration running down his spine. Cecily watched him but didn't move. Philip felt bad leaving her, but they wanted him and if he disappeared, they'd leave. Now Uncle Byron had arrived and he'd make sure nobody hurt his sisters.

He reached the door and his mother said something. He slipped through the doorway. The gunman shouted at him to stop and Philip's heart jerked. Then he realised he wasn't speaking to him and continued. He waited in his father's study and tried to control his pulse. After a few moments he crept towards the French windows leading into their garden. Voices rumbled behind him, sounding like they were arguing.

The click as he opened the lock made him jump. He froze, waiting for the blast of a shotgun in his back. When nothing happened, he exhaled and eased the door open. Once outside, he pushed the door to, afraid to close it in case it made a noise. If anyone came into the room, they'd notice.

He hesitated. Should he run for help or stay and make sure his family was safe? He'd check first, but remained ready to run into the darkness if anyone should follow him. His pulse still racing, he worked his way towards the kitchen window and peered in, trying to see into the hallway.

"Hello, Philip." Mugisa's voice made him jump; then a cold, sharp blade pressed against the back of his neck.

CHAPTER 9

The man ripped The Boy from the room where his mother was being violated. Unable to take in what he'd seen The Boy didn't struggle. The powerful grip on his windpipe prevented air entering his lungs.

His mother, galvanised by the sight of the man seizing her baby son, increased her struggles. Although weakened by her wounds, she managed to dredge up the strength to dislodge her attacker. Caught by surprise, the man fell back. She rolled over and rose from a kneeling position. The man recovered and, seeing his prize escaping, grabbed his assault rifle from the corner where he'd left it.

Not wanting to waste bullets, he hefted the weapon, and brought it crashing into the back of her skull. She fell in a tangle of limbs, a puppet with its strings severed. Her killer, frustrated at having his pleasure curtailed, kicked out at her lifeless body.

In the next room, his captor held The Boy by the scruff of his neck and showed him the body of the man who had defiled his sister. The giant who held him glared at The Boy. Despite confronting the biggest man he'd ever seen, The Boy remained unmoved and returned the stare, challenging the man to do his worst. The man produced a knife and held the point to The Boy's throat.

Byron stood on the doorstep watching the four men walk away from the house, relief at their departure mixed with concern they would return. McLaughlin wouldn't let the matter go; especially as he'd blame Byron for his humiliation.

His case lay on the drive but he waited until their car left before retrieving it. When he returned, his brother held Cecily while Rebecca soothed her. A second girl he recognised stood at the bottom of the stairs and surveyed the scene.

"Wow, what's gone on here?" she said, surveying the hallway. "Uncle Byron!" she yelled in surprise.

"Lucy?" Both girls had grown so much since he'd last seen them.

She smiled before coming over to give him a hug.

"Samuel, Rebecca," he greeted her parents.

Rebecca looked at him coolly. "Byron."

Samuel loosened his hold on Cecily and nodded a greeting. "What are you doing here?"

Byron said, "Good thing I came."

"I'm sorry, I meant…"

"Philip called me." He jerked his thumb towards Samuel's study. "He said you had an unwelcome visitor at lunchtime. The same gang I presume."

Rebecca nodded. "Just one, the one I…"

"Did you recognise him?" Byron asked his brother.

"Should I have?"

"Ritchie McLaughlin. Two years above me at school. He's got — had a twin brother. A nasty piece of work, even then." The memory of their last confrontation still haunted Byron and no doubt McLaughlin recalled it vividly.

"He'd have been a few years below me." Samuel looked around and asked, "Where's Philip?"

"In here." Byron entered the study and switched on the light.

The draft hit him before he saw the open doors and he stepped outside, peering into the darkness and calling the boy's name. He dismissed his apprehension. McLaughlin's men couldn't have got hold of Philip. Byron had seen them get straight into the car and the only thing on their minds was to escape and get their boss patched up.

He returned to the study where the rest of the family waited. "Do you have any outside lights?"

Lucy flicked a switch beside the doors and harsh white light filled the garden.

"We've got sensors, but we disabled them. The cats…" Samuel explained.

Byron took a few minutes to check the garden, his apprehension growing as he searched. Rebecca joined him with a torch and they checked under the hedges and the small orchard at the far end. The shed and greenhouse were locked and looked undisturbed. The rest of the family gathered round the doors, looking worried. Byron returned and shook his head in answer to Samuel's unasked question.

"He's probably made a run for it. He wasn't to know those men would leave like they did. That would have been the sensible thing to do." Despite his unease, Byron attempted to sound reassuring.

"Where would he have gone?" Samuel didn't sound convinced.

"If it was me, I'd wait on the streets near the house. I'll have a quick look."

"I'll come with you." Rebecca gripped her husband's shoulder, and he stroked her hand. "I'll get my coat and another torch."

Adam returned from the X-ray department to the waiting room, to await the next stage of the battery of checks he'd been sent to take. Two pumps sat idle in the hospital car park until their crew members re-joined them. The other three were no longer in the waiting room. Getting a can of Vimto from the vending machine, he took a seat. The clock on the wall clicked as the minute hand moved. Gone midnight.

Footsteps echoed on the tiled floor and Julie arrived. "You finished?"

"I've had the x-rays but someone's going to check my respiratory function."

"Pain, isn't it? We weren't exposed to anything."

"I suppose they've got to cover their backs." He remembered training with tear-gas in the marines. They'd told him to wash his burning eyes out with cold water and given him a mug of tea.

Julie bought a cup of something from the vending machine and sat next to him. A sweet chocolatey smell temporarily eclipsed the overriding whiff of disinfectant and stale urine. They sat in uncomfortable silence.

Julie broke it before he did. "You're wondering how long I've been with Wayne."

"It's a surprise. More of a shock really." He grinned. "Astonishing, startling—"

"Astounding."

"Staggering."

"Stunning." Julie's grin became a laugh, and they both relaxed. "He's all right once you get to know him."

"Hmmm, I'm sure."

"That sounded shit. He's a really nice guy, but he hides behind a big bad wolf persona."

"We're all hiding something." Adam drained his can and crushed it.

"He worried about you finding out."

"Why?" A sense of dread tugged at his guts. "You weren't together when we were?"

"Of course not. We've only been an item for three weeks. He thought you might be upset and mention…" She hesitated.

"He saved my life."

"You saved his."

"Yeah, but I value mine a lot more than I do his, so I'm still in his debt."

She returned his smile. "But you covered up for him when he missed that woman."

"It's a mistake anyone could have made."

"But you didn't, and you know what people are like."

Adam did. "Yeah, but I only found her because I *knew* she was there. I'd have ripped the walls apart."

"Thanks. I told him you'd say that." She gripped his hand, hers still hot from the drink.

He returned the pressure. "I'm glad you've moved on, found someone…"

"What about you?" She studied him from under her auburn fringe, her big brown eyes seeming to see his innermost thoughts.

"Nobody special."

"Not someone you want to start a family with?"

"Nah."

"You're still only twenty-seven, Adam. I'm not even going to think about kids 'til I hit thirty."

The reminder of the circular arguments they'd had in the lead up to their breakup broke the spell and brought a return to the awkward atmosphere. Adam squeezed the already flat can, deciding whether to have another, just to get away.

"Adam Sterling?" a nurse said.

With a surge of relief he stood and followed her.

Byron searched every garden he could get into, marvelling at how many people didn't lock their gates. He ignored barking dogs and security lights as he examined dark corners. His thoughts strayed to McLaughlin. He'd hoped to have time up here before McLaughlin found out he'd come back, so he could confront him on his own terms. Now he'd have to be on his guard from day one, but first they needed to find Philip.

A figure jogged towards him out of the darkness. "Philip?" Rebecca called.

"Afraid not," Byron said.

For a moment her disappointment almost brought forth tears but Rebecca was made of stern stuff. "Did you search every garden?"

"Those I got into—"

"Which ones did you miss out?"

"Did you want me to break into the houses as well?"

She glared at him for a second before deflating. "Sorry."

"He may have gone further afield. Do you want to get the car?"

She started for home, not waiting for him. He caught her up as they reached their drive.

"He might have gone to Jenna's, his girlfriend," she said.

"Which way would he go?" Byron said.

"Why?"

"If he's taking the trouble to stay out of sight, he might not have arrived yet, but if he has, he'll be safe and comfortable until we get there."

She hesitated. "Okay."

Rebecca followed a route from her house, pausing at each junction for Byron to check the side roads and alleyways.

Ten minutes later, she pulled up outside a semi slightly smaller than her house. "This is where Jenna lives."

Byron opened the passenger door.

She stopped him. "I'll go."

"I'll come with you."

"No need." She slammed her door and strode to the house.

Byron suppressed his irritation and waited. Although Jenna's parents must have liberal views to allow her to go out with Philip, the sight of a strange six-foot-five black man at their door at this time of night might be too much. Rebecca returned two minutes later, her body language telling Byron what he needed to know. She sat in the driver's seat fiddling with the keys.

For the first time in his memory, Byron felt sorry for his sister-in-law. "Is there another route he might have taken?"

"Hmmm. Possibly." She started the engine, and they returned by a different route.

They fell into the same routine, Byron ducking out to search at each junction. Ahead, he saw the first of the many parks in the vicinity, its gates locked. She pulled up and killed the engine.

"What are you doing?" Byron asked.

"I'm going to see if he's in there." She crossed her arms.

"How will we search such a big area in the dark?"

Anger flashed in her eyes but after a few seconds she started the engine. They returned home in an uncomfortable silence. Byron didn't think he'd ever spent so long in Rebecca's company, even before…

Samuel and the girls looked at them expectantly and Byron, although sure something had happened to his nephew, felt the pressure to be positive. "I bet he's gone to one of his mates."

"There's Mugisa, he spends a lot of time with him," Samuel said.

Byron remembered the phone call. "He wouldn't go there."

"Why not?" His brother frowned.

"He's right, Dad, they've had a row," Cecily said, "Mugisa came round this afternoon and Philip threw him out."

"Why would he do that? They're so close," Rebecca said.

Byron struggled to frame his reply, conscious of his promise to Philip. But this changed everything. "This Mugisa's involved in what happened to Philip's friend last night."

"The murder? But Philip wasn't involved!" Rebecca's eyes filled with tears.

"No, but he knows the identity of the killers."

The second pump pulled out of the hospital car park with a full crew and the sub booked them available. Adam slumped in the back, thinking about his conversation with Julie.

"What's happened to the two lads we got out, Sub?" Mal asked, sticking his head through the gap into the front cab.

"One's got concussion and the other's has a dislocated ankle, plus they're not sure if the lad with the damaged suit has been exposed to chemicals."

"Someone will be doing a lot of paperwork."

"They've only had the new suits a few months. They'll have to explain why they didn't use the older ones."

"Yeah, that *will* be the focus of any investigation." Mal gave a wry smile and returned to his seat. "You had a good chat to Julie."

"We're still mates."

"I've never stayed mates with an ex. Just doesn't work, too much baggage to get in the way."

Maybe he was right. Adam checked the watch on the BA board. Ten past one. He should ring Byron, explain why he'd let him down. "Sub, can I use the phone?"

"You're not ringing your family in Hong Kong are you? Everyone over here will be asleep."

The comment reminded him he'd not spoken to his mother for a few weeks. "Directory enquires, then a local call to Didsbury."

"Sure, you still want the night off?"

"That's why I need to make a call."

Back at the station, he left Mal to change their cylinders and used the phone in the station commander's office. After getting the number for the only Dr Mason in Didsbury, he scribbled it on a message pad. He dialled the first few numbers, then hesitated. A vision of waking up a sleeping household flashed into his mind. But a GP would be used to calls at all hours.

Samuel answered on the second ring. "Dr Mason's residence."

The deep voice ignited the memory of meeting a large, vigorous man who moved like an athlete. "Hello, Samuel, it's Adam Sterling, is—"

"Byron's friend. How are you, Adam?"

"Fine, thanks. Is Byron there?"

"He's … out. When did he tell you he'd be here?"

"He rang from the train, told me he was worried about Philip."

Samuel didn't speak for a few seconds. "Philip's gone missing. That's where Byron is, looking for him. I hoped this call was to tell me they'd found him."

"I'm sorry. Byron asked me to come over but I'm on nights…" A surge of guilt made his throat close up. "I'll come round—"

"I'm not sure what you can do now. Shall I get Byron to ring you when he gets back?"

Adam ended the call. The feeling he'd let Byron down weighing heavy.

Byron held his finger on the doorbell until a light came on. An angry voice muttered, and the door opened, revealing a thick chain and, behind it, the sleep-rimed eyes of a middle-aged man.

"Mr Walcott?" Byron asked.

"Yes, what do you damn want?" He swore like a man unused to the act.

"Can I speak to Mugisa?"

The man looked puzzled for a moment. "Matthew you mean. He's asleep. What do you want with him?"

Byron hesitated. If the boy was in bed, he couldn't have taken Philip.

Rebecca pushed past him. "Mr Walcott, it's Rebecca Mason, can you please check my son Philip's not with him?"

The man gave an exasperated sigh. "I'm not disturbing my son at this time of night. Now go, before you wake the whole house, or I'll call the police."

The door slammed and Byron returned to the car. Rebecca stared at the door for a few seconds, but then followed him and they set off for home. Byron clung to the hope Philip was hiding out at a friend's house. They'd left Samuel with the job of phoning them, but at this time in the morning, the calls wouldn't be welcome.

Rebecca gripped the steering wheel like a lifebelt in a hurricane. She looked close to losing control and Byron searched for something positive to say.

"I'm sure we'll find him. I bet Samuel already has, and he's staying with one of his other mates."

"He'd have rung."

Yes, he would. "Philip mentioned places they used to hang out. It could be worth searching them."

"What do you plan to do?" Rebecca's voice betrayed her tension.

"I'll have a look round in the morning."

"I still don't understand why we shouldn't tell the police."

"If we report what happened with McLaughlin, we'd spend tomorrow under the microscope being questioned and making statements. We need to be free to search for Philip."

"But if we tell them he's gone, the police would help search for him."

"They won't do anything unless he's missing for over twenty-four hours. Let's see what his friends say first."

Rebecca opened her mouth to speak, but changed her mind, and they continued the journey home in frosty silence. Until he knew the full extent of Philip's involvement in his mate's murder, Byron didn't want to speak to the police. Experience told him that what the boy had said over the phone wasn't necessarily the whole truth, or even part of it.

As soon as they walked through the front door Byron could tell Samuel had been unsuccessful.

Rebecca looked ready to collapse. "You spoke to all of them?" Her question held a note of desperation.

Samuel nodded. "Eventually. Three of the boys didn't want to talk to me, but nobody's seen him."

"Have you got the names of the three lads?" Philip had mentioned three others but Byron didn't recall their names.

Rebecca looked at him. "You don't think they had anything to do with his disappearance?"

"No, but if he's scared, he might hide with them, and they're not going to just tell anyone who rings up he's there." He didn't believe his own words but wanted Rebecca to accept it. She couldn't take much more tonight.

"Yes, but they all know my voice," Samuel protested.

"How can they be sure you're not sat here with the thugs who came for him holding you at gunpoint?"

The boy's parents greeted this with silence.

Byron realised how exhausted his brother was. "I think you should both get some sleep. It won't do Philip much good if you're too knackered to help when he needs you."

An objection formed on his brother's lips, but Samuel studied his wife and nodded. "By the way, your friend Adam rang. Apologised for not being here."

"I'll ring him." Adam must have had failed to get the night off, but why wait so long to ring? Exhaustion seeped into Byron's bones — he needed to get some sleep if he wanted to function tomorrow but he'd need Adam's help to find his nephew.

A grumpy sounding stranger answered the phone and summoned Adam. Byron's irritation grew as he waited.

"Byron. I'm really sorry—"

"Why didn't you ring to tell me if you couldn't you get the night off?"

"We had a bit of a nightmare, I didn't get back from hospital until I rang your brother." Adam sounded like he was stifling a yawn.

"You okay?" Byron regretted his tone.

"Just a check-up, I'll tell you about it tomorrow."

"Don't worry, mate. I know you'd have come if you could. Are you free tomorrow?"

"When and where do you want me?"

"Here, at my brother's place. Can you make it for first light?"

After a moment's silence Adam said, "Yeah, no problem. I don't finish till nine, but I'll get off early — as soon as someone gets in from the day crew. See you in the morning."

Byron ended the call, the happiest he'd been since he'd arrived at his brother's house.

The boot of the old car Mugisa forced Philip into stank of old rubber and carpet mixed with exhaust fumes. Scrunched up in the small boot, Philip's arms and legs cramped. After an eternity, the car came to a halt and Mugisa opened the boot. Holding the machete at his side, he stepped away and gestured for Philip to get out.

Philip pulled himself up, wincing as he lowered himself to the road and stretched his aching muscles. His vision grew accustomed to the light, and he checked his surroundings. With a sense of dread he recognised the building next to them. The memory of bringing Liam there twenty-four hours earlier caused his insides to flutter.

"Why are you doing this?"

Mugisa ignored him and gestured with the machete. Philip walked towards the gate into the courtyard, shivering in his shirt and jeans as the frigid air chilled his skin. Once in the dark basement, they shuffled forward, the blade touching the back of his neck. Mugisa's other hand gripped his shoulder, the fingers digging into his flesh like steel claws. With every step, sensation returned to his limbs. As they moved forward in the darkness, his left foot hit something. He stumbled but Mugisa stopped him from falling.

"Pick it up," Mugisa commanded, his voice devoid of emotion.

Philip realised he'd kicked the chair they'd used for Liam. Terror made his bladder leak. He bent forward and fumbled for the chair, finding it with his hand. He gripped the sides of the chair. Mugisa shuffled his feet and moved the blade from his neck. Philip seized his chance and lifted the chair, but the handle of the machete crunched into the top of his head. Lights flashed and he lost control of his limbs, falling into a heap.

Mugisa straightened the chair and lifted Philip's unresponsive body onto it. Seized by panic, Philip tried to resist as Mugisa wrapped tape round his torso and arms, securing them to the back of the chair and fastened his ankles to the chair legs. Feeling returned, the taste of blood first then the cold. A shocking pain radiated from the top of his head.

Mugisa spoke from behind him. "I'll come back this evening and we will have a trial."

Philip realised what that meant. He would get the same treatment as Liam. "Let me go and I won't say anything about this. I know you didn't mean to kill Liam."

Mugisa didn't reply.

"With your background, what you've been through, anyone would understand. They'll probably let you go."

After a long silence Mugisa spoke, his voice cold and distant. "So you're sorry for me?"

"No, I just meant, what happened to you…" Philip tailed off, wishing he could take the words back.

Mugisa's feet shuffled closer. Tape wound round Philip's head, jerking it back. He gagged as the tape covered his mouth. Mugisa finished, then his footsteps receded. Philip tried to call out to him but only managed an incoherent mumble. A door scraped across the floor, then silence.

Above his laboured breathing, Philip heard the noises of the building. The walls and floors ticking and groaning as the temperature dropped further. But above that came the sounds of the rats, returning to claim their territory. Philip's skin crawled. At least he wasn't on the floor.

As the cold seeped into him he shivered. He should try to get free. He tested his bonds, pulling at each limb, but Mugisa had done a good job. If Asif had remembered the rope Liam wouldn't have got cut and none of this would be happening. With a roar of frustration and rage Philip tensed his muscles.

The chair creaked and moved. Could he break it and get free? Philip rocked. There, the back leg was loose. Infused with hope he rocked again, moving the loose joint more each time, until with a crack, the chair collapsed.

He fell backwards, slamming onto the solid floor. His head bounced, landing on the wound the machete had caused. The pain paralysed him and blood dripped from the injury. Then, as sensation returned to his limbs, he realised he hadn't freed himself. All he'd done was placed himself at the level of the rats. Ears straining, he listened for their return.

CHAPTER 10

The knife pressed into his throat, but The Boy remained impassive. The man glared for many seconds and The Boy, resigned to his fate, didn't react. Convinced the man would kill him, he was surprised when the man's expression changed. A huge grin split his face and he laughed before handing The Boy to a second man who grabbed his arm and dragged him out.

The second man took him to a hut where other boys and girls from his village waited. The attackers had by now overrun the village and more bodies lay between the huts. Most were old men and women, too slow to escape and others the mothers, who had fought to the death, defending their children.

Screams and moans came from several dwellings and flaming brands from a blazing hut filled the air. Other huts smouldered and smoke drifted between the remaining homes. The scene they presented would have been familiar to medieval churchgoers in Europe.

The terrified children stared at the destruction of the only world they had ever known. In shock at having witnessed the violent deaths of friends and family, and unable to take it all in, they stared in bewildered silence. Eyes, bright with excitement and joy a short while ago, became blank as their young minds shut down.

Adam studied Samuel's house as he waited for someone to answer the doorbell. Byron's brother must be doing well. He'd been a junior doctor last time Adam saw him but he must be a consultant by now to afford something like this. Rebecca came to the door, looking older than the last time they'd met, and she didn't appear to have slept much.

"Hi, Rebecca, isn't it? I'm Adam." He thrust out his hand.

She returned his grip. "Hello." Recognition bloomed. "Sorry, Adam, I didn't recognise you for a second. You didn't have..." She gestured at her nose.

"Oh, yeah. I broke it a few months after we last met."

"Please come in."

Byron stood behind her, a mug of coffee in one hand, and half a slice of toast in the other. Despite his obvious tiredness he grinned then shoved the toast in his mouth and placed the mug on a side table. Adam stepped towards him and they embraced.

"Good to see you, mate." Adam broke away and prodded Byron's torso. "Fatherhood's put a few pounds on you. It's not a sympathetic pregnancy?"

Byron swallowed the rest of his toast and cuffed his shoulder. "Cheeky young pup, I'd still whup you in a gym test."

Rebecca hovered at one side, excluded from the easy camaraderie of the two men. "Do you want coffee, or breakfast?"

Adam wouldn't have minded a bacon butty but could see Byron wanted to go. "No thanks, Rebecca, I ate at work. Ready to go, Byron?"

Byron pulled on a coat and they said their goodbyes. Once outside, he produced a list of three addresses. Adam recognised them.

At the car, Byron did a double take. "Something you want to tell me?" He gestured at the child seat in the rear of the SUV.

Adam grinned. "Not yet, mate. I borrowed this from one of the lads. I didn't think my TR6 would cut it." He became serious. "Have you decided where we should go first?"

Byron pointed to an address on the list. "This one. Shall I look it up for you?" He reached for a battered street atlas in the door pocket.

"No need. I know it." Adam passed Byron the list and started the car. Byron looked tired and Adam detected a tension behind his usual easy manner. "Do you want to fill me in?"

Byron outlined the events of the past two days, explaining what had happened and why McLaughlin had tried to snatch Philip. As his friend relayed Philip's account of Liam's death, Adam's mind returned to the discovery of the young man's body.

"I found the body."

"What do you mean?" Byron asked.

Adam explained.

"Shit, I didn't realise. They must have put the body in the house after Philip escaped."

"You sure he had nothing to do with it?"

"Yeah, I believed him."

Adam didn't know Philip, so couldn't comment. "So, who are we visiting?"

"These are the other three lads who were with Philip on Sunday. Samuel rang them last night, but they seemed evasive, like they were hiding something."

"How come we're not going to see this Mugisa? If he's the ringleader?"

"Rebecca and I called round last night, straight after Philip went missing. Mugisa was in bed, so I want to check these three first."

"You think one of them has Philip?" If Adam had wanted to get rid of a witness to a murder, he wouldn't bother snatching him, and if he had, he'd make sure he silenced him soon after.

He hoped he was wrong, but he guessed Byron shared the same thoughts.

"It's a possibility. If they haven't, we have to go to plan B."

"Okay. So what exactly is plan A?"

"I'll pose as a welfare officer from college, checking to make sure the death of their friend hasn't traumatised the boys."

"Not bad," Adam said. "Unless, of course, the college has already sent somebody."

"Unlikely. I don't think the police identified the body until late yesterday so the college might not know one of their pupils is dead and even if they do, they won't have had time to organise anything."

"What about McLaughlin?"

Byron made a gesture of dismissal. "No need to worry about him."

"Oh yeah?" What Adam knew of the man suggested he'd be a big threat, especially with their history and after Byron had thwarted him last night.

Byron drummed his fingers against the car seat, a sure sign someone better beware, but Adam wasn't sure if Byron realised what forces McLaughlin now controlled.

Siobhan had arrived at work early and although pleased the team had updated the incident board, she found the failure to find CCTV evidence disappointing. Maybe they would find something today. She'd brought her team to Liam's college at the earliest possible time, eager to press on. The admin building with its smell of candle wax and its stained-glass windows made her think of boring Sunday mornings listening to interminable sermons. She checked the time again as she waited for the receptionist to return with the principal. As she waited, she relived her embarrassment when she'd mistaken her drunk neighbour for a burglar. At least he'd taken it in good spirit. She heard voices and adjusted her expression.

A tall thin man with rounded shoulders and wearing a business suit walked ahead of the receptionist. His receding hairline, prominent Adams apple and beaky nose brought to mind a vulture.

"Chief Inspector." He held out a bony hand. "I'm Stephen Hughes and I'm in charge here, for my sins."

"Chief Inspector Quinn," Siobhan said as they shook hands, his withdrawn almost before they'd made contact. "Do you have somewhere we can talk in private?"

"My office." He looked past Siobhan to her entourage. "But I'm afraid you won't all fit in."

"That's fine; it will just be the two of us." She introduced Eddy.

The principal led the way to his office and, although shocked when he learned of the murder of one of his pupils, he soon recovered.

"That's dreadful news, Chief Inspector. Do you know who might have done it?"

"Not yet, sir. We want to interview Liam's friends. Find out if anyone saw him on Sunday so we can build up a picture of his movements in the hours before he died."

"Of course. I'm sure they'll be only too glad to help." He frowned, repeating, "Dreadful news. Have you told his mother? Of course you have. How's she bearing up?"

"She seemed to be coping, sir," Eddy replied. "We have a superb team of counsellors."

"Do you have somewhere where we can speak to Liam's friends?" Siobhan asked. "Somewhere private, where people can talk without being overheard? If you have more than one room…"

"Of course." He produced a timetable and studied it.

"We need to borrow a few of your staff. Some of the people we want to speak to are minors and will need to have an appropriate adult with them."

The principal nodded and reached for the phone on his desk. Siobhan prepared herself for a long and distressing morning.

"Chief Inspector Quinn?" A tall, muscular youth stood at the door with a friendly, but serious expression.

"Matthew Walcott?" she asked.

Walcott nodded.

"Come in." Beside her Eddy picked up his pen. The college welfare officer shifted in her seat and gave a tight smile.

Walcott didn't look at all nervous and strode to the desk with a confident, easy manner. "Good morning," he said, including the other two.

She recognised his accent as African, although she didn't know from which part of the continent. "Please sit down, Matthew. Can I call you Matthew? Or do you prefer Mugisa?"

Surprise made his eyes widen.

"I'm called Matthew in college."

As they'd agreed, Siobhan let Eddy take the lead.

"Okay, Matthew. I'm Sergeant Arkwright. There's nothing for you to worry about. We just need to trace Liam McLaughlin's movements on Sunday evening."

"I heard someone killed Liam," Walcott said. "Who would do such a thing? He was very popular. What happened?"

Eddy ignored the questions and asked his own, establishing Matthew's identity and personal details. This usually helped to relax witnesses, but Siobhan didn't think this witness needed help.

"We're trying to build up a picture of his movements over the weekend," Eddy said. "When did you last see him?"

Walcott looked pensive. "Friday. We had a history class together."

"You haven't seen him since?"

"No, sir."

Siobhan insides fluttered as one strand of Philip's alibi fell apart.

Eddy expression didn't change. "Can you tell me where you were Sunday night?"

"Is that when he died?" Walcott's look of concern returned.

Eddy studied him.

"I was with some friends; we were meant to go to Philip's, to work on a project." He gave a conspiratorial smile. "We didn't go."

"Philip?"

"Philip Mason."

"So he was with you Sunday night?"

"Until about eight."

Siobhan felt disappointed, but Philip still had to explain why he said Liam was with them.

"And you didn't see Liam?" Eddy asked.

"No, sir."

"Where did you hang out?"

Walcott mentioned local landmarks, which Eddy seemed to recognise.

"Can you tell me the names of the other people with you?"

Eddy noted the names. The same ones Philip had given the night before.

Siobhan took over. "Thank you, Matthew. You've been very helpful, but we might need to talk to you again, just to clarify a few points."

Walcott pushed his chair back and stood. She saw him deciding whether to shake hands with her before settling on a nod to each of the room's occupants.

Siobhan addressed the college welfare officer. "Do you want to grab a cup of tea? We'll take a break." Siobhan waited until the woman left. "What do you think of Matthew Walcott?"

"Pretty cool, very believable."

"I agree, but we know he's an accomplished liar. He lied to his parents about being at Philip Mason's house last night."

"What do you want to do next?"

"I think we should interview Philip Mason now. Get him to explain the discrepancy with his version of what happened on Sunday evening."

Eddy pushed his chair away. "I'll get him. Do you want a brew?"

"Yes please. Milk no sugar."

As she waited, Siobhan replayed the interview. Something about Matthew wasn't right, but she couldn't pinpoint the cause of her disquiet. She left the idea alone; it wouldn't come if she chased it, but she would put Matthew Walcott on the list of people to re-interview.

The door opened and Eddy returned, wearing a frown. "Philip Mason's not shown up today."

Although she shouldn't have been surprised, alarm bells rang. "I'll sort out the paperwork and visit him at home. Matthews and Khan can come with me and you take over here. Let me know if anything else crops up."

Byron returned to the car and waited for Adam to return. Their failure to find Philp weighed on him. The confidence he'd started out with drained away with every setback and they were running out of options. And he still had to decide what to do about McLaughlin, something he couldn't put off for too long.

Adam jogged out of an alleyway and returned to the car. "Any joy?"

"Anthony's mother claimed he stayed home all evening. She said he's been withdrawn since the weekend and hasn't been out, except to go to college."

"That figures, if he took part in the killing."

They sat in silence for a few moments, each remembering the first time they'd seen violent death at close quarters.

"Alternatively," Adam said, "he could be genuinely upset about the murder of a close friend."

"Nah, there's no question he's involved." He didn't want to consider the alternative, that Philip had lied to him. "You find anything round the back?"

"Another row of houses. They've got a small back yard with no outbuildings and nowhere you could stash someone."

It was a world away from where Philip lived. "Any boarded-up houses?"

"Not that I could see. They all overlook each other, so it would be a big risk to take a prisoner there."

"Okay." Byron tried not to let his frustration show; Adam would help him regardless, but he didn't need to make it any more unpleasant. "Mugisa's next, you know the address?"

Adam nodded and started the car. Byron realised he couldn't do the next call. Much as he wanted to speak to Mugisa's parents, it would be a stupid risk for him to see them.

"Can you go in on this one?"

"Yeah … sure…"

"The father will recognise me from last night so if he's in…"

"Of course, I'd make a great welfare officer." Adam gave a goofy grin. He didn't fancy doing it but he could see how stressed Philip's disappearance made Byron and could imagine how he'd feel if it one of his sister's kids went missing. He parked a few doors from their target and waited for Byron to vanish down the alley leading behind the houses before he got out.

As he waited at the door, he ignored the uneasy sensation in his gut and rehearsed his patter, determined not to let Byron down. The middle-aged woman who answered studied him with a frown.

"Hello, Mrs Walcott." He gave her his best smile. "I'm Steve, the welfare officer from the college. We're concerned about the effect recent events might have had on our pupils. Could I come in and have a chat about Matthew?"

"Call me Miriam." Reassured she gave his Fire Service ID a cursory examination before leading him into a comfortable kitchen smelling of fresh baking and insisted he sample the brownies cooling on a wire tray.

"So, the death of his friend hasn't affected Matthew?" Adam asked, reaching for another piece of cake.

"I don't think he knew the boy well. He only heard about it this morning — on the radio."

"Didn't the police come round last night?"

"Oh yes, they did, but he was at Philip Mason's house." She frowned. "He might have found out there, I suppose."

"Didn't he mention it when he came home?"

"We were asleep. We're early-to-bed kind of people." She gave a conspiratorial grin. "And once we go to sleep, it's the devil's own job to wake us."

Adam's pulse quickened, but he tried to keep his voice casual. "So you didn't see him when he got home last night?"

Miriam opened her mouth before closing it and narrowing her eyes.

Bugger! He complimented her on her baking, and she relaxed, pushing the laden tray across the table. He took another piece and chewed as he considered his next question. He wanted to ask if Matthew had a den, somewhere he went to be alone, but already suspicious, she'd probably throw him out, or worse.

"Do you have any pictures of him?" he asked then realising his mistake added, "One of him as a youngster." Come on Adam, why would the welfare officer need a photo.

She considered the request before answering. "We haven't many. We only got him at fourteen."

"He's adopted?" Adam couldn't hide his surprise.

"The principal knows all about it." Her suspicion returned.

"That's not information he shares with all the staff." She appeared to accept this and Adam exhaled, relieved he'd guessed the gender of the principal.

"I'll get them," she said, leaving the room.

Perspiration soaked Adam's torso and he told himself to get a grip before he blew it. She returned with a leather-bound album. The first page displayed three creased and faded prints.

"These are from before we rescued him."

The images showed a skinny black youth squinting in the bright African sunshine. He wore tattered fatigues, two sizes too big for him and stared fiercely at the camera. In one image he carried a Kalashnikov. Adam looked at the prints with growing unease. He'd seen pictures like this.

"These are from after we found him." Miriam turned the page.

These photos showed the same youth in some sort of transit camp. He looked better fed and clothed but his eyes still held the same fierce anger.

"You went to Africa to get him?"

"Oh no. When I say we, I mean our church. We rescue lots of young people from that terrible place."

The later images showed the youth growing taller and filling out. He wore a smile in most of them but behind it Adam sensed a hidden sadness. Miriam and a small middle-aged man appeared in many of the pictures.

She pointed at the man. "That's my husband, Joseph."

"Very distinguished looking."

She smiled and preened. "Yes he's a very good man."

Adam memorised the most recent images of the youth, making sure he'd know him if they ever met and refusing offers of more refreshments, he thanked Miriam and left.

Byron waited in the car. "You took your time."

Adam offered a smile of apology. "Did you find anything round the back?"

"Nah." Byron sounded despondent. "There's space where you could keep someone but you'd need a car to get them in and out unseen and I doubt these boys have one. So, how did you get on?"

"He's our man. The parents were in bed when he came in last night. He could have come in at any time."

Byron studied him. "There's more isn't there?"

Adam nodded. "Our friend Mugisa is adopted. He was a child soldier. I saw photos, twelve and carrying a Kalashnikov. Do you remember Sammy Lee?"

"The ex-Ghurkha you served with in Kuwait?"

"Yeah. He'd fought in Sierra Leone and said they were the meanest soldiers he ever fought. No fear, no compassion; didn't know when they were beaten."

"Yes, but whoever placed him for adoption must have made sure they rehabilitated him."

"He might have slipped through the net."

Adam started the car and pulled away from the kerb. They remained silent. If Mugisa had him, Philip was in more peril than they had thought.

CHAPTER 11

A shout from the driver guarding their vehicles alerted the attackers. The men and older boys from the village, away tending their animals, saw the smoke and returned.

With shouts and blows, the invaders drove their young captives towards the waiting vehicles. Crammed into the rear of a small truck like animals on the way to market, the prisoners stood. They set off in convoy, back to their camp. The men from the village appeared in the distance. Most carried hand weapons or sticks. A few bore ancient Lee Enfield rifles, over half a century old.

In anger and desperation the men from the village fired these, releasing puffs of smoke from the barrels. The invaders were now almost out of range and most of the bullets missed. By a savage irony, one bullet found a target, passing through the head of one of The Boy's footballing companions. Blood and brain matter splashed The Boy. Constricted by the crush of bodies, he couldn't raise his arms to wipe it away.

Pressed against his friends' bodies, the victim remained upright as the convoy made slow progress along rough roads, every bump making the body lurch into The Boy. Unable to comprehend any more horror, he stared out at something visible to nobody else. In the months that followed, The Boy thought of his dead friend as 'the lucky one'.

Siobhan waited outside the Mason house for a response to the doorbell. She should have sent two of her men round the back in case the lad tried to do a runner but she'd not got the impression he would from yesterday's meeting. Anyway, too late now, a figure approached the door.

"Mrs Mason, I'm—"

"That was quick, Detective Chief Inspector." She greeted Siobhan with a look of surprise. "And call me Rebecca, please."

"What do you mean?"

Rebecca gave a puzzled frown. "Aren't you here to investigate Philip's disappearance? I've reported it at the local station."

Siobhan cursed. Someone should have told her. "I'm sorry Mrs Mason, we weren't aware of this. We're here investigating the murder of Liam McLaughlin." She produced a document. "This is a search warrant for your address and my team are here to carry it out."

The boy's mother scrutinised the piece of paper, not seeming to take in the words.

"Mrs Mason, I will have to insist you let us in."

Rebecca noticed the officers behind Siobhan for the first time. "I suppose you'd better come in." She pulled the door open.

Siobhan led her team into the house and they filled the hallway. "I'd like to make a start on the search. The sooner we begin…" Siobhan studied Philip's mother, who seemed to age before her. "Are any of the rooms locked?" she continued in a gentler voice.

"No," Rebecca whispered.

"We'll need access to the whole house. If we have to take anything away, we'll give you a receipt. Please show me to your son's room. I'll start there." She addressed the rest of her team. "Youssef, start at the top and Debbie, search this floor."

The two detectives each led off a small group of uniformed officers to carry out Siobhan's orders. As she followed the still silent Rebecca up the stairs, Siobhan told herself to forget her disappointment at not finding Philip at home and concentrate on locating evidence. She wondered if he was really missing.

Rebecca showed Siobhan into her son's room and waited in the doorway. "Can you tell me what you're looking for?" she asked, rediscovering her voice.

Siobhan studied the room. A smell of deodorant and trainers reminded her of her brother's room, although his had been nowhere this size and the posters on his wall showed Man United players, not motorbikes and what look like African tribal art. "I'll need the clothes he wore on Sunday night for a start."

Rebecca glanced away before replying. "They're in the basement."

"Take me to them." Siobhan suppressed her unease and followed Rebecca back down the stairs.

They walked through the kitchen and towards the basement stairs, her trepidation increasing with every step. As they descended, she smelt the distinctive aroma of detergent, fabric softener and damp clothing. Rebecca reached the bottom of the stairs, switched on a light and led Siobhan into a large chamber. Clothes hung from a drying rack and a washer with matching dryer stood along one wall. Rebecca pointed at the drying clothes.

"You've washed these?" Siobhan said, glaring at Rebecca.

"They were soaking wet: he'd been out in the rain." Rebecca avoided her gaze.

"What about his footwear?"

"They're still damp; they're over there, drying."

"Show me."

Rebecca led the way and Siobhan picked up a large pair of top-of-the-range running shoes. "You've also washed these."

"Of course, they were muddy."

Siobhan's hands trembled with anger and she struggled to control herself. She thrust the trainers into a large evidence bag, then gathered the clothes off the rack and bagged them.

An hour later, they'd completed a thorough search of the premises. Siobhan returned to the kitchen where Rebecca sat, having a cup of tea. Still angry, she slapped a sheet of paper on the table in front of her.

"This is a list of items we have removed," Siobhan said. "When I came yesterday, I told you we wanted to examine your son's clothes from Sunday night. I believe you washed them to destroy any evidence which may be on them—"

"There wasn't any *evidence* on them," Rebecca protested. "My son has done nothing wrong."

"I haven't decided yet what action to take but we may charge you with attempting to pervert the course of justice. Your son is wanted for questioning about the murder of Liam McLaughlin. If you know where he is and fail to tell us, I'll make sure you're charged. Do I make myself clear?"

Rebecca nodded.

Siobhan pointed to the list. "I'll tell you when you can have these items back."

Rebecca nodded again and appeared to shrink. Siobhan stifled any compassion she felt towards her. Liam and his family deserved her sympathy, not whoever had killed him or shielded his killers.

Philip woke with a start. He took a few seconds to get his bearings. Someone whispered in his ear. Had Mugisa come back already? But it couldn't be, he wouldn't whisper. Awareness of his surroundings returned, and he realised the source of the whispering. He screamed through his gag. With squeaks of alarm, the rats feasting on his spilled blood scattered.

He jerked away from them but an unbearable pain almost made him pass out. He lay still until it faded. Bile rose into his throat but he fought to control it. If he allowed himself to be sick, he'd drown in vomit. A violent shudder seized his body as the cold hit him and his teeth chattered.

When his headache subsided, he tested his bonds again, but they hadn't loosened. The rats drew closer and he jerked his body, scaring them away. But they weren't his main worry — he had to escape before Mugisa and the others returned. How long did he have?

He had to get off the floor. He struggled to turn over, but with his arms and legs secured and with his torso taped to the back of the chair he couldn't do it. Unable to right himself, he realised he was trapped, like a giant beetle. Despite the pain caused by any movement, he struggled until exhausted. The cold and fear the rats would return kept sleep away.

The light intensified until Philip could see the walls of the basement. By spinning round, he got a good idea of the layout of the room. He lay in a large chamber. Metal pillars supported the floor above and the nearest walls were thirty feet from him.

Further away he saw an old circuit board attached to the wall. Broken ceramic insulators hung from it. Could he use them to cut his bonds? His headache had faded and the improving light raised his spirits, reviving the belief he might escape. He spent a few minutes investigating the best way to cross the floor. He discovered if he used his legs to push himself along, the back of the chair acted like a sled.

Weakened by the cold and inactivity, his leg muscles didn't react well and each push covered a depressingly small distance. After a few trial lurches, he calculated it would take one hundred steps to reach his destination. He counted and, after thirty, he grew warm. He'd soon be at the wall.

The euphoria lifting his spirits dissolved in an explosion of pain. Philip's head smashed into a cast iron pillar. A shock wave travelled along his spine and he lay stunned. The pain faded and he tried to move, but the pillar stopped him. Inch by inch, he rotated his body until he cleared the obstacle. He looked around, realising he'd gone off target. He needed to aim to his right. At least forty feet of floor still separated him from the board. His recent optimism evaporated, replaced by a sense of despair.

After a few minutes, he gathered himself and started again. With each step, pain infused his body. But he must get free before Mugisa returned.

Adam's borrowed car idled at the traffic lights on the northern edge of Manchester city centre. Next to him, Byron related Philip's version of where they'd taken Liam.

Adam tried to picture it. "That's not a lot to go on, Byron. Do you know how many disused mills there are round here?"

"Yeah, a lot." Byron exhaled and ran a hand over his cropped hair.

The absence of his friend's normal confidence distressed Adam. "Don't worry, I know this area like the back of my hand."

"Oh yeah, you've been living up here how long now? Three years?" Byron gave a strained smile.

"Plenty of time to get familiar with it. Don't forget I work round here."

The lights changed and they set off. The journey revived unwelcome memories for Adam. They drove along the road where he'd discovered Liam's body and he didn't need the distinctive police barrier tape to identify the house. Scorch marks disfigured the brickwork above each opening and Adam recalled the conditions they'd endured within those rooms.

Adam drove past and headed towards nearby Ancoats where he expected to find the building they sought. They stopped outside a large mill and Adam parked near the corner. They got out and examined the red brick hulk. A few of the upper floors displayed signs in the windows, proclaiming the identity of the occupants.

"I'm not sure, Adam, he described it as disused."

"There's nobody down here." Adam pointed to the lower floors where peeling plywood and rusty wire-mesh covered the windows. "You said he took the lad to a basement." He peered in through a grimy window and beyond the cracked glass he could make out a large room, empty except for a broken workbench and piles of rubbish. Byron nodded and they split up to circle the building. An hour later they pulled up in front of yet another large building, occupying a whole block, and with a low gate across the entrance to the courtyard.

"Shall I go in?" Adam dismissed the weariness which had descended on him. He always hit a wall after nights if he didn't get to bed.

Byron's spirits hadn't improved as they drove from one disappointment to another and he nodded. "I'll check the other side."

Adam vaulted over the barrier and circled the courtyard. He checked all the doors but they either led to small rubbish-strewn alcoves stinking of urine or had rusty padlocks securing them. He approached the final door where a barrel held it closed. As he reached for it, a shout came from the gateway.

"Oi, what you doing?"

Adam at first assumed this was the owner, but then noticed the man's uniform. "Good afternoon, Officer."

The policeman had a pockmarked face and straggly moustache. "I said, what are you doing?"

Adam clenched his jaw but before he could answer Byron returned from his search of the outer perimeter. The policeman focussed his attention on him.

"Are you with this gentleman?" he asked.

"Hello, Officer. Is there a problem?" Byron's smile didn't reach his eyes.

"I asked you a question."

A second officer appeared from the opposite side of the building, burly but carrying a few too many kilos his demeanour made it clear he hadn't come to exchange pleasantries. He stopped a few metres behind Byron, his hand resting on the hilt of his baton.

"The owners have asked my company to provide security for this building." Byron produced his business card. "We're just looking around to find out what's involved."

"Oh yeah, and what about the others you were looking at?" The policeman read the details on the card. "Do you have any proper ID?"

"Are we in a police state now?" Adam demanded.

"It's fine, Adam." Byron produced his driver's licence.

The officer examined it, taking it out of the plastic wallet.

"I don't think you're allowed to do that."

The constable bristled but returned it to the wallet before noting the details in his notebook and giving it back to Byron. "And you, sir?" He held a hand out to Adam.

Adam considered refusing but he didn't want to waste any more time. He jumped over the gate, making the policeman take a step back. "Here." He retrieved his Fire Service ID card from his wallet and thrust it at the policeman.

"You moonlighting?"

Adam snatched the card from the officer. He got on with most of the coppers he met but these two were going out of their way to be obnoxious.

The officer scowled and asked Byron, "You got any proof the owners have approached you?"

"Not with me, Officer. The letter's in my office. Do you want me to get a copy faxed to you?"

Adam tensed — what if he said yes?

"Oi, which one of you owns this car?" The other policeman stood by Mal's car, their own vehicle parked behind it.

"What's the problem?" Adam said.

"This tyre's below the legal tread depth." He tapped the nearside wheel with his baton.

Adam strode to the car. Mal fastidiously checked his car every week. "You tested it with a depth-gauge?"

"So, is this your car, then?" The man squared off to Adam.

"It belongs to one of my colleagues. I've borrowed it for a few days."

Triumph gleamed in the policeman's eyes. "In that case you won't mind if we check—"

"Be my guest. His name's Malcolm—"

"Back at the station, I'm afraid, *sir*. Both you and Mr Mason."

"Is that necessary, Officer?" Byron said.

"Are you refusing?" The policeman lifted the baton to the horizontal.

"No, but I will make a complaint about you and your colleague."

The policeman shrugged. "Suit yourself."

Byron exhaled a frustrated breath. "Right, we'll follow you to the station."

"Sorry, sir. The car's not roadworthy."

Adam had had enough. "There's no way I'm leaving that car around here. You either let us drive it to the station or you can arrest us."

Instead of arguing, the officer turned away. "Fine, we'll follow you. You know the way to Longsight nick?" He walked to his car and his colleague joined him.

"Fuck's sake!" Byron muttered under his breath as he marched to the passenger seat and got in.

Adam started the engine. "The bastard's enjoying this — you see him grinning when he got into his car?"

"How did he know we'd looked at other places?" Byron said, frowning.

CHAPTER 12

Twenty of the children seized made it to the invader's camp, a large settlement hidden in acacia trees. Within three weeks, their number reduced to fifteen. The children, none older than twelve, stayed in enclosures with captives snatched from other villages. Their captors expected them to work to earn their meagre rations.

In between work and sleep, they attended classes where they forgot their past and learned of a new future. The girls, even the youngest, were used as concubines and personal slaves for their guards. The slightest misdemeanours led to savage beatings and the weak or sick didn't survive long.

The numbness The Boy experienced lasted many weeks before his feelings returned. A protective shell formed at his centre, keeping a small part of him safe. In it, he stored memories of his mother and sister. He thought of his father and brothers, people who loved him and would welcome him back. He realised their grief must be greater, they had lost not only their mother and sister, but also the beloved youngest of the family. The Boy began to think of escape.

Byron sat in the airless interview room at Longsight police station, waiting for the officers to question him. Every minute they wasted here meant they weren't looking for Philip, but making a fuss would only lead to them taking even longer. The door opened and the officer with the pockmarked face came in, bringing with him the odour of stale tobacco. As he entered, he turned his head and Byron caught his distinctive profile. A certainty he knew this man struck him.

"Sorry to keep you, sir." A few crumbs, which hadn't been there before, clung to the edge of his moustache.

Byron took a few deep breaths. "Why are you keeping me here?"

"I need to ask you a few questions." He produced a notebook and placed it on the table. "According to your driving licence you live in London. Where are you staying while you're up here?"

"What business is that of yours?" Byron racked his brain — where had he met him?

The policeman gave a lopsided smile. "You were trespassing and if you want to be difficult—"

"I was on the public highway when you demanded my ID. We're here to clear up a minor issue with the car my friend borrowed. Something you could have done with one phone call."

"How we choose to investigate a suspected car theft is our business."

"Yeah, it is." *Don't antagonize him, remember you need to get out there looking for Philip.* Then a memory flooded back. "How much does McLaughlin pay you?"

The blood drained from the man's face and his mouth fell open but he recovered. "Who's McLaughlin?"

"Does he still call you Beaky?"

Colour flushed the policeman's cheeks.

"Well, Beaky, I'm going to walk out of this door and wait in reception. If Adam doesn't join me in ten minutes, I'll be having a word with your inspector and suggesting he looks into your finances."

The policeman's expression of hatred could have struck Byron down but with an effort he controlled his emotions. "I think we've finished now, *sir*." He snapped his notebook shut and, pushing the chair back, strode to the door and pulled it open.

Byron took his time and sauntered out, the skin on his neck crinkling as he walked in front of the policeman. At the door to the reception area, Byron made a show of checking his watch. Ten to two — they'd been here over an hour. The door slammed behind him and he paced the entrance.

Two uniformed officers came in and studied Byron warily as they passed through. Byron checked the time. The ten minutes were almost up. He glanced towards the reception desk where the constable on duty avoided looking at him. Byron started towards him and the officer picked up a phone and punched buttons.

The door from the station opened and Adam strode out, followed by the other of the officers who'd brought them here.

"Okay, mate?" Byron said.

"Let's go." Adam continued past him, adding in an undertone, "Before I kill the bastard."

Byron followed, and they both got into the car. "What did he say?"

"Not a lot. Left me stewing in an interview room while he got lunch. Didn't even hide the fact. I expected to be there all afternoon, but the other guy came in and told him to let me go. He didn't seem happy. Was that your doing?" Adam started the car.

"I recognised him from school. He was one of McLaughlin's posse. A hanger-on who decided to be a gofer rather than keep getting picked on."

"You reckon McLaughlin put him up to this?"

"They'd obviously followed us before picking us up. They must have been hanging about outside Samuel's place when we went back."

"Sorry, mate, I haven't been checking for tails."

"Don't worry about it. At least we now know McLaughlin's got at least one copper in his pocket."

Siobhan held the phone to her ear and listened to the account of Mrs Mason's visit from the desk sergeant at Didsbury. Eddy appeared in her doorway holding a sheaf of papers and she gestured to him to come in and sit. He closed the door and sprawled in the nearest chair.

"She said Ritchie McLaughlin 'invaded' their house?" Siobhan said and Eddy sat up, paying attention. "Did she say why they didn't report it at the time?"

"Apparently, once he left she didn't see the urgency." The sergeant's tone of voice told Siobhan what she thought of this explanation.

"But today she thinks he's responsible for her son's disappearance?"

"Not exactly, Boss. She suggested he's hiding from McLaughlin."

From what Siobhan heard it seemed a sensible course of action. "Did she say why McLaughlin left?"

"Sorry. She wasn't very forthcoming."

"Thanks Anne, keep me informed if you hear anything."

Eddy looked at her, eyebrows raised. "Whose toes has Ritchie stepped on?" he asked.

"Mrs Mason claims he called round there last night."

"Brave man. I'd think twice before I tangled with her."

"She's a bit less fierce today." Siobhan's anger had abated and she allowed herself some sympathy for the woman. She gave Eddy an edited account of the search of the Mason house and her conversation with the desk sergeant.

"So, she didn't say Ritchie took the boy?" Eddy asked.

"No. Is he capable of kidnapping?"

"Kidnapping is right up his street."

Siobhan massaged her temples. "That's all we need — a vicious vigilante. Do we have anyone inside his gang?"

The gesture from her sergeant told her they didn't. "A few figures on the periphery, but most of them are too scared of the bastard."

Siobhan wasn't sure what this development meant to her case and put it to one side for the moment, asking, "How did the interviews go?"

"They're getting typed up, but nobody saw Liam after Sunday afternoon. Two girls met him for a drink and they watched the football. After that nobody apart from Philip Mason admits to having seen him. Although one lad said he thought Liam intended to meet up with Philip on Sunday evening."

"One of the lads Philip claims to have been with?"

"No. *They* each claimed Philip was with them until eight but none of them mentioned seeing Liam."

"That's interesting. Do you think they might have rehearsed their story?"

"I didn't speak to all three but I'll check the exact wording."

"I still can't shake off my unease about Matthew Walcott. There's something about him that doesn't feel right."

"The accent you mean? I noticed that."

"Of course. His mother spoke with a local accent didn't she?" She chided herself for not making the connection earlier.

"Quite a few lads adopt an accent, often West Indian or American, but why not African? His dad might come from Africa."

"Something else about him bothered me, but I can't put my finger on it."

"Do you want to speak to him again?"

"Keep him on the back burner for now, I want to get hold of Philip Mason first, especially if McLaughlin's looking for him. In the meantime, let's have a word with Mr McLaughlin."

"Good idea. Shall I get him to come to the station?"

"No, we'll visit him in his lair." She looked at her watch. "I'd hoped the PM report would have arrived by now."

Eddy held up the printed sheets in his hands. "Sorry, Boss," he said, looking sheepish. "It just arrived by fax."

Siobhan took the sheets and scanned them. The report detailed the violence visited on Liam's body, but she read on until a sentence checked her.

"It says here he'd consumed chips and cola about an hour before he died."

"There aren't too many chippies round there," Eddy said. "I'll get the team to check the nearest ones and work outwards."

The door opened and Debbie Matthews stuck her head in the room. Siobhan frowned at her.

"Sorry, Boss, it's important, I've found footage of Liam on the CCTV."

A surge of excitement energised Siobhan and she followed Debbie and Eddy to the comms suite where a technician finished rewinding a section of film.

He looked up, brows furrowed. "The lighting's crap," he apologised. "But I've done my best to improve it."

Debbie thanked him and took the proffered remote-control. She pressed play and a washed-out image flickered on the screen. The scene showed the corner of a wall, overlooking a yard full of building materials. A road junction lay beyond the wall surrounding the yard. A lone figure ran from the right, glancing behind him every few steps. By slowing the footage and zooming in, they could see the distinctive jacket Liam wore.

Adrenaline rushed through Siobhan. "Well done Debbie," she said.

Eddy's grin reflected hers. Debbie ran the film on and seconds later a blur of movement shot across the corner of the screen.

"What the hell's that?" Eddy asked.

"A car. I'll check the closest traffic cameras to see if they've picked it up," Debbie said.

"As a matter of urgency, please," Siobhan said.

"Will do."

The technician restarted the film until another object flashed past the screen.

"Another car?" Siobhan asked.

"Someone on a bike. Probably more than one of them."

"Can we clean it up and identify them?" Her excitement grew.

"Unlikely. The resolution's too poor." He looked at her and smiled. "I'll see what I can do."

Her exhilaration ebbed but, despite her and Eddy's obvious disappointment, Debbie's manner didn't change.

"There's more," she announced with a smile and ran the film on again.

Another figure appeared on foot, two minutes behind Liam. The figure got to the corner, stopped and looked around before staring at the camera.

A fuzzy image of Philip Mason looked out of the screen at them.

Mugisa waited for the others at the main entrance to the college. Had he done enough to deflect suspicion onto Philip? The woman and her ugly sidekick couldn't hide their excitement when he told them he'd not seen Philip after eight on the Sunday. He needed to find out what the others had said. Although he'd coached them, he wasn't confident they would hold things together. As they came out of the building, his stomach clenched. They still looked like three antelopes caught in the headlights of a truck.

"Hi, boys," he said. "Do you fancy a pizza? I'm buying."

The lacklustre response irritated and concerned him but he led them, not towards their usual diner, but to the pizza restaurant sitting amongst the Asian eateries that proliferated in this area. The pizzas from here were several notches up from those the diner served and the other boys brightened. After ordering, Mugisa studied each of them. Anthony appeared the most subdued. Usually the most enthusiastic, he often chided the others for their timidity.

"What did they ask you?" Mugisa asked in a low voice.

"Just about Sunday night. If we saw Liam or Philip," Ryan said.

"What did you say?"

"What you said." Anthony shrugged. "We saw Philip until eight, but not Liam."

Mugisa hoped they'd sounded more convincing than they did now. The food arrived and by the end of the meal, helped in part by Mugisa's encouraging banter, they became less despondent.

Mugisa paid and left them outside the restaurant. He found the act of cajoling them a strain. He'd never had to do this in his last life; his people knew to obey orders. The weakness of his followers worried him — they'd need careful handling.

Ignoring the heaviness in his limbs, he yawned and made his way to his den: a disused lockup he'd commandeered. He stored everything important to him here, including his weapons and the few mementoes of his past life. He also kept the car he'd borrowed there and, after checking he wasn't observed, he undid the large padlock he'd fitted to the door.

After collecting the items he needed, he considered his position. The police weren't much of a threat unless one of the others cracked. The fact they were concentrating on Philip made it less likely they would look at them, but he needed to get rid of him quickly. If Philip committed suicide, the police would take it as confirmation of his guilt and they would be safe. He decided not to wait for the others. If he used the car, he'd be there in less than twenty minutes and he could finish this.

Byron switched on the courtesy light above the passenger seat and finished marking the road map. Outside, dusk fell and streetlamps flickered. His fear they wouldn't find Philip grew stronger with every unsuccessful search. "Are you sure there aren't any more?"

"Not within walking distance of where we found the body."

"What about this area?" Byron pointed to a section of the city on the other side of the burnt-out house. "We haven't looked around there."

Adam checked the map. "That area's all yuppie flats and boutiques — there aren't any disused mills left. He *must* be in here." He indicated the neighbourhood they'd just searched with his index finger.

"You're the one who's supposed to know the area." Byron immediately regretted his tone.

"And you're the one who's supposed to know what the building looks like. I've taken you to all the ones matching the description you gave me."

The uncomfortable silence stretched for several long seconds until Byron said, "Yeah, I know you have. Sorry." He ran his hands over his head.

"Could he have come from further out?" Adam pointed to an area on the edge of the page. "There's a few here."

Byron placed his forefinger on the road containing the burnt-out house. "It has to be between here and the place where they got off the bus, further south." He moved his hand down the page.

"We've done the lot then," Adam said, looking as frustrated as Byron felt.

Byron checked the time. Mugisa would have finished college by now and might be on his way to wherever he'd hidden Philip. If it hadn't been for that bloody crooked policeman they might have found him by now. He tried to ignore the gnawing feeling in his guts. "Is it worth following Mugisa? See if he leads us there?"

"We don't know where he is, and he could be there already."

Byron punched the dashboard in frustration. "Let's retrace our steps in case we've missed anything."

"Yeah, okay." Adam didn't protest this time and started the car. "We could go back to the one where the coppers picked us up."

"We had a good look at that one, but a couple of the others might be worth revisiting."

"I didn't check the last door. They arrived before I finished."

Byron didn't need to speak and spent the drive to the mill willing the car to go faster.

CHAPTER 13

The Boy and his new companions received barely enough food to keep hunger at bay. This made him weak and listless, but he realised the recruits receiving military training got better food. He also noticed they had more freedom. Before he could join them, he needed to show he'd completed his indoctrination.

Intelligent and quick to learn, he took a more prominent part in the re-education classes and soon came to the notice of the instructors, always volunteering to recite the propaganda they learned. He rarely saw the giant who had captured him; the man only came to the camp with new recruits. On these occasions he made a point of seeking out The Boy and seemed pleased at his progress.

His interest and The Boy's own efforts led to him being fast-tracked into military training. Here, they taught him the rudiments of fighting as part of a disciplined force. They used basic weapons but learned to use them to good effect. Firearms, rare and expensive, were reserved for those with combat experience. The trainee soldiers still received indoctrination training, but this took a small part of each day. Once he started on the improved diet, The Boy grew stronger.

Philip reached the wall and paused. The sense of panic that accompanied his crossing of the last few feet left him out of breath and he sucked air in through his nostrils. He manoeuvred himself beside the wall and pressed his right shoulder against the bottom bricks. Taking a deep breath, he gritted his teeth and rocked away from the wall. As he lifted off the floor, he pushed off with his left leg. The chair slid towards the wall and, as he fell back, his muscles tensed. The pain was worse than he'd feared and he lay panting, tears leaking from under his eyelids.

Philip realised the right side of his body now rested against the brickwork and he gave a snort of laughter: his plan was working. The second step would be harder. He must make sure he didn't slide down and end up where he'd started. The next attempt finished with him in the same position, but then he got his shoulder higher. Boosted by his success, he contemplated escape for the first time.

The right side of his body remained six inches off the floor but would it be enough? Not knowing if he had the strength to get higher he decided to go for it. By coordinating his exhausted muscles he put in an enormous effort and rotated his torso. At the apex of his movement he knew he'd make it. Visions of escape and re-joining his family flashed through his mind.

After teetering for an age, he fell backwards but refused accept his failure until he landed with a crash. A red-hot needle of agony almost made him black out. He lay gasping, waiting for it to go. The pain receded and he opened his eyes, confirming what he'd feared: he lay flat on the floor again.

Tears of frustration flowed as he lay on his back. Outside, darkness closed in and he realised he would run out of time. He couldn't tell how long he lay on the floor, trying to gather his strength for another attempt. Shivering as the cold reasserted itself, he thought of his family and decided to try again, determined not to give up.

He adjusted his position, pushing himself close to the wall but when he moved, he realised something had changed. What had happened to his bonds? He tensed his arm and it pulled free. Unwilling to believe it, he moved his other arm, with the same result. The tape binding him must have worn through as he pushed it across the rough floor. He lay back; his muscles jelly and more tears came.

He tore away at the strips securing him and they unravelled. In under a minute he'd freed his limbs and he rested, letting the circulation return to his arms. He rolled over onto the filthy floor and rose to his knees. He stayed there, swaying, until his body got used to being upright. Then, with a final effort, he got to his feet and ripped the tape from his mouth, before gulping down lungful's of cold air.

After a minute or two, he took tentative steps. He staggered but stayed upright. There wasn't much time, so he started for the doors, but as he moved towards them he heard a new sound.

He paused and held his breath. The right-hand door creaked open and a pair of legs appeared at the top of the stairs. The newcomer continued into the room. Even in the gloom he recognised the figure at the bottom of the steps.

Unable to find a parking space near McLaughlin's flat, Siobhan left her car in a loading bay.

"Put this on the dashboard." Eddy produced a laminated card with POLICE BUSINESS printed under the GMP crest. "Unofficial but effective — I'll get you one, Boss."

"Thanks, Eddy." Siobhan got out and stretched her back.

"How do you want to play it?" he asked.

"I'm here to pay my condolences," she said, pausing for a moment. "I'll also tell Mr McLaughlin to leave the detecting and punishing to us." She smiled. "Especially the punishing."

Their warrant cards got them past the concierge and they found themselves outside the door to the penthouse flat which opened after she rang the bell for the third time.

"What?" the man in the doorway demanded. He was smaller than she'd expected.

"Hello, Kieran," Eddy said.

"What do you want?" Kieran studied them, arms crossed.

"Chief Inspector Quinn." Siobhan showed him her warrant card. "I'm here to see Mr Ritchie McLaughlin."

Kieran scowled at her. "I'm not sure if he's available." He stepped away.

"I suggest he makes himself available."

Kieran stared at her but he blinked first and retreated, slamming the door behind him.

She winked at Eddy and he smiled in response. The door opened again to reveal a bigger and better dressed man in a suit, gleaming white shirt and silk tie.

"I understand you've been throwing your weight about," he said, looking her up and down. "Not that there's much of you."

"Don't concern yourself, Mr McLaughlin. There's plenty for what I need." She studied the bandage on his ear. It looked like a new injury. Could it be from his visit to the Mason household? She couldn't imagine anyone she'd met there doing that to him. Maybe the missing Philip did it and it would explain his disappearance.

"I cut myself shaving. Now, what do you want?" Any semblance of civility vanished.

"We're investigating the death of your nephew. Please accept our condolences."

His expression softened.

"Can we come in and ask you a few questions?"

"What sort of questions?"

"Can we come in please?" Siobhan regretted her decision not to make him come to the station.

He hesitated before stepping away. "Come in," he said, pointing at the doorframe. "You're the first of your kind to cross this threshold."

The large corner room he led them into offered panoramic views over the city and distant hills. Two large white leather sofas made an 'L' shape at the outer corner and they followed him to these.

"Coffee, Chief Inspector?"

She shook her head.

"What about you Sergeant?"

Eddy declined and McLaughlin shouted over to the far corner where Kieran sat at a counter, sulking. "Kieran, bring me a Turkish will you?" He pointed to the sofa overlooking the city centre. "Please sit."

McLaughlin took a seat on the other sofa, draping an arm over the back. Siobhan saw he had no intention of breaking the silence and exchanged a look with Eddy before speaking.

"Can you tell me what you know about your nephew's death?"

McLaughlin bared his teeth. "I know some fucking toe-rag butchered him and you're not doing anything about it."

"I can assure you we're conducting a thorough investigation into Liam's death." Siobhan's cheeks grew hot.

"Oh yeah? So how come you've not arrested him yet?"

"Arrested who? Do you have any evidence against anyone?"

"No, but you…" His gaze dropped. "No I haven't."

"We're speaking to Liam's friends but do you know of anyone who might have had a grudge against him?"

"Liam? You're joking."

"He's not involved in your 'business' dealings?" Eddy drew quote marks in the air.

McLaughlin glared at Eddy. "Behave. He was a kid, still at school."

"What about someone who knows he's your nephew? I imagine you've got enemies," Siobhan said.

McLaughlin hesitated for a few seconds, seeming distracted by an idea but then dismissed it. "We both know who he was with Sunday evening."

"You might believe you know, but I don't want you to take the law into your own hands."

McLaughlin stared out of the window at the fading light, looking annoyed. Siobhan tried to hide her unease and studied his damaged ear until he became uncomfortable, using his hand to hide the bandage.

"Do you mind telling me how you got injured?" she asked. "It looks very recent."

"I told you, I cut myself shaving."

"So if I check a certain house in Didsbury, I won't find a piece of your ear in the rubbish?"

Anger flared behind McLaughlin's eyes and he shot out an arm towards her, finger extended. Her insides fluttered, but she held his gaze and beside her Eddy stiffened. The coffee arrived, releasing the tension.

Siobhan sat forward. "If I hear you've taken the law into your own hands, or are even considering doing it, I'll make sure you regret it."

The sneer McLaughlin attempted wasn't a success and he still couldn't meet her eyes. But he'd soon pull himself together. Time to leave.

"Thank you for your help Mr McLaughlin. I may need to speak to you again so don't take any trips." Siobhan signalled to Eddy, rose and started for the front door, forcing herself not to hurry.

"Is that it?" McLaughlin shouted at her back.

At the door Siobhan smiled at him before letting herself out. In the lift on the way down, she let out a long, slow breath. Perspiration soaked her armpits.

"Bloody hell, Boss, I've never seen him like that." Eddy laughed. "I thought he'd go for you when you mentioned his ear, but when you stared him down…"

"Mr McLaughlin's had a nasty experience at the hands of a woman and a man in a wheelchair and I suspect it's knocked his confidence."

Siobhan studied Eddy and contemplated McLaughlin's blunder. The idea one of her team might be leaking information to him appalled her, but she'd make sure she found the mole. She hoped it wasn't Eddy; she was beginning to like him.

The dark bulk of the mill loomed ahead and, checking nobody had followed them, Adam parked the car outside the entrance gate. Byron jumped out before the car stopped moving. After locking the car, Adam vaulted the gate and caught up with Byron as he removed the drum from in front of the door at the far end of the courtyard.

A musty smell of damp masonry and decomposing timber rose up from the opening. The torch they'd found in Mal's glove compartment illuminated a set of stairs going down. Feet had cleared a path through the sludge of rotting leaves on each step. Had they belonged to Philip's captors? Or just rough sleepers looking for a secluded shelter?

Byron descended and Adam followed. The stink increased and the stairs opened into a large space. They paused and studied their surroundings. The torch threw out a narrow cone of light which didn't reach the edge of the room. A figure moved at the far wall. A surge of adrenaline prepared Adam for action. Then the figure cried out and staggered before slumping to the floor.

"Philip!" Byron ran across the rubbish strewn floor.

Adam followed, almost tripping on the remains of an old broken chair. Byron grabbed Philip and lifted him upright, holding him in his arms.

Philip sobbed, speaking incoherently between taking gulps of air. Adam kept watch on the entrance, aware they needed to leave in case his captors came back. After a few moments Philip's breathing returned to normal and Byron introduced them.

"Nice to meet you, Philip." Adam took his cold, damp hand. "Shall we get out of here?" He gestured towards the stairs.

Byron supported his nephew until his legs steadied. Philip struggled to climb the gate but between them they got him to the car. A small old-looking car had stopped at the corner of the next street. Adam hadn't noticed it before and approached it. He couldn't see the driver, but he thought someone moved in the shadows behind it. He stared at the spot until Byron called him. Adam jogged back to the car and helped put Philip on the back seat. As he drove past the other car, he checked it and memorised the number plate. The shadow he'd taken for a person still hadn't moved.

"What's up?" Byron said.

"Nothing." Adam gestured at Philip with his thumb and studied him in the rear-view mirror. Philip sat, head lolling and hunched up in his uncle's jacket, overwhelmed by the exhaustion of two days without sleep. Now the euphoria of his rescue had passed, he didn't look too well. They rounded a corner and he fell into the child seat, jerking awake. Adam pulled up into a layby, got out and removed the booster seat.

"Lie down." Byron ordered and Philip complied.

Adam stowed the seat in the boot and found a rug which he laid over Philip. They closed the doors and got into the front.

"The poor lad must be shattered," Adam said.

Byron wore a thankful grin. "Thanks, Adam. I couldn't have done it without you."

Adam shifted in his seat. "It wouldn't have taken as long, you mean. We were there hours ago." His relief at finding Philip matched Byron's.

"It's not your fault, mate. If those bloody coppers hadn't turned up… Anyway, we've got him now. I'll ring his parents and tell them he's safe." Byron took out his phone as they pulled away. "Rebecca," he said, "we've got him."

Byron listened to Rebecca's response and ended the call. "We'll have to stick him in a hotel. The police have searched the house and taken his clothes. Rebecca's worried he'll get arrested."

Adam considered this for a few moments. "He can stay at my place. I've got plenty of room."

"You sure?"

"What are mates for?" Adam hoped he wouldn't regret it.

Byron sat at Adam's kitchen table, washing his cheese sandwich down with a mug of coffee. Adam chopped onions for the evening meal, seeming unbothered by the acrid fumes.

"You sure you don't want me to make you some?" Adam said, scraping the contents of the chopping board into a spitting frying pan.

"I'd better see Philip's parents, tell them how he is."

Steps sounded in the hallway and Philip walked into the kitchen. Although looking bruised and exhausted, the shower had done him good. He wore one of Adam's tracksuits, the legs and sleeves too short. Adam wasn't small but Philip might even eclipse Byron's six-foot-five frame.

"I'll get you some clothes when I go round."

"Thanks, Uncle Byron."

"You're old enough to dispense with the uncle. Do you want to tell me what happened?"

Panic and bewilderment crossed Philip's features as he related his abduction and imprisonment. When he finished, tears rolled down his cheeks.

"Did Mugisa say why he abducted you?"

"He thinks I've betrayed him and the others. Like Liam did."

Byron exchanged a glance with Adam. *We know how that ended.* "I'd better go and put your parents' minds at rest."

Half an hour later, Byron sank into the armchair in front of the fire in Samuel's study, a glass of red wine in his hand. He drained the glass and put it on the table. Samuel still kept a great cellar. Philip's parents had listened in silence as he related the account of their son's abduction and subsequent rescue.

"Even if he thought Philip let him down, I don't understand why Mugisa would do such a thing. They're such good friends." Rebecca sounded bewildered.

Byron couldn't recall ever seeing her like this. "He was a child soldier. These kids are seriously damaged; there's no accounting for how they'll behave."

"Surely they would have rehabilitated him and undertaken psychological evaluations before letting anyone adopt him?" Samuel said, outraged.

"It doesn't always work." The warmth and wine made Byron sleepy and he yawned.

"Where's Philip?" Rebecca frowned at him.

"He's safe, but it's not a good idea for you to know where he is."

"Why not?"

Byron considered how to phrase his reply.

"I'm concerned about the police. If you don't know, they can't do you for obstruction."

Rebecca broke the silence. "I told the police he's missing…"

Both brothers stared at her. "Why the hell did you do that?" Byron demanded.

She held his gaze. "I. Was. Worried. About. My. Son."

"Let's not fall out," Samuel said.

It was way too late for that, but they needed to maintain this fragile truce until they sorted out Philip's problem. "Like Samuel says, we also have those gangsters to worry about."

"Do you think they'll return?"

"I don't expect them to hurt you, but they'll still be looking for Philip." *And me*, he neglected to add. "Unless we make them reconsider."

"And how do you propose to do that?" The challenge in Rebecca's voice returned.

Byron wouldn't rise to it. He had no idea what he would do, but he needed to come up with something soon. They might have found Philip but Mugisa hadn't gone away and McLaughlin wouldn't stay quiet forever.

CHAPTER 14

His determination to return to his father and brothers grew as his strength increased. The Boy knew if he escaped, he could find his way home using the old tracking skills his father had taught him.

The camp sat in a deserted part of the country, and he would have to travel far before meeting outsiders. Experience told The Boy he could survive many days without food but he'd need water and would have to take some with him. Guards watched the children at all times, never leaving them alone. He must be cunning, ready to take advantage of any slip on his captors' parts.

Amongst the other captives was an older girl of twelve or thirteen. Beautiful and vivacious, she reminded him of his dead sister. She had been in the camp about a year and belonged to an officer. Because of his status, the soldiers treated her with deference.

Siobhan pursed her lips, as she read the fingerprint analysis from the fire. "So, we haven't got either print on the database?"

"No, Boss." Eddy looked disappointed. "But there's no question they're from two different people. One of whom was pretty big."

"Philip Mason's pretty big, and his prints aren't on record." Siobhan smiled. "Can you check if they can get any prints off the gear we got from his house? The trainers had patches of shiny material on the tongue. It will save us going back."

Eddy frowned. "Those prints could come from the firemen who moved the security grille."

"They wore gloves."

Eddy left and constables Stefan Dabrowski and Debbie Matthews arrived. Stefan strode to her door, grinning.

"You're looking pleased with yourself, Stefan."

His grin widened. "I've found a witness putting the Mason lad together with the victim at around ten on Sunday night. A shopkeeper who saw them said he remembers them because the black lad looked nervous." He held up a videocassette in an evidence bag.

"Well done, Stefan — and you, Debbie. Good work. Let's have a look at it."

In the comms suite, Siobhan remembered they were still waiting for the final analysis of the last video and she collared the technician. "Any joy with the cyclists in the other video?"

"Err, not on the bikes, Ma'am. There's at least two, maybe more, but we can't see any detail. I'm trying to sharpen it up, but..." He tailed off before adding, "One thing I can tell you — they were going in the opposite direction to the two lads on foot."

Siobhan tried to quell her disappointment. "What about the car, Debbie?"

"I've checked the cameras on the main roads, Boss, but I kept it to a narrow window, fifteen minutes either side of the sighting we got. The good news is there weren't many cars. We've tracked down all but four and spoken to the owners."

"And the four?"

"Still working on it, but one doesn't even appear on the database. I tracked it but lost it when it turned off the main road near Ashton."

Was it significant? The evidence led to the Mason lad and his friends. She couldn't ignore the car but mustn't waste too much time on it. "Keep on it. Follow up the other three then widen the timeframe and see if we can find the fourth one heading into the area. We might be able to discover where it came from." She studied the screen which showed a fuzzy image of a small shop.

"Is the time stamp correct?"

"Yes, Boss, within a couple of minutes," Stefan confirmed.

The time showed 22.03. Two faces filled the screen as the figures stepped in front of the camera. Both lads ate from a bag of chips. Liam smiled, looking relaxed. Philip, in contrast, looked tense and shifty. They bought two cans of cola and walked out. By the time the scene ended, Siobhan's disappointment had changed to quiet satisfaction. She had Mason.

Adam finished his coffee and placed his mug on the worktop in his kitchen. Footsteps sounded on the tiled floor of the entrance hall and he greeted one of his guests. "Morning, Byron. Coffee?"

"Yes please, mate." Byron looked around the smart kitchen. "Nice place you've got here. I won't ask how much you paid; it'll make me sick."

Adam poured the coffee. "It needs a lot of work. I only finished the kitchen and bathroom before Sarah…" He changed the subject. "Is Philip okay?"

"I've let him sleep. He needs the rest." Byron frowned. "I've been thinking about McLaughlin, and how to get him off our backs."

"Any ideas?"

"One or two." Byron hesitated, before asking, "Can you look after Philip this morning? I need to call on someone."

"No problem, mate. He can help me strip the dining room."

Footsteps clomped down the uncarpeted staircase and Philip appeared in the doorway, looking like he'd barely slept.

"Morning, Philip. You want a coffee, or breakfast?"

"Have you got any juice?" He nodded a greeting to his uncle. "How's Mum?"

"Okay. She and your dad are both worried about you but they're holding up. How are you?"

He shrugged. "Okay, I suppose." Philip caressed the cut on top of his head and he winced. The ugly lump in the centre of his forehead looked sore.

"I'll get going." Byron strode to the door, a suppressed energy in his movements. "I'll see you both later."

Adam couldn't remember ever seeing Byron so wound up. He prepared breakfast and Philip began sobbing. Unsure how to react, he ignored the young man and adjusted the heat under the griddle. By the time he'd cooked the bacon, Philip had his emotions under control.

"Tuck in," said Adam. "There's plenty more if you want it." He pushed the plate of bacon sandwiches across the table. "Brown sauce?"

"Thanks," Philip mumbled and opened one of the sandwiches, squeezing a generous dollop of sauce on the strips of streaky bacon.

Adam recognised the expression in the youth's reddened eyes and swallowed his mouthful. "Do you want to talk about it?" he asked.

Philip didn't reply and Adam took a swig of his cooling coffee. He got up to refill his mug and Philip started to speak.

"I didn't know they intended to kill Liam. We were just going to scare him." His lower lip quivered. "Mugisa said he'd betrayed us and we had to punish him. It was an accident."

Adam sat back down. Images of the dead youth's body sliding out of the fire-damaged bin returned. Hell of an accident. But he recognised someone rationalising their actions and tried not to judge Philip too harshly. God knows, he'd made mistakes often enough in his youth.

"How did you get involved with Mugisa?"

Philip assumed a faraway look. "I suppose he was exciting. The other lads all looked up to him. I'm just a doctor's son from the suburbs and he was a genuine African who'd fought in a war. I wanted to be like him. When he asked me to join 'the brotherhood', I was flattered."

Adam remembered how it felt to be the exotic one in his school, coming from Hong Kong and looking as he did. "What did this 'brotherhood' do?"

"Not a lot. It sounded exciting, but we didn't do much." His gaze flicked away from Adam's. "We sometimes nicked stuff. The first time they made me do it I was terrified, but it made me feel alive. I know we shouldn't have done it. But we didn't nick anything from houses, just businesses. Mugisa said most businessmen are cheats..." Philip's voice tailed off.

If Adam hadn't joined the Royal Marines, would he have become part of a similar gang? He'd gone off the rails in his teens, especially after his mum returned to Hong Kong and he'd stayed with his dad and 'the wicked stepmother'. "So what happened with Liam?"

"We nicked laptops from a retail park, but Liam kept a few for himself." Philip sounded outraged. "He'd taken an oath. We all had. Why the hell did he do it?"

He began crying again. Adam sat uncomfortably for a few seconds before placing his arm across Philip's shoulders. The youth leant into him, the sobs making him shake. Adam searched in vain for words of comfort. Even if he and Byron could keep him safe from McLaughlin and Mugisa, he would have to live with his actions, something Adam knew all about.

Siobhan sat at her desk, stifling a yawn and took another sip of coffee. Eddy looked exhausted.

"How are you coping, Eddy?"

"Youngest is teething, Boss. I keep suggesting to the missus we let him sleep in the cellar, but she won't hear of it."

Siobhan smiled, glad she didn't have those worries. "Get everyone who gave Philip an alibi for Sunday night brought in for questioning." She noticed his expression. "You don't agree?"

"The girl's lying, but he might have been with the other four until eight."

"You're right, but I'm not happy with the stories of the four lads. And you know my feelings about young Mr Walcott."

"Shall I bring them here?"

"Yes. Get uniform to do it. Make them realise how serious we are. Can you ask the college to provide an appropriate adult and we'd better have a solicitor standing by. I don't want any criticism from the CPS."

Forty minutes later, Eddy returned. "They're here, Boss. How do you want to play it?"

"Let's take Jenna Young first," Siobhan replied. "There's a possibility she's been in touch with Philip and can help us find him. Do we have an update on the fingerprints we got from the items we recovered from Philip Mason's bedroom?"

"We got some good prints off a glass from his bedside and a photo frame. They're comparing them now."

"Right, let's get Miss Young and see what she has to say for herself."

Siobhan led the way to the canteen where the pupils waited. When she walked into the room, she sensed something wrong. The girl sat with the welfare officer but the four boys clustered round a table away from everyone else.

Matthew Walcott spoke in a vehement undertone, fixing each of the others with his gaze as they listened. Conscious of her watching him, he looked over and, for a second, his eyes blazed with a fierce anger. Unease made her insides flutter as the youth's expression changed and he looked at her with amusement. This unsettled her more and she glanced at Eddy, receiving confirmation he'd seen the same transformation.

Where were the officers who'd collected the students? A group of them loitered at the counter chatting and waiting to get served. Despite the urge to wade in and tear a strip off them, she kept her temper under control.

"Find out who's in charge," she hissed at Eddy and taking a deep breath, she approached the students. "Thank you for coming in to help us with our enquiries. Mr Walcott, can you follow me?"

At least she now knew for certain who pulled the strings.

Mugisa sat across from the two police officers in the interview room. Alongside him sat a solicitor and the welfare officer from the college. The airless room felt crowded.

The Chief Inspector studied Mugisa and he gave her a friendly smile, to no effect. Realising he'd made a mistake in the canteen, he believed he could recover the situation. He studied her sidekick, who'd changed from the friendly figure he'd spoken to at college.

Nobody said anything for a long period. The solicitor looked bored and gazed around the room, doodling on the pad in front of him. The welfare officer cleared her throat, looking uncomfortable with her role.

"Mr Walcott, you realise you're not under arrest and you may leave whenever you want?" the sergeant said.

Mugisa nodded. "Yes, sir, I understand."

"We need to clarify what happened on Sunday evening. Last time, you told us you spent the evening with four people." He read out the names.

"Yes, sir."

The policeman asked him the same questions as yesterday, wanting to know where he went and who he saw. Mugisa gave his answers enough attention to make them convincing, while at the same time trying to work out how he could get to Philip.

"What happened once Philip left?" the sergeant continued.

"What do you mean, sir?" This new question made Mugisa uneasy, but he'd covered the whole evening with the others, so it shouldn't be a problem.

"Philip left about eight — what did you do then?"

"Oh, right." Mugisa smiled at them. "We hung around Dimitri's for a bit and then to the amusement arcade and the park." Because they were in there so often, the staff wouldn't remember if they'd seen them Saturday or Sunday.

"So the four of you stayed together?"

"Yes, sir."

"What time did you go home?"

"Eleven or later, I'm not sure." Mugisa showed them a bare wrist.

"The others didn't have a watch?"

"No, sir. Sorry."

"So if we speak to your parents, they'll confirm your story."

"Mr and Mrs Walcott were in bed, but you can ask them." They would have no idea what time he'd came home. Mugisa glanced at the woman officer who hadn't spoken since they sat down. She'd just stared at him, but he recognised her tactics and smiled at her.

"Do you own a bike, Matthew?" she asked.

Thrown by the question, he replied without thinking. "Sorry, sir?"

"There's no need to call *me* sir, Matthew. Chief Inspector will do." Her smile didn't touch her eyes. "Well, do you?"

"Yes, Chief Inspector." Puzzled, Mugisa tried to work out what she wanted.

"Do you mind if we examine it?"

Mugisa's thoughts raced. He couldn't remember what had happened to his bike. He'd left it at the side of the alley, away from Liam, but he hadn't checked it for blood. Had he wheeled it through any?

"No." He forced himself to hold her gaze, knowing he needed to concentrate.

"Where is it?" she asked. "At college?"

"No, it's at home." He thought of a perfect solution and relaxed. He would let them take Mr Walcott's bike.

"We'll get someone to pick it up once we've finished here. Would you mind letting us have your fingerprints and a DNA sample?"

The solicitor paid attention and opened his mouth but Mugisa stilled him with a gesture. "Chief Inspector, I have nothing to hide." They couldn't think he was stupid enough to have left fingerprints.

"Where were you born, Matthew?" the policewoman asked.

Thrown by this change of tack, he hesitated. He didn't want to discuss his past with anyone, least of all this woman.

"It's not a secret," she continued in a gentle voice, "I can easily find out, I'm just interested."

"Kampala," he replied. Nobody, even people from Uganda, had ever heard of his actual village.

"I don't think I've met anyone from there before." Her smile seemed genuine. "So, the Walcotts, they're not your real parents?"

Mugisa shook his head and studied his hands, thinking back ten years to when he'd last seen his mother. Despite the surroundings, he imagined he could feel empathy from this woman but he caught her exchange a look with the sergeant and cold anger surged through him.

She saw him and blushed. "Now, you said you didn't see Liam at all on Sunday."

"No, I didn't." He needed to control his anger. It was just a game, and she had almost tricked him.

"You said in your statement you hadn't seen him since Friday. Do you want to change it now?" She picked up a sheet of paper in front of her.

"No, I meant I didn't see Liam." He glared at her. Is she laughing at me?

She dropped the paper. "A witness told us Liam was with you on Sunday night."

"Philip?" He saw he'd guessed right. "Sometimes Philip lies to make himself seem important."

"He's not the only one," she snapped.

"Sorry, Chief Inspector?" He concentrated, waiting for the next trick.

"You told your mother you were at Philip's on Monday night. Where did you go?"

"I went to Philip's house." He took a gamble. "But I saw you and left. I didn't want to get involved." Mugisa read her disappointment and realised he would be all right.

Byron sat in a greasy spoon he used to frequent after his boxing lessons a lifetime ago and sipped his coffee. It tasted as bad as he remembered. He'd hoped someone here would direct him towards friends he used to come with but the owner had died a few months ago, leaving the place to a nephew from Bradford. The man wanted to help and suggested Byron returned later when one of the old waitresses he remembered came in for her lunch.

Thoughts of how to keep his nephew safe from Mugisa whirled round Byron's head. He didn't have a handle on what motivated the young ex-child-soldier. And he still had to deal with McLaughlin. His phone rang, but he didn't recognise the number. It could be about work — he'd neglected his business since arriving in Manchester.

"Hello, Byron Mason. How may I help you?"

"Well, Mr Mason. It's more a matter of how I may help you."

It sounded like a sales call, but the American twang intrigued him. "Go on?" he said.

"I understand you've had a few problems with some…" the caller hesitated, searching for a description. "Bad people."

Byron didn't respond. It wasn't a sales call, but what the hell did he want?

The caller continued, "How much to find out what they're planning?"

Byron still didn't reply and heard the caller breathing.

"Mr Mason?"

"How would you know what McLaughlin's planning?"

"Call me a disgruntled employee. The guy's an unprofessional psycho. I'm not into settling personal vendettas."

"You're not scared of what he'll do if he finds out you've spoken to me?"

"Petrified, but I'm going stateside ASAP and could do with a bit more capital to start again."

"Okay, why don't you just tell me how much you want?"

"Five thousand."

Byron laughed. "Sling your hook."

"You wouldn't want anything to happen to Cecily or Lucy, would you?"

The mention of his nieces made Byron want to rip the man's head off. "What do I get for the money?"

"Don't worry, it will be worth it."

They agreed to meet in a bistro near his brother's house in an hour. Byron ended the call and drained his mug, grimacing as the bitter liquid assaulted his taste buds.

He arrived early and checked that the layout of the restaurant hadn't changed since he'd last visited. He took a table in a corner, facing the window. The gloomy interior meant passers-by couldn't see him, but he had a good view of anyone arriving.

A man approached the front door and Byron paid attention. He'd built up a mental picture of the mysterious caller and this man fitted. The man did a double take before he spun on his heel and hurried away. Byron stepped towards the window and scanned the road. Outside the bakers across the road a hard-looking man sat in the front of a dark SUV. A second man, carrying a paper bag, joined him. He opened the passenger door and stared straight at Byron.

I should get out of here. Then the man threw his bag into the car and said something to the driver. Byron didn't wait and rushed through to the back room. Two doors on the left wall displayed the silhouettes of a man and a woman. A door on the opposite side led to a fire-exit which he remembered came out near the front of an alleyway by the side of the building. He ran towards a doorway in the back wall, leading to the kitchen.

As he reached it, a waitress carrying a tray of plates came out and just missing her, he charged through the opening. Steamy air, laden with the odour of rosemary and garlic, enveloped him. Four people stopped chopping food and cooking to stare at him.

"Staff only." A bulky man wearing a stained apron said.

"Can I get out this way?" Byron started for a doorway in the far corner.

"You no hear me?" The man picked up a large knife and stepped towards Byron. A scar from below his right ear disappeared down his thick neck into the mass of black curly hair sprouting out of the top of his shirt.

"I just want to—"

A scream from the restaurant distracted the man and Byron ran for the back door. It opened outwards and, barely slowing, he charged through it, smashing it against the side wall. It led into a courtyard enclosed on two sides by buildings. To the front, a padlocked gate led to the alleyway where the fire-exit opened. The back wall consisted of concrete panels topped with three strands of barbed wire supported on metal poles. Behind him a pan clanged to the floor and angry voices shouted.

Two wheelie bins stood in front of the back wall and running at the nearest one, Byron vaulted onto the lid. It bowed under his weight but held. He peered over the barbed wire. Thick holly bushes grew at the base of the wall and the ground fell away towards a disused railway line.

A figure appeared in the doorway and levelled an arm at Byron. Metal glinted. He grabbed the top of the nearest pole and leapt over the barbed wire. The top strand caught his jacket but with a ripping sound he was over. The ground rushed up to meet him. He ploughed through branches and wet leaves, landing on the rubble-strewn ground. His left ankle gave and he crashed to the earth, landing on a lump of concrete.

Dazed, he lay still for a moment. Feet landed on the lid of the bin with a hollow clang. He searched for a weapon and picked up a half brick, then glanced at the top of the wall, waiting for the gunman to appear.

CHAPTER 15

One morning the girl appeared, covered in bruises. A surge of anger seized The Boy, but he did not remark on it within the guards' hearing. At lunch, he sat near her in the shade of an acacia tree.

"Are you alright?"

She stared at him, wide-eyed, before nodding and finishing her meal.

"Who did that?" He indicated her bruises. "Did he do it?"

She checked nobody could overhear before answering. "Yes," she replied in a whisper.

"I will kill him," The Boy announced.

Despite her obvious pain, she laughed. The Boy, now eight, was less than half the size of the officer who'd beaten her.

She covered her mouth with her hand. "I am sorry to laugh at you." She reached out and gripped his shoulder. "Thank you, but please don't get into trouble. It was my fault he hit me." She lowered her head and continued to eat.

The Boy meant what he said and from that day forward they became friends, eating together and sitting near each other in the classes. His natural athleticism, revived by his better diet, allowed him to thrive in this new environment. His captors gave him more freedom, allowing him to wander further afield.

Siobhan and Eddy followed Walcott out and watched him walk away.

"Cool bugger isn't he?" observed Eddy. "You think he's got anything to do with it?"

"I'm not sure. Philip must have had help, so why not the cyclists?"

"But they were going the wrong way."

"Maybe, but if they were searching for Liam..." She didn't need to finish. "I thought we had him when I asked about the bike." Siobhan recalled his momentary panic. "Make sure someone takes him home and collects it."

"I'll get them to take him in a van; they can bag it and shove it in the back, although he didn't seem too worried about the fingerprinting or DNA."

"Probably wore gloves, but it's worth a try."

Eddy nodded. "Shall we do the other boys now or the girl?"

"The girl. Let the others sweat."

Jenna Wilson sat in the seat between the solicitor and welfare officer and smiled at Siobhan but she didn't return it. Nonplussed, the girl's gaze flicked to the solicitor who'd stopped doodling and was studying his new client with interest.

"Jenna, do you know why you're here?" Siobhan asked.

"You want to ask me about Liam?" The mention of the dead youth seemed to upset her.

Siobhan studied her, trying to gauge her sincerity. "We're not happy with your account of what happened on Sunday the twenty second: the evening you spent with Philip Mason. You do realise lying to the police is a serious matter?"

"Of course. I wouldn't... I haven't lied." The girl blinked, looking less assured.

"So you don't want to change anything you told us yesterday?" Eddy used a grave tone.

"No," she whispered and glanced towards the solicitor who looked like he wanted to intervene to save her, if he could only think of a reason for doing so. "No, I don't want to change anything," she said with more conviction.

Siobhan detected fear behind the confidence. "What would you say if I told you we have evidence Philip was in Ancoats at the time you said he was with you?"

The girl examined her immaculate fingernails.

"That's near where the firefighters found Liam's body, as you no doubt know."

Tears created two tracks down her cheekbones and she sniffed. The solicitor produced a handkerchief, handing it to the girl as he favoured Siobhan with a look of censure. Jenna whispered something to him.

"Chief Inspector, can I have a private word with my client?"

Siobhan concealed a smile of triumph and gathered her notes. "We'll wait outside."

A key clicked in the lock of his front door and for an instant Adam imagined Sarah walking back into his life. He'd not thought of her for months but now she seemed to be haunting him.

"I'm just going to get changed, Adam," Byron called from the hallway.

Adam strolled out of the kitchen. A bedraggled Byron stood inside the front door. Dead leaves clung to his stained trousers and the insulated padding poked out through a rip in his jacket. A small twig with three holly leaves on it stuck out of his hair. "Bloody hell, what happened to you?"

"Long story. I'll get changed first." Byron limped to the stairs.

"What have you done?"

"Turned it, but I don't think it's too bad."

"Sit, let's have a look."

Byron sat on the third step and stretched his left leg out, rolling up the mud-spattered cuff of his trousers. His sock left a deep indentation in the flesh.

Adam prodded the swollen flesh. "Can you flex it?"

Byron moved his ankle, grimacing as he did so. "It feels like a strain."

Adam hoped so and bandaged the joint then put the kettle on while Byron changed into clean clothes. He returned to the kitchen with a less pronounced limp.

"Go on then, what happened?" Adam plonked a mug of tea on the table in front of him.

Byron pulled the mug towards him. "I got a call from someone with information about McLaughlin and agreed to meet him." He related what he'd done. "When he turned up, he saw two of McLaughlin's heavies and did a runner. They saw me. I had to make a quick exit. At least one was carrying."

"What?" Adam's mind flew back to a car fire where they'd found the driver with a bullet hole in his head. That had only been three miles away.

"A handgun. One of them took aim at me but I jumped over a wall and did this." He gestured at his ankle. "I was waiting for him to poke his head over but his mate shouted him and he ran off. Then I heard the staff saying he had a gun."

"Why didn't you tell me? I'd have come as backup."

"And leave Philip?"

"Nobody knows he's here."

Byron shook his head.

"You sure they're McLaughlin's men?"

"Who else. They guy who rang knew my nieces' names so I'm betting McLaughlin has briefed his crew to look out for me."

"So what do you want to do about him?"

"Take him out."

Adam swallowed. "That's a big step."

"He's talking about my family. His men have my nieces' names."

"If you're serious, I'll—"

"Nah." Byron exhaled in frustration. "It's too risky, although I'm tempted."

Relief made Adam's hands tingle.

"McLaughlin's pragmatic, or he used to be, and I reckon if I give him a bloody nose he'll conclude it's too much trouble to continue."

"So, what's the plan?"

"Not sure yet — I need to do some research. A mate from school who I used to box with is involved in the same life and he'll know everything about his operation. I don't even know how many men he's got working for him."

"Where does your mate live?"

"That's what I was trying to find out." Byron checked the time. "I'd better go — I'm supposed to be seeing someone who might be able to tell me."

"You need to rest the ankle."

"Yeah." Byron stood, wincing as he took the weight on the injured joint. "I shouldn't be long."

Byron arrived at the small housing estate built alongside the park. The Victorian cotton-barons' mansions which once lined the streets surrounding it had long gone from this side, replaced by mean council houses, built with tiny windows.

Three large new cars huddled outside a house at the end of a cul-de-sac. He parked Adam's borrowed vehicle alongside them. The sensation of being watched accompanied him as he approached the front door which opened before he reached it. An athletic young man with a roll-up hanging from the corner of his mouth stared at Byron with blank eyes.

"I'm here to see Cyrus. He's expecting me," Byron said.

The man looked him up and down for a few seconds. He exhaled, blowing smoke towards his visitor. Byron smiled in response, not willing to let this arsehole get to him.

"Lynton, let the man in." A familiar voice came from within the house.

Lynton waited a few seconds before moving aside. Byron stepped forward, but Lynton placed the palm of his hand against Byron's chest, gesturing to him to raise his arms so he could frisk him. Byron ignored the instruction. Movement came from a room off the small hallway.

"Lynton, why you playing the fool? Byron's a brother."

Without taking his attention off their visitor, Lynton let Byron into the room. In the dim light, Byron could make out bare white-painted walls and an ugly green polyester carpet. Two cheap black leather sofas and a chair took up most of the floor space. In the corner, a massive silver television occupied pride of place. The thick haze spoke of prolonged and dedicated smoking by the occupants. Cyrus greeted his old school friend with a complicated handshake routine Byron, surprisingly, still remembered.

Cyrus dismissed the two young women, sprawled on one sofa and offered Byron the seat. A third man, who could have passed for Lynton's brother, emerged through the beaded curtain hanging across another doorway. The newcomer ignored Byron and handed bottles of Red Stripe to Cyrus and Lynton.

Cyrus raised his bottle to Byron. "To our schooldays. Best days of our lives, don't they say?"

"I believe they do." Cyrus had worn well, but Byron suspected his old school friend had done nothing which could be described as hard work.

The newcomer stayed in the doorway and Lynton sat on the arm of the sofa, glaring at Byron, who ignored him.

"So, Byron. You said when you called you want to know about Ritchie McLaughlin?" Cyrus stretched each syllable of the name.

Byron nodded.

"Why you want to know?" Cyrus's accent veered between broad Mancunian and Jamaican.

"He's threatening my family and I want him to stop."

"You was always big on family, Byron. That brother of yours still boxing? Man he was fierce, he should have turned pro." He looked at his two companions. "His brother had it all: speed, power, aggression. Like a young Muhammad Ali."

The other two didn't seem impressed but Byron guessed it took a lot to impress them. The words transported Byron back eighteen years as he and Cyrus watched a teenaged Samuel batter grown men, some of them seasoned professionals, in the gym he sneaked off to in Moss Side. Being the bright son of a prominent brain surgeon, he had to make sure his father never knew of his activities. The responsibilities of early fatherhood soon made sure he finished, long before he ended up in the wheelchair.

"No, he stopped when he got into medical school."

"Oh yeah. I forgot he also had a head full o' brains. So how did your family upset Ritchie?"

"Something to do with my nephew — my brother's son." Byron didn't want to get into details.

Cyrus chuckled. "Chip off the old block, eh?"

He handed Byron a sheet of lined paper torn out of a school exercise book and he wondered if it belonged to one of the two girls. It contained a list of addresses inscribed in small, neat handwriting. Byron read them in the gloom.

"Top one's his pad; fancy apartment in the city." Cyrus leant across and pointed to the first address. "The others are places he owns."

Byron tapped an address on the sheet with his forefinger. Unlike the others, which bore the names of bars and restaurants, the building occupied an unfashionable part of the city.

"What's this one?"

"Lynton found that. It's where he keeps his gear before he moves it on."

Byron nodded his thanks to Lynton who just grunted, obviously still upset at being rebuked. He folded the list and slid it into his pocket, trying to work out how he could use it.

"There's rumours he's got half a million quid's worth of dodgy gear in there on a lorry, just waiting for him to ship it out." The man in the doorway spoke for the first time.

An idea occurred to Byron. "What security does he have?"

"He's got four of his men guarding it round the clock, two on site and two on call."

Lynton came out of his sulk. "You thinking of hitting it?"

Byron ignored the question; he didn't intend to share his plans with Lynton.

"How many men you got?" Cyrus cut in.

"Two: me and one other."

Lynton chuckled and the man in the doorway joined him.

"Man, Ritchie has at least twenty men," Cyrus said.

"It should be fairly even then," Byron said.

Cyrus laughed and flicked his fingers at his former schoolmate's riposte. Byron had hoped the crew he'd taken on at his brother's formed the bulk of McLaughlin's forces. Without the element of surprise he already faced an uphill task.

Mugisa watched Rebecca come out of the house, with the two girls following her. The alarm beeped as Cecily locked the door. He would need to change his plans. Rebecca reversed her car out of the drive and set off towards the main road. A surge of hope improved his spirits. Was she taking them to see Philip?

Rebecca, a careful driver, took her time in the heavy late afternoon traffic, enabling Mugisa to keep up with her. While he drove, he wondered how the others had got on with the police. He'd have to meet up with them later.

Rebecca parked the car and Mugisa realised he'd visited this house before. Philip's grandmother lived here and he'd come with him once. This must be where he'd gone to hide. Mugisa looked for a place from which he could observe the house.

A row of red brick terraces ran down each side of the narrow street. Most of the houses looked occupied but a few parking spaces remained and he chose a spot outside a house with no curtains and a For Sale sign nailed to the front wall. The car he'd borrowed from one of Mr Walcott's friends blended in with the others in the street.

An old newspaper lay on the back seat and he opened it out onto the steering wheel, pretending to read while he watched the house seven doors away on the other side.

Rebecca left half an hour later and Mugisa waited, discarding the paper as darkness fell. The temperature dropped, but he ignored the discomfort. The door to the house opened and Cecily came out and walked towards the small parade of shops on the main road. He tracked her in the mirror until she returned with a bag of groceries, but still no sign of Philip.

Mugisa decided to wait until it got darker and, if their brother wasn't there, he'd make them tell him where he was. Failing that, he'd use one of them for bait: a goat to catch a hyena.

Byron drove past the building, pulled over and studied it, pretending to read his road map in case anyone saw him. The single-storey warehouse had two openings in the front, both protected by roller shutters, a door for pedestrians and a larger opening, big enough to accommodate a lorry. A dark SUV sat in front of the bigger gate, confirming the presence of guards.

The roadworks he'd passed gave him an idea of how he could get in, but he'd need help. If he planned to do it tonight he didn't have much time. As he drove past the roadworks he slowed and studied the excavators before continuing on his way to buy the equipment he needed.

Three hours later, he arrived at Adam's house, having bought the various items in different shops and paying cash for them. Before he went in he called Louisa.

"Hi, Baby. How are you doing?" he said.

"Great. We went to Mum's, and she sends her love. How is Philip and the family?"

He hesitated. "They're fine."

"Are you sure?"

"Yeah, just teenage stuff." He squirmed in his seat.

"Any idea when you'll be able to come home?"

"Not long, hopefully by the weekend."

"Oh." She imbued the sound with her disappointment.

"How's Lilly?" he asked, trying to keep his voice bright.

"She's lovely, as ever. I've just put her to bed. She misses her daddy though. She wouldn't sleep last night, so I brought her in with me."

His heart constricted. "Look Louisa, I'd better go. I'll call you later."

Byron ended the call and sat for a few moments, wanting to go home and get on with his life. The sooner he got

McLaughlin off his family's back, the sooner that would happen.

He let himself into Adam's house calling, "Honey, I'm home."

Adam emerged from the back room. "Hi, Byron. I thought you'd abandoned us." He carried a stripping knife and wore a paint-stained sweatshirt over an old pair of jeans.

"Sorry, mate. It took longer than I expected."

"Did you get everything done?" Adam said, fishing for information.

"Yeah, sure." Byron remained vague, not wanting to involve his friend. "Philip okay?"

Adam held up his hand, palm down, and wiggled it. "Sometimes he seems okay, but … you know."

Byron nodded. "He'll need plenty of time. Where is he?"

Adam pointed upwards. "He gave me a hand for a bit but he's tired out. He's having a nap."

"Can you take a break?"

"Yeah, sure. I need one. Wallpaper stripping ain't my favourite activity." He put down the stripping knife and led the way into the kitchen. "Have you had lunch?"

Byron realised he'd not eaten yet. "I could eat, if you've got anything in?"

"How does home-made leek and potato soup and fresh bread sound?"

"You serious?" Byron's surprise lasted until he remembered Adam cooking for their unit.

"Sit, and I'll get it."

"You'll make someone a great wife someday." Byron tucked into the steaming soup, his mind on his plans, thinking of a way he could execute them on his own.

Adam laughed. "Eat up you cheeky bleeder." His expression became serious. "What are you planning?"

"That transparent, eh?" Byron paused for a few seconds. "I intended to do it alone but I might need help."

"I'm not doing much at the moment."

"Cheers, Adam. I wouldn't ask, only…"

Adam held up a hand. "Just give me a rundown."

"McLaughlin's got a warehouse with a forty-foot trailer full of stolen gear in it. If we can get hold of it, we can use it as collateral to persuade him to leave my family alone. I'd let him have it if he backs off."

Adam frowned and played with a few breadcrumbs on the table before replying. "Do you think it will work? You knew the guy."

"If I'm honest, I have to say I'm not sure." Byron put down his spoon. "He always loved money and half a million is a lot to lose."

Adam whistled. "That's a lot of persuasion."

Byron nodded. "Yup and I think it'll be enough."

Adam rounded up the crumbs on his plate.

"I can't just sit here and wait for McLaughlin to attack my family." He held his breath until Adam looked up, wearing a big grin.

"Okay, mate. I'm in."

Byron smiled and pushed his bowl away. "Thanks, mate."

"I'm assuming you've checked the place out," Adam said.

"I have. It's a single-storey brick and steel warehouse, ten metres by twenty with two doors at the front—"

"Roller shutters?"

"Unfortunately."

Adam made a face.

Byron nodded. "Yeah, but I have a plan." He wiggled his eyebrows. "There's also an alarm and security cameras."

"Anti-ram barriers?"

"I saw none. Oh, and they have between two and four guys on site."

"Oh." Adam frowned.

"Yeah, oh. If you decide you don't want to get involved, I'll understand."

"And leave you to make a hash of it?" Adam's expression didn't leave him in any doubt.

"Cheers, mate."

Half an hour later, they'd finalised their plans, Byron dismissing the small voice telling him they didn't stand a chance.

CHAPTER 16

The Boy woke one morning to find the camp almost deserted. Most of the soldiers had gone on a big raid, leaving just a few guards. He resolved to escape that night — he'd take the girl with him. They had become close and he regarded her as a sister. At lunch, he sat with her, away from the others.

"I'm running away," he said. "Why don't you come with me?"

She looked at him, her eyes wide with shock. "If they catch you, they will kill you."

"They will not catch me," he announced, with total conviction. "Come with me."

She looked even more horrified.

"Don't you want to go home?"

Her eyes clouded and she looked down at the forest floor. Tears ran down her cheeks for several moments before she wiped them and sniffed.

"All my family are dead." She looked around at the camp. "This is my home now."

"All of them?" She nodded and a surge of sympathy made The Boy's want to hold her. "Come with me. You can live with my family."

She shook her head. "Go alone. No decent family would want me now."

He wanted to protest, but her expression told him she wouldn't change her mind. Disappointed, he ate some of his food, but saved most for the journey. She offered him hers and he thanked her, putting it with the water he'd hidden.

Siobhan shivered, her office needed one more radiator, or just one which worked, although Eddy didn't seem bothered by the cold. She examined the report comparing Philip's fingerprints with those found at the fire and tried not to let her disappointment show. "It was a long shot Eddy, but at least we still have the CCTV and the eyewitness putting him with Liam just before he died."

"You're right, Boss, but finding his fingerprints would have been the first bit of physical evidence linking him to the scene."

Siobhan determined not to dwell on the setback. "Has the bike gone off to forensics?"

"Yes, it was a bone-shaker. I'm surprised at a young lad having such a tatty bike. What do you want to do about the girl?"

"I'll let the CPS decide. We'll concentrate on the investigation."

"Good idea. What about the other lads?"

Siobhan exhaled in frustration. "It's clear they're all lying. It sounds like they're reading from a script and I know who wrote it. We'll speak to the parents and find out what time each boy got home."

"Do you want them brought in?"

"Not yet, I want them on-side at the moment, but we'll reconsider if any of them become difficult." She suspected Mr Collins would be the most likely to give them trouble.

Eddy nodded. "The lads didn't object to us taking their prints."

"Yeah, I know." Her limbs felt like lead and she exhaled.

"Don't worry, Boss. We'll get something. I've got a good feeling."

"Was my frustration that obvious?" She laughed. "Anyway, isn't it me who should have intuitive thoughts?"

"Did you hear the news about Ritchie's man?"

She shook her head and waited for him to continue.

"Someone beat Darren Riley, one of Ritchie's soldiers, half to death outside his house. They're not sure he'll make it."

"Any ideas who did it?"

"It's got all the hallmarks of Harris and his boys."

Siobhan frowned in confusion.

Eddy explained. "Old man Harris and his two sons hate McLaughlin and the feeling is mutual. They're involved in stolen cars, drugs and prostitution but McLaughlin's been treading on their toes."

"That's the last thing we need now — a turf war. Although I suppose it might keep McLaughlin too busy to harass the Masons."

"You could be right, Boss." Eddy didn't sound convinced.

Byron glanced at Adam as he reversed off the road leading to McLaughlin's warehouse. His friend wore a grim expression: his combat face. Adam switched the lights off and killed the engine. The warehouse lay six hundred metres away. The road served an industrial estate and they hadn't seen another vehicle since they'd left the main road.

Byron got out and examined the two JCBs at the roadworks before going to the rear of the car where Adam joined him. Both men wore navy-blue overalls, black heavy-duty boots and work gloves. Black ski masks, now in their pockets, completed the outfits. Adam retrieved a large pair of bolt cutters and approached the biggest and most powerful digger.

A heavy metal plate protected each window, and he snipped the solid-looking padlocks securing these. Adam climbed aboard and using the universal key he'd borrowed, started the engine. As the digger drew alongside the car, Byron threw a bag of tools into the cab and climbed onto the footplate. Byron expected McLaughlin's men to be armed but hoped the element of surprise would give them enough of an edge. He welcomed the tingle across his scalp as a sign of his body getting ready for action.

They set off for the building and Byron checked he couldn't see the car from the road. Nearer their target, each put on his ski mask. Byron grabbed the bag of tools and jumped off before vanishing into the shadows to make his way to the main entrance.

The warehouse lay in darkness, and a wire mesh fence enclosed most of the perimeter. Although a black Range Rover sat in front of the goods entrance, the two roller shutters remained closed. As he waited an emptiness invaded Byron's stomach, but he knew it would pass once the action started.

Adam revved the digger and with a roar the vehicle lurched forward, crashing into the black SUV. The bucket bit into the side of the car with a screech of metal. An ear-splitting wail of the alarm followed. The bucket lifted, then closed on the roof of the car and Adam dragged it clear of the shutter.

Muffled shouts came from inside the building and Byron prepared for action, adrenaline surged through his bloodstream and his mind cleared. An electric motor whined and the roller shutter on the front door lifted. The door banged open against it as those inside tried to get out, too impatient for the motor to finish its job. Angry voices grew louder.

The note of the motor changed as the shutter approached the top of its travel and the door, released from the shutter, sprung open. He glanced at the JCB, now facing the door, and shielded his eyes as Adam switched on the spotlight.

Two men ran out, yelling. Byron hit the nearest one and the man grunted and fell. The second spun towards him but, dazzled by the light, he couldn't see. Byron grabbed him, smashing his head into the wall, and the man dropped.

Byron signalled to Adam and the lights died. The engine quietened and Byron rushed into the building, searching for more guards. Beside the door, he found a bank of light switches and an orange glow filled the space. The warehouse comprised an open space, almost filled by a tractor unit attached to a forty-foot trailer. A small glass-fronted office occupied the back corner next to the toilets. Byron checked these while Adam dragged the first man into the building.

"Can you manage?" Byron asked him.

Adam nodded and Byron approached the main roller shutter. He switched the motor on and pressed the up button. With a click and creak, the shutter rose. It stopped and the motor screeched. Two large padlocks, too hefty for the bolt cutters, secured the door to bolts set into the floor. *Fuck*. He switched the motor off and rushed to the office, returning with the keys for the truck but none for the padlocks.

"Search their pockets, Adam."

Adam finished securing the second man's legs with cable ties and searched his pockets. "Nothing here."

Byron frisked the other man with the same result. With the truck so near the barrier, he didn't think it would build up enough momentum to break out.

Adam straightened. "Keep away from the gate."

Byron finished securing the two prisoners and waited at the doorway. He checked the time. Having driven the route from the nearest of McLaughlin's other properties, they'd allowed five minutes for the raid and had already used three. If the guards had raised the alarm before coming out, or they had another base closer, they could be in trouble. He took a deep breath. Sweat ran under his ski mask.

Adam started the digger and manoeuvred it in front of the roller shutter before raising the bucket until it aimed at its centre. He let out the clutch, the vehicle leapt forward, and the bucket struck. With a shriek of tearing metal, the shutter bowed. The bolts securing it to the ground ripped free, and the shutter lifted. Then it jammed, and the JCB came to a sudden halt. The force of the impact knocked Adam off his off his seat and the engine stalled.

"Adam, you okay?" Byron's voice sounded loud in the silence.

Adam struggled into the seat and shook his head to clear it. He waved to Byron and pressed the starter. After a couple of attempts, the engine fired, filling the night air with thick black smoke. Byron checked the time again. The sensible thing to do would be to abort the raid now and leave.

Adam reversed the vehicle and regarded Byron with a grin before he charged forward again. This time, the blade ripped the gate free of the side runners. The blade came to a halt less than two feet from the front of the truck and Byron gave Adam the thumbs up.

Adam slammed the digger into reverse, ripping the shutter away from the entrance. The metal slats hung from the bucket like pieces of torn curtain. Byron ran to the cab: their five minutes were well and truly up.

Mugisa left the freezing car and made his way towards the small parade of shops round the corner from Philip's grandmother's house. Even the convenience store which boasted opening hours ''til late', had now closed and the pavements were empty. He headed for the alleyway behind the shops, searching for the bins. A few minutes' scrabbling about in the stinking debris enabled him to locate what he needed.

He returned to the house carrying his find and made his way to the yard behind the old woman's house. The gate opened with ease and two pairs of luminous eyes observed him. He remembered their owners but doubted if they would recall him.

He opened the container of out-of-date cream, placed it on the ground and retreated, waiting just out of reach. After checking to see what the intruder wanted, the cats came to investigate and, reassured by his passivity, feasted from the carton. Mugisa reached out a hand to touch them. At first they recoiled, but eventually they allowed the stranger to stroke them.

The purrs of contentment made their bodies vibrate under his hands. Mugisa gripped each cat by the scruff of its neck. Yowls filled the air as they slashed at him with needle-sharp claws. Held by the scruffs of their necks neither could reach the hand seizing it.

The orange sack he'd also rescued from the bins lay at his feet and holding a spitting cat in each hand, Mugisa lowered one to the mouth of the sack and attempted to open it with his foot. He'd got the animal half in when the back door opened. Startled, he relaxed his grip on the other cat and it shot out of his hand, disappearing with an indignant wail.

"Seraphim? Margo?" the old woman called.

Mugisa grabbed the sack in his left hand and got to his feet. In his other hand he now held the machete which he'd used on Liam. The old lady peered into the darkness then shuffled out into the freezing night. Mugisa stepped towards her and she gasped in alarm.

"Young man, I don't have any money but you can take the television."

He didn't reply and held the weapon at her throat. The memory of the kind old woman who welcomed him into her home and fed him fish stew and dumplings made his throat close up. Unable to speak, he used the blade to back her into the kitchen. He slammed the door behind him and held the weapon at shoulder height. The smell of fresh baking made him salivate.

"Where's Philip?" he demanded.

Her eyes widened behind thick lenses. "He's not here."

"Where are the girls?"

She shook her head. "What girls?"

Mugisa, angered by her lie, lifted the machete. She cringed and opened her mouth, but before she spoke, Cecily walked into the kitchen.

"Nana, it's freezing, what's—" Her mouth fell open and she stared at him.

"Hello, Cecily. Fetch your sister."

The old woman came to life. "No, dear, run. Take your sister." With surprising speed she moved between him and her granddaughter.

He hefted the blade at her grandmother.

"No, Mugisa." Cecily's voice rose in horror.

He halted his blow mid-strike and she left.

Recognition bloomed in the old lady's eyes. "You're Philip's friend."

Guilt made his chest tighten and he watched her until the girls returned. Lucy rushed in. Her expression of contempt made him weaken, but he must be strong.

"Where's Philip?" he asked again, stripping his voice of emotion.

The girls looked at one another. "We don't know," they said in unison.

He brought the blade closer to the old woman's throat. "Old woman, tell me."

She shut her eyes and shook her head. "I'm sorry. I haven't seen Philip for over a week."

He reached into the bag, grabbed the cat and let the sack fall to the floor.

"Seraphim! You're hurting him." She reached out for her beloved cat.

Mugisa waved the blade at her. "Where is he?"

"I don't know!"

She looked at him beseechingly, tears flowing down her cheeks.

Mugisa threw Seraphim into the air and swung the blade. It caught the cat behind the neck.

"Girls, look away," the old lady shouted then let out a wail of grief. The girls screamed.

The smell of blood gave Mugisa courage and he grabbed a sobbing Cecily and held the blade to her throat.

"Old woman, tell me now."

Adam waited in the car, having returned the digger. He exhaled through pursed lips. What the hell had happened to Byron? He should have been just behind him in the truck. The guards couldn't have got free and overpowered him. Adam started the engine but headlights approached from the main road. A car raced past, towards the warehouse, and his pulse raced.

He checked for other cars before pulling out and heading for the warehouse. As he rounded the bend, he saw the car had pulled over. Two men stood in front of it gesturing towards the damaged gates and wrecked SUV. The darkened truck and trailer still sat in the warehouse but he saw no sign of Byron.

One man took a phone out of his pocket as they walked towards the building. Adam assumed Byron hadn't left yet. He put the main beam on and drove forward, revving the engine.

As he got closer, he realised the car was the twin of the one he'd wrecked. This must be the backup crew. Adrenaline surged through him. He stopped behind their vehicle and got out as the two men focussed on him.

Adam put on a comedy Chinese accent. "What happen here?"

"Nothing to do with you. Get back in your car and bugger off." The man gestured at him to go.

"Look, accident. Someone hurt." Adam ignored the man and approached the damaged car he'd left at the side of the yard.

"I said leave it." The man's voice rose.

"Someone inside." Adams voice grew excited and he pointed towards the wrecked SUV. He didn't need to do much acting.

He'd reached the car. The man came closer and Adam saw the small automatic he'd taken for a phone. The man's companion said something in a low voice and grabbed at the armed man's elbow. The armed man shook off the hand and advanced.

Adam pointed into the crunched vehicle. "Driver in there, bleeding."

The second man swore and started towards the car, his more aggressive friend now less than six feet away. Adam hoped Byron was nearby. While he knew he could take the first one out, he wasn't sure if the other also carried a gun.

Behind them the lorry roared into life and both men froze. Adam hit the armed man with all his might. His fist smashed into the back of the gunman's head. The man gave a surprised grunt and fell — unconscious before he hit the ground.

Lights blazing, the lorry leapt out of the warehouse and headed straight for the newcomers' car. The second man vacillated, torn between helping his mate and trying to protect his car. He chose the latter and took a shot at the cab.

By the time the man realised the danger, Adam hit him. He drove his shoulder under the man's ribs and heard the air leave his body. The impact lifted the man off his feet and he crashed into the concrete of the yard. Adam slammed the man's head into the ground and something crunched. Footsteps came from behind him and he scrambled to his feet, ready to confront a new threat.

"Mickey Skinner would have been proud of that." Despite the smile, Byron's voice betrayed his anxiety.

"You okay?" Adam asked.

"Yeah. Dead man's handle. Took a while to suss it out." Byron studied the unconscious newcomers. "We'd better get going."

Heart still pounding, Adam jogged to the car.

CHAPTER 17

The afternoon dragged by and The Boy's mood swung between eagerness and despair. The thought of seeing his father and brothers again was tempered by the realisation he would never see his new sister. He kept looking at the horizon, worried the others would return before he could escape. The perils of his forthcoming journey didn't worry him.

As evening drew in, he relaxed. The others would be away until tomorrow. At their evening meal, he sat with the girl, intending to persuade her to join him. After they sat down, her officer arrived and summoned her. Without a word to The Boy, she went to him. The Boy's gaze followed her, emptiness growing inside him.

Once the other children in the hut quietened down, The Boy lay awake, listening to the sounds of the night. The yap of jackals as they scavenged round the camp contributed the most common noise. Although small, many carried rabies and a bite from an infected animal would lead to a terrible death. The whoop of hyenas on their nocturnal rounds sounded less frequently and came from a greater distance. These dangerous predators would make short work of a small boy.

The Boy decided he should leave before he lost his courage. He had hidden a short spear after the afternoon's class and would take it with him. He crept out of the hut and collected the weapon and his concealed provisions without incident. As he approached the perimeter of the camp, he moved more carefully. Guards patrolled every night, both to protect them from intruders and prevent people escaping. He slipped between the bushes as his father once taught him.

A cough sounded behind him and he froze: animal or human? A voice replied, confirming its identity. The two guards conversed in low voices and one of them laughed. The Boy used their sounds to avoid them and continued outwards.

Siobhan picked up the phone on her desk and listened for several seconds. "Yeah, I'll attend. Can you confirm the address?" She wrote it on a notepad. "Thanks. Sure, I'll liaise with the officers in attendance." She strode out of her office. "Eddy, get your jacket."

She briefed him as she drove and he navigated. They took the main road past one of the city's major football clubs, heading south west. Eddy directed her into a warren of narrow streets lined with red brick terraced houses. They looked well cared for, unlike the ones where they'd found Liam's body. Most showed lights in the lower windows and blue screens flickered behind open curtains. She saw the patrol car and parked behind it. The inhabitants of the normally quiet street followed their progress to the house.

The front door stood ajar and she pushed it open, calling out, "Hello, anyone home?"

A uniformed constable appeared in the kitchen doorway. "Chief Inspector Quinn?" he said in a strong Geordie accent.

She showed him her ID.

Eddy recognised him. "All right, Allan?"

"Sarge." He gestured behind him. "It's a bit of a mess in there, I wouldn't go in." He moved aside to let Siobhan have a look.

The smell of blood and guts mingled with the odour of baking hit her. The small kitchen had walls painted a bright yellow, and old-fashioned cupboards lined two sides. Spots of blood flecked their doors and more, mixed with entrails, covered the floor. Marks showed where feet had slipped in this and a machete lay by the back door. Siobhan wanted to grab it. What were the chances of it being the murder weapon?

"Do we know what's happened here?" she asked.

The Geordie constable gave her a summary of what he'd gathered from speaking to the witnesses. Siobhan listened with growing concern. There must be a connection between the attacks on this family.

"Where's the family?" Eddy asked.

"Next door with the neighbour, Mr Jessop." He jerked his thumb over his shoulder.

"Make sure nobody goes into the kitchen or the back yard until SOCO gets here," Siobhan said. "Eddy, let's have a word with Mrs Mason."

Mr Jessop let them into a small, neat living room. Rebecca and her daughters sat on the sofa sipping tea. The two girls had been crying but looked unhurt. Rebecca wore a determined expression and held the hand of an old woman sitting in an armchair, staring into space.

Siobhan said, "Mr Jessop, is there somewhere I can talk to Mrs Mason in private?"

"Through here." He opened another door to show a similar sized room containing a large silver television, a sofa covered in brown fabric and a comfortable-looking armchair. He bustled in and folded up a newspaper scattered on the sofa.

"Mrs Mason, are your daughters okay? Do you want an ambulance?"

"No, they're fine, Chief Inspector; physically at least." She gave Siobhan a fleeting smile. "Thank you." She patted her mother's hand and got up.

In the next room, Siobhan and Eddy took the sofa and Rebecca faced them from the armchair. Under Siobhan's questioning, Rebecca related her account.

"When I arrived Lucy screamed. Mr Jessop heard her and came to the door." Rebecca paused.

"How did you get into the house?" Siobhan said.

"I have a key. Lucy was in the doorway to the kitchen and I ran to her, then Mum cried out and I rushed into the kitchen. Mugisa ran out the back door—"

"You saw him?" Eddy interrupted.

Rebecca hesitated then shook her head. "He spoke to the girls. Who else could it have been?"

"So your daughters recognised the intruder?" Siobhan said.

"Of course." Rebecca looked irritated. "I told you, it was Mugisa."

"I'm sure you're right, but we'll have to ask them."

"After what they've gone through, surely you don't—"

"Not immediately." Siobhan's mind raced, trying to understand why Mugisa would do this. She remembered his fierce expression from the morning and didn't doubt he was capable of it.

"Did they say why he did it?" she asked Rebecca.

"He wanted to know where Philip was."

"Did they tell him?"

Rebecca glared at her. "We. Do. Not. Know. Where. He. Is. How many times do I have to tell you?"

Siobhan held her gaze for a few seconds. "Okay, I believe you."

Although Mugisa had subjected the girls and their grandmother to an unpleasant ordeal, at least he'd hurt nobody, and with any luck the machete he'd dropped would be the same one used to attack Liam. In which case, she needed to refocus the investigation. Her insides shrank as she realised once the press heard of this attack they'd crawl all over it. Madmen with machetes, dead pets and pretty girls held hostage. Just the story ingredients they loved.

Mugisa observed the two police officers leave the house next to the old woman's. He still felt angry with himself for leaving the machete but hearing the man's voice had startled him. He should have anticipated at least one of the men who'd freed Philip would have been there. It was another sign he had become weak and soft.

The police would be looking for him. He had enough money to start again somewhere else, but he'd made a big mistake trusting these people, letting them get close. He wouldn't do so again.

After the policewoman drove off, he studied the house. The other police car remained and the man who'd startled him hadn't left. Dismissing his fear, he walked towards his car, forcing himself not to hurry. Heart hammering, he started the engine but stalled as he tried to pull out. He closed his eyes and inhaled; he needed to stay calm.

By the time he reached his den he'd decided on his next move. He would collect the few items he kept at the house and leave. He felt guilty about leaving the Walcotts like this — they'd been good to him — but he couldn't afford the luxury of sentimentality. After loading the car, he drove to the house, but he saw the policewoman and her assistant waiting on the doorstep. He recalled the policewoman's attempt to trick him and was angry that he'd almost trusted her. He drove on, leaving behind another home which he could never return to.

A slight middle-aged man with short grey hair answered the door after Siobhan knocked.

"Mr Joseph Walcott?" she asked.

"Yes, can I help you?"

She made her introductions and he led them into a neat living room smelling of furniture polish. The three-piece-suite looked in showroom condition and the carpet, a patterned Axminster, bore no signs of wear. A dark-wood sideboard contained a full, 32-volume leather-bound Encyclopaedia Britannica. She remembered the day her father returned home with the set he'd rescued from a skip. Missing volumes 24 and 26, thereby undermining her knowledge of Metaphysics and Pre-Columbian Saints, it had formed the backbone of their home education.

Miriam Walcott looked pleased to see Siobhan again and produced a plate of home-made cakes to accompany tea in bone china cups. Eddy couldn't get his oversized fingers through the handle and gave up, picking the vessel up in both hands before lifting it to his lips like a chalice.

"I'm sorry Chief Inspector but Matthew isn't here," Miriam said, smiling. "You keep missing each other."

"I didn't expect to find him here." Siobhan regarded the couple with sympathy. "We have reason to believe he threatened an elderly lady and her grandchildren with a machete."

In the ensuing silence, Joseph stared, open-mouthed, but Miriam seemed uneasy and she recovered first. "There must be some mistake. Matthew has never been violent."

"He's never been in any trouble," Joseph confirmed.

"There's no mistake," Siobhan said. "The two girls know him well. They're Philip Mason's sisters." She studied them as she continued. "It's vital we find him before anyone gets hurt. Can you tell me where he might be?"

Tears formed in Miriam's eyes and Joseph shook his head. "He doesn't have many friends." He mentioned the three lads who'd been with him on Sunday night. "And of course, Philip Mason…" His voice tailed off.

"Is there somewhere else he might go?"

They named the places Mugisa mentioned in his alibi. Siobhan had already arranged for patrols to search there.

"Matthew told us he isn't your biological son," Eddy stated. "What can you tell us about his background?"

Joseph opened a locked drawer in the cabinet and produced a legal envelope. He withdrew papers from it and handed them to Siobhan. She read them and the couple regarded her, their wariness suggesting they feared what else she might have to say.

"I don't know this organisation." She read out an acronym.

"They rescue child soldiers," Joseph said, his voice above a whisper. "They rehabilitate them and find them homes."

"So Matthew is — was — a child soldier?" She shared a look with Eddy as she absorbed this information.

The Walcotts both nodded. "He spent nearly a year in a transit camp being rehabilitated before we met him," Joseph said. "He still sees a counsellor every month, but he doesn't have any problems."

"Do you have a recent photo of Matthew?" Siobhan asked, realising they'd have to organise a manhunt.

Joseph rummaged in the drawer for a few seconds. "Miriam, I can't find the album?"

Miriam left the room and returned with a small leather-bound photo album. "I showed it to the welfare officer from the college."

Siobhan raised her eyebrows. "When did she visit?"

"It was a he; a lovely young man — Chinese," Miriam said.

Siobhan made a note to check with the college. They studied the pictures. The images of the small boy moved and disturbed Siobhan in equal measure. She pointed to the most recent picture. "Can we have this? We'll return it."

"It's okay, we've got a copy," Miriam said.

"Would you mind if we searched Matthew's room?"

Joseph started to object but his wife silenced him and led them upstairs. The immaculate room contained none of the usual paraphernalia teenage boys accumulate. They retrieved two pairs of trainers and the clothes he'd worn on Sunday night.

"Does he have any heavy boots or shoes?" Siobhan asked.

"I keep telling him he needs good waterproof shoes but he always wears trainers," Miriam said.

Siobhan thanked her and left the devastated couple in peace.

In the car, Eddy examined the copy of the most recent photo of Mugisa. "Where does it leave us with Philip Mason?" he asked.

"I've been thinking the same thing since we found out about the attack on the grandmother. We know it would have taken at least two to carry the bin across the yard and into the house. I think they're in this together. We've heard how close they are."

"Were," he corrected her. "They've obviously fallen out?"

"Yes, big time, and I think it's got to do with whatever happened on the night Liam died."

"You could be right." Eddy looked pensive. "Think he'll come back?"

"Here?" She jerked her thumb behind her. "No, I doubt it, but he seems determined to get to Philip."

"So all we need to do is find Philip."

"Exactly. Can you speak to someone at the college? Find out if they have a Chinese welfare officer."

She couldn't imagine why anyone would visit Mugisa's parents pretending to be from the college, unless they already suspected his involvement in Liam's death. Maybe she needed to speak to McLaughlin again.

Byron reversed the lorry into the courtyard, shut off the engine and sat in the cab. The sudden silence echoed in his ears. The euphoria of their close escape from the warehouse had worn off and he questioned the wisdom of his actions.

By the time Byron joined him Adam had secured the gates with a padlock. "Are you sure it will be okay here?" Byron asked.

"It's been empty for years and nobody comes here." Adam indicated the padlock. "Unless someone tries to open it, they can't tell I've changed the lock and, even if they do, they'll probably think it's just rusted up."

"Great."

"Let's go. I know Mal's with Philip but I don't want to take advantage."

Byron nodded. He couldn't read his friend's expression but suspected what he'd done troubled him. Adam didn't have his ability to compartmentalise. "Thanks, mate. I owe you." Byron gripped Adam's shoulder.

"Yeah, whatever," Adam said in a gruff voice and started for the car.

As they neared Adam's house Byron's phone rang. Rebecca said, "Is Philip with you?"

Byron hesitated. "No, but he's safe."

The silence stretched until she asked, "What do you mean?" Her tone was icy.

"He's safe," Byron repeated. "What's happened?"

"Why isn't he with you?" Her anger reached across the airways.

"Has something happened?"

"Mugisa showed up at my mum's. He threatened her and the girls with a knife."

"Stay there, I'm on my way."

"No!" Rebecca hesitated and Byron heard her breathing. "No, you stay with Philip — he's who Mugisa wants. Call me when you're with him, and Byron … if anything's happened to him…"

Byron passed on this news and the car surged forward as Adam put his foot down. Despite that, the journey to Adam's took an age and Byron leapt out of the car when they arrived. He opened the front door, calling to his nephew. Loud voices came from the lounge and he charged into the room. Philip jumped out of the sofa in alarm. The sound came from a music video playing on the television.

The tension in Byron's chest released. "You okay, Philip? Where's Mal?"

"Hi, Byron," A quiet voice from behind him replied.

The door swung closed and Mal faced him, a hefty steel poker in his hand. "Hi, Mal." Byron gazed at the implement.

"I recognised the car but you can't be too sure." Mal returned the poker to the fireplace.

"Has something happened?" Philip asked.

"Nothing. I just had a bad feeling." Byron hesitated. "Have any visitors been round?"

"Nope," Mal said.

The front door opened and Adam walked into the room. "Cheers, Mal, thanks for stepping in."

"Anytime, mate." Mal offered Philip his hand. "I'll see you again, young man. And next time, we'll play *my* music." He shook Byron's hand and left the room.

"I'll get going now Byron," Adam said. "You know where everything is." He waved towards the kitchen. "I'll see you both in the morning."

Byron followed him out into the hallway and locked the door behind him. He wasn't sure they should split their forces, but he didn't want to leave the rest of his brother's family unprotected.

CHAPTER 18

The Boy planned to travel as far as possible before daybreak and the discovery of his escape. A thin crescent moon and bright stars shone above him. He concentrated on the constellations. At first, the profusion of distant suns confused him, but gradually he recognised the patterns his father had shown him. Once he identified the star he sought, he wondered how he'd missed it. Taking care not to walk into any hazards, he pressed on, away from his captors and towards home.

At the camp, the girl cowered in the corner of the officer's hut. He'd been drinking and, as sometimes happened, could not perform. He lashed out, angry at her failure to arouse him. The blows rained on the girl, knocking her to the floor. He stood over her, kicking her. Terrified, she curled up into a ball.

He grabbed her by her neck, lifting her to her feet and held her against the wall as she struggled to free herself. She'd never seen him this angry and fearing for her life, she told him of The Boy's planned escape. The officer threw her to the ground and rushed out to investigate. The shame of her betrayal tempered her relief.

Adam replayed the incident at the warehouse as he drove to Byron's brother's house. Would the two men recognise him if they saw him again? He didn't think they'd report him to the police, but Manchester wasn't such a big city and he'd likely bump into them. He'd have to make sure he stayed alert. He parked on the road outside the Masons' house. Rebecca answered the door, looking surprised.

"Where's Philip?" she demanded.

"He's fine. Byron's with him. Can I come in?" The lines round Rebecca's mouth had deepened since Adam had last seen her.

"Sorry." She stepped back.

"We thought I should stay with you, in case Mugisa returns."

A shadow passed behind her eyes. "That's very kind of you, but the police are sending someone."

"Shall I wait until they get here?"

She gave him a strained smile. "I'm sorry, Adam. I'm being rude. Shall we start again?"

"No need. I understand."

"Shall we wait in the lounge? Samuel's finishing a report for a patient but I'll tell him you're here. He's looking forward to seeing you again."

"I'd better have a look round."

Her lips trembled and she opened her mouth.

"I'm sure there's nothing wrong, but it's best to be certain."

She showed him the back door and lent him a torch. Adam inspected the perimeter, then checked the ground floor openings and, reassured, he returned to the house and bolted the back door. He entered the lounge and Rebecca reacted like a startled deer.

"Everything okay?" she asked, her voice unsteady.

"Sure. I told you it was just a precaution." Adam smiled, trying to reassure her.

"Adam." Samuel's voice boomed from the doorway. "Good to see you again. It's been a long time."

Adam started, but recovered to respond, "Hello, Sam … Samuel. How are you?"

Samuel shook his hand then patted the wheelchair. "I wasn't in this last time, was I? I've been in it seven years. Didn't Byron tell you?"

"Yes, of course. It's just slipped my mind." He recalled something had happened when Byron returned home on leave but didn't remember the details.

"Unfortunately it can't slip our minds." Rebecca's bitter tone and Samuel's expression made it clear the subject still caused them both a lot of pain.

The uncomfortable silence stretched until the front door bell rang.

"That will be the police. I'll get it." Rebecca's relief reflected Adam's.

Once the police patrol took over Adam returned home.

"It's only me," he announced as he opened the door.

"Through here," Byron said from the lounge. The sound of the television died as Byron muted it.

"Has Philip gone to bed?"

"Yeah, he's still shattered."

Adam indicated the bottle of lager in Byron's hand. "Shall I get you another?"

"Better not, I've drunk two and Rebecca will kill me if she finds out I had too many."

Adam took off his coat and fetched a beer from the kitchen. He sat in the armchair and drank half the bottle in one swig.

"Looks like you were ready for that." Byron laughed.

"No mistake." Adam studied the bottle.

"Something on your mind?" Byron asked.

"I saw Samuel. I'd forgotten about the wheelchair."

Byron's frowned. "Yeah, I should have reminded you. Sorry, mate."

Adam pulled at a corner of the label. "Remind me what happened."

Byron cleared his throat. "I'd returned home on leave and he took me out on his new bike, a Honda Goldwing. I was twenty-two, full of myself and he was a responsible family man. He took it over the Snake Pass, showing off." Byron stared at a spot on the far wall. "I think he wanted to show me he wasn't past it. He'd been such a hero to me when I was growing up." He paused. "I think I'll have that beer."

Byron returned with two bottles. He handed one to Adam and, sitting down, took a drink. "Anyway, he overtook a lorry, going uphill and a caravan came the other way. He'd have made it but the lorry had a trailer and we couldn't see it until we drew alongside. The bike left the road and Samuel broke his spine." Byron touched his lower back. "Spent two weeks in a coma, but yours truly got away with just a few cuts and bruises."

"Shit, Byron. How awful for you."

Byron had his eyes shut.

"So why the problem with Rebecca?"

"Rebecca." Byron snorted. "And Mum. She didn't speak to me for three years. If it wasn't for my sisters, I'd have been an outcast."

"It wasn't your fault," Adam protested.

"I was driving when we set off, so everyone assumed it was 'the young tearaway'." He laughed bitterly. "We changed over about ten minutes before the accident, but I was the one who got done for reckless driving."

"Surely you told them?"

Byron studied his bottle. "I couldn't. By the time Samuel came out of his coma it had become the accepted version. I was back with the unit and we were on our way to Kuwait. I hoped he'd tell them the truth but he must have found it too difficult." Byron gave a bitter smile.

"I'm so sorry, mate." Adam's chest tightened. "Why didn't you tell me?"

"No point. You couldn't have done anything." Byron flicked a hand towards the television. "Anyway, second half's started. Turn up the volume."

The next morning, Siobhan sat at her desk and read the report comparing the fingerprints taken from the grille at the house fire with those of the suspects. Disappointment and elation vied for supremacy and she pushed it across to Eddy.

"Bad news?" he asked, picking it up.

"Yes and no."

Eddy finished reading. "Good news on the smaller print. Were you hoping the other belonged to Matthew Walcott?"

"Hoping, but not expecting." Siobhan dialled an internal number. "Youssef, take Debbie and pick up Anthony Lees. He should be in college." She hesitated for a second. "Fetch the other two, Asif Malik and Ryan Collins." She'd have to send someone to collect their parents.

"Shall we arrest them, Boss?" Youssef asked.

"Not unless they refuse to come."

Eddy smiled at her. "The fingerprints are a good breakthrough and I reckon Lees will fold like a rusty bucket once we put pressure on him."

"Nice picture, Eddy, but after seeing them with the Walcott boy, I'm not so sure."

"You might be right. I've never seen anyone change so completely."

An hour later Siobhan led Eddy into the interview room. Anthony Lees, a long-limbed youth with a coffee-cream complexion and short, tightly-curled hair, studied her across the table. Alongside him sat an angry woman Siobhan assumed to be his mother, and next to her a court-appointed solicitor.

Eddy switched on the recorder, made the introductions then read Anthony his rights. The young man folded his arms and leant back in the chair, but his sullen expression couldn't disguise his fear. His mother, wearing too much perfume and what looked like her Sunday best outfit, glared at him but he kept his attention from her.

"Anthony, do you understand why you're here?" Siobhan asked.

"Something to do with Liam?"

"We're trying to clarify a few minor points on your statement. When we spoke to you yesterday, you said you didn't see Liam on Sunday. Are you sure?"

"That's what I said, didn't I?"

"I want to make sure you haven't made a mistake. Do you want to reconsider any of your statement?"

He shook his head. "Why should I?"

"Okay, can you tell me if you've ever visited Argyle Street?"

"Never — been — there. I've never even heard of the place."

"Really? That's where we found Liam's body. Haven't you seen the reports on the news?"

Anthony reddened. "Oh, yeah, I meant I don't know it."

"Do you want to reconsider your answer? You've never been there? I don't mean just on Sunday night." Siobhan kept her voice even, concealing the importance of this question.

"No, I told you."

The solicitor leant forward but Anthony dismissed him with a gesture. Siobhan didn't allow herself a sigh of relief but let Eddy take over.

"Can you explain how we found your fingerprints in number 32?" Eddy produced photos from a folder in front of him and slid them across the table.

Anthony stared for a few seconds. "You can't have."

"Why not, Anthony?"

"Because we wer—" He closed his mouth.

"Because you were what, Anthony?"

"Because I weren't there." He seemed to have trouble controlling his breathing.

"Maybe your friends weren't, but you were. Your fingerprints confirm it and they don't lie."

Siobhan could almost see Anthony's mind working and guessed he was replaying the events of the evening. His breathing grew faster and sweat leaked from his forehead.

"The story you told us was a pack of lies, wasn't it?" Siobhan said.

Anthony shook his head.

"Your friends are next door," she continued, "speaking to my colleagues, and they've told us the same lies. I'm sure they've only done it to help you out because we didn't find their prints. Just yours."

Anthony's eyes darted and his mouth moved but no words emerged.

His mother stared at him, open-mouthed, then the solicitor coughed. "Chief Inspector," he said. "Can I have a word with my client?"

Siobhan knew she had him and checked the time. "Interview suspended at ten twenty-three."

After switching the cassette recorder off, she led Eddy out into the corridor. She wanted to punch the air but Anthony's mother had joined them. A pang of sympathy for the bewildered woman made her ask, "Would you like a drink?"

The woman nodded.

"Come on, love," Eddy said, "I'll take you to the canteen where you can grab a brew and a sit down."

Siobhan returned to her desk but her blood fizzed with anticipation and, unable to concentrate, she flitted between jobs until a constable arrived to informer her that the solicitor had finished. Siobhan arrived in the interview room before Eddy and Anthony's mother, and studied the youth. The veneer of cockiness he'd exhibited had disappeared. Eddy returned and gestured Anthony's mother into the room. The woman appeared to have aged ten years in the last half hour. The anger she'd displayed earlier had gone, leaving her with a haunted air.

Siobhan wondered what effect the change in his mother's demeanour would have on the youth. Anthony stared at his hands, motionless on the table in front of him. Siobhan switched the tape recorder on and reminded Anthony he was still under caution.

The solicitor picked up a sheet of paper. "Chief Inspector, my client wishes to make a statement. He has no idea how his fingerprints ended up on the door of 32 Argyle Street. He has never been to Argyle Street and he stands by his account of what he did that evening."

Although Siobhan wanted a confession, this presented the second-best outcome. The solicitor must know the risk of adopting this strategy and she saw he wasn't happy. "Are you sure that's what you want to say, Anthony?" Siobhan thought he nodded. "You'll have to speak up for the tape."

"Yeah," he mumbled.

They had enough to charge him but she decided to have one more attempt. "Anthony, you know we've got Ryan and Asif here. According to your statement, you spent Sunday evening with them. We know you were at the house where we found Liam's body but it doesn't mean you killed him. I know he was a good friend of yours. If the others made you help them get rid of the body, it doesn't make you guilty of murder."

The youth didn't respond but his mother brightened.

"If you're scared of them, don't worry, we can help protect you."

Anthony snorted but didn't speak.

Siobhan decided to take a break. They would have another try with him later, once they'd questioned the other two and he'd spent a few hours in the cells. She signalled to Eddy.

"Anthony Lees," he said, "you are under arrest, in connection with the killing of Liam McLaughlin."

Anthony looked on vacantly as Eddy continued, whispering, "Yes," when Eddy asked him if he understood.

Weariness tempered Siobhan's satisfaction. At least she could give the Chief Super something.

Mugisa arrived at the cul-de-sac lined with small scruffy houses and drove to the end of it before parking half on the pavement. He recognised Lynton's flash BMW and tried to remember which of the houses he lived in. The door to the house at the end opened and a young man left, calling his goodbyes. Mugisa recognised him as a low-level drug dealer who often attended student parties and he waited a few seconds before going up to the door.

An aggressive black man answered the door. "What you want, man?"

Mugisa studied him. He was one of the men who hung around with Lynton, so he had the right house.

"I'm here to see Lynton."

The man relaxed. "Lynton! Someone to see you!" he shouted through to the back of the house.

Lynton arrived wearing a sour expression but brightened on seeing Mugisa. "Hey, man. Come in." He showed Mugisa into the lounge. The other man slunk off upstairs.

Mugisa closed the door. "I need a handgun."

"Just like that?" Lynton couldn't hide his amusement.

"Can't you get one?" Disappointment made Mugisa's limbs heavy.

"Yeah man, no problem," Lynton reassured him. "But it'll cost you."

Mugisa hid his relief. "How much?" He'd brought a thousand and had more, but knew he'd need it to start a new life.

Lynton thought for a moment before replying, "For you, a monkey."

Was Lynton mocking him? He scowled.

Lynton licked his lips and sighed. "Okay, four hundred."

Much less than he feared, but he should haggle. "Three."

"Three fifty."

"What can you get?" Mugisa doubted if Lynton could get him a Glock. He'd taken one off an officer he'd killed and preferred it to the Type 77 his own officers had carried.

"Makarov, nine mill."

Mugisa had never fired one, but he'd heard they were okay. "I'll need bullets. A full magazine and a spare."

Lynton sighed again. "Okay, man. You drive a hard bargain."

Mugisa smiled and they bumped fists.

"When you need it?"

"Now."

Lynton checked the time. "Give me an hour and ring me on this number." He handed Mugisa a creased piece of card with a mobile number printed across the centre.

Mugisa wondered if Lynton was leading him on, but he didn't have many other options. Once he'd got the gun, Mugisa would finish Philip, then leave this city behind.

CHAPTER 19

The Boy listened to the vehicles, wondering why they were out, then he realised they'd come looking for him. Gripped by fear he moved further into the bush, but in his haste he stumbled into a burrow — home to a warthog and her litter. The enraged female shot out, tail upright, and rounded on him. He let out a cry and ran. The mother, satisfied she'd seen off the danger, trotted back to her den and took up her former position.

The Boy's pursuers heard his cry and the experienced trackers amongst them found signs of his passage. Fear gave The Boy strength and he pushed his way further into the bush and, at first, he stayed ahead of them. But the weeks of ill treatment and poor diet soon told and he tired until his hunters, bigger and stronger, cornered him.

He waited for them to attack, determined to take as many as possible before they overpowered him. His legs trembled with exhaustion and his lungs struggled to fill. The first man to reach him received a wound in his arm as The Boy stabbed out with the small spear he carried. The remaining men overwhelmed him and, after giving him a beating, trussed him up.

Despite the exhilaration at having charged Anthony, the lack of progress in locating the ringleader frustrated Siobhan. "How's the search for the two lads going, Eddy?"

"Not great. Matthew seems to have few friends and no family. Nobody's seen hide nor hair of him."

"And Philip?"

"He's a local lad." Eddy held out his palms. "With lots of friends and an extensive family network."

"So, plenty of people who could protect him?"

Eddy nodded. "Do you want to try an appeal?"

Siobhan wasn't sure. "We could consider it."

"Are you worried about McLaughlin?"

"I don't want him to go sniffing around the Walcotts. We haven't the resources to protect them and the Masons."

"Why don't we do a missing person's appeal? We don't have to say why we're looking for them."

"I don't think so. Can you imagine the message? 'These lads are missing and their families are worried about them. By the way, don't approach them as they might take a machete to you.'"

"I see what you mean, Boss." Eddy frowned. "You could do one for Philip, or do you think he's dangerous?"

"I'm not sure, Eddy." The mention of machetes nudged her memory. "I wonder if they've found anything on the weapon recovered from Mrs King's house."

She picked up the phone and called the forensics lab. She listened with growing excitement.

"Thanks, I'd really appreciate it," she said, ending the call.

Eddy looked at her with raised eyebrows. "They've got something?"

"Matthew's fingerprints, hardly a surprise. They've analysed the blood. Most of it's from a cat but they've found traces of human blood between the blade and the handle. They're checking it against the DNA samples we took." She smiled at an idea. "Can you get hold of one like it?"

Eddy's brow furrowed. "I think there's one in the evidence room we can borrow."

"Great — can you get it?" Siobhan checked the time. "I think it's time we spoke to Anthony again."

A few minutes later, Siobhan followed Eddy into the interview room. Anthony's determined expression surprised her. His mother's red-rimmed eyes and haunted air suggested she'd suffered more. Eddy placed a plastic-wrapped machete on the table in front of him, started the recorder and repeated the caution. The jerking of Anthony's right knee gave him away.

Let's see how tough you really are, young man. Siobhan smiled at him. "Anthony, do you know Matthew Walcott? You might know him as Mugisa?"

Looking wary, Anthony didn't answer.

"It's a simple enough question."

After checking with his solicitor he nodded. "Yeah, I know him."

"What would you say if I told you we know he attacked Liam?"

Anthony took a sip from the plastic cup of water in front of him. "I'd say you're bullshitting." His mother tutted, but he ignored her.

Siobhan didn't let her smile falter as Anthony's gaze flicked again to the parcel on the table. "Anthony, you seem very interested in this." She picked up the bag and smoothed out the plastic so he could see the object. "Have you seen it before?"

Panic froze on his features. "No."

"So it's not the weapon used to attack Liam?"

"No, it isn't." His knee jigged faster.

"How do you know?" she asked.

He closed his eyes and muttered inaudibly then said, "I don't. I don't know what happened to him..." He reached for the cup, spilling water on the table.

"Don't you want me to tell you how we got hold of this?"

He shrugged, but his chin trembled.

"Matthew used a machete to threaten Cecily and Lucy Mason."

Anthony blinked and his breathing grew louder. His knee knocked the underside of the table, then his eyes rolled up into his head.

"Anthony!" his mother screamed.

The youth slumped sideways, his head rebounding off the solicitor's shoulder and bouncing onto the table.

Siobhan caught the cup before the water soaked her.

"Please step back, Mrs Lees. Give him room." Eddy took charge and laid Anthony out on the floor. His mother, upset even before he'd collapsed, stood wringing the life out of a handkerchief.

"Interview suspended at 14.42," Siobhan announced and switched off the tape. This wasn't the dramatic breakthrough she'd hoped for.

Adam made his way to the gym, glad to get away from the house, and if he was honest, Byron. Although in the past, they'd spent weeks cooped up on operations, his friend had changed. His only interest now was his family, specifically his 'little angel' Lilly. Adam loved being her godfather but hearing her every achievement lauded as if she'd won an Olympic medal soon palled.

As usual on a Thursday afternoon, the changing room was almost empty. The lunchtime crowd had gone, leaving behind damp patches on the floor and the fruity odour of shampoo and shower gel, and the early evening mob hadn't arrived. The few occupants comprised a few shift-workers and dedicated trainers who seemed to live on the premises.

He changed into his kit and after a quick warm up, hit the rowing machine, covering a steady five K in eighteen minutes. The exercise cleared his mind, and he threw himself into a series of power circuits before a twenty-minute session on the heavy bag.

He finished and after changing went to the café attached to the gym. He leant back in his chair, enjoying the exhaustion following a good workout. A name which had haunted his last hours caught his attention.

"...Ritchie's offering good money, it's short term, but I'd take it."

"Why's he need extra bodies?" a Brummie asked.

"His own lads are busy sorting out the shine who ambushed him."

"I heard he lost a couple of his lads — did the same guy take them out?"

The other one laughed. "Ritchie offed one of them himself. He shoved his head down the toilet after they caught him talking to the shine."

"That's a bit drastic, but that's Ritchie for you." The Brummie laughed. "I wouldn't want to be the black lad. Was it one of the Gooch Close mob?"

"Nah, someone said he's from London, but he'll be going back in a box, from what I've heard."

"Good, it's been quiet and we don't need a turf war."

Adam's good mood evaporated. He hurried out of the café but stopped at the newsagent and bought the early edition of the *Evening News*. He let himself into the house. The low rumble of Byron's voice carried through the open door of the living room.

Adam carried the paper through to the kitchen. He found the report on page five and read it. While he waited for Byron, he scanned the rest of the paper but didn't see a report of their escapade last night. McLaughlin's men had obviously not reported it.

Byron walked into the kitchen but his grin faded on seeing Adam. "What's up?"

Adam slid the paper towards him. "Is this the guy you saw yesterday?"

A photo of a balding man with a bushy moustache and prominent eyebrows sat beneath a headline, 'American computer hacker killed by intruders'. The article mentioned his links to organised crime and detailed his gruesome death.

"Looks like him."

"You were right then, he wasn't setting you up."

"So, McLaughlin killed him for talking to me."

The latest forensic evidence arrived and Siobhan wanted to use it straight away. To her relief the doctor certified Anthony fit to continue and his solicitor didn't object. Anthony looked haggard when they resumed and the sight weakened his mother's already tenuous hold on her composure. Siobhan experienced a pang of sorrow for the poor woman. By the time this was over, it would rip her family apart and Siobhan hoped the woman had a good support network.

Eddy reminded Anthony he was still under caution and she began: "Anthony, I want you to show me your wrists."

The youth checked with his solicitor, seeming to have abdicated his decision-making. Siobhan wasn't a psychologist, but she suspected his personality led him to look for people to follow. Anthony held out his hands and turned them over. A small, fresh scar ran just below the ball of his right thumb.

"Can you tell me when you received this injury?" Siobhan asked.

He shrugged. "No idea," he whispered.

Eddy produced a machete in a sealed bag and placed it on the desk between them.

"Do you recognise this, Anthony?" Eddy asked before describing the item.

"I suppose so." Anthony checked with the solicitor again. "It looks like the machete you showed me before."

"Can you explain why your blood's on the handle?"

He stared and opened his mouth to speak but closed it again. His eyes glazed over but he recovered and said, "No."

"Could it have been when you cut yourself?" She pointed at the nick on his wrist.

"Yea—" he shook his head. "I mean no."

"We also found traces of Liam's blood on the handle and we're certain this was the weapon used to attack him. So, I ask again, can you explain how your blood ended up on it?"

She wasn't sure he'd heard her but eventually he said, "No."

"Anthony Lees," she said, "I'm charging you with being an accessory to the murder of Liam McLaughlin."

Anthony's mother cried out and buried her face in her hands. Tears ran down Anthony's cheeks and the solicitor leant over him, whispering into his ear.

The solicitor addressed Siobhan. "Can I have a few minutes with my client?"

Siobhan signalled to Eddy who made the announcement and switched off the recorder. He led the boy's distraught mother from the room, leaving Anthony with his solicitor. Instead of the usual euphoria she experienced at charging a murderer, Siobhan felt a profound sadness.

The information Adam overheard confirmed what Byron suspected but the fact McLaughlin had beaten one of his own men to death for meeting him, made him pause for thought. He needed to make contact and force him to back off.

Cyrus didn't have his phone number, but Lynton suggested the names of people who might. Leaving Philip with Adam, he got a cab to a pub in in the east of the city. The afternoon light was fading when it drew up in the potholed car park.

The driver studied Byron in the mirror. "You sure you want to go in there."

Byron's already tight nerves stretched further. "I'm meeting someone."

"You want me to wait?"

"Cheers. I shouldn't be long." Byron paid him, adding an extra ten, and walked towards the scruffy building. Built in the sixties to replace an even more decrepit predecessor, it needed more than a coat of paint. He pushed open the scarred outer door and stepped inside.

The smell of stale beer and cigarettes enveloped him. In the dim light he made out the dark swirls on the patterned carpet which must have been there since the pub opened. Two bulky figures sat at the bar. From Lynton's description, these must be Tom and Trev Harris. Drinkers sitting round the edge of the room fell quiet as he approached the bar, every one of them seemed to have missing teeth, prison tattoos and skin the colour of lard. The hair on his forearms stood up.

Alerted by the barman, the two men turned. Both wore long leather jackets and grease-stained jeans tucked into steel toe-capped boots. If they hadn't been clean-shaven and crop-haired, he'd have taken them for bikers. Although obviously brothers, Trev, who had his name tattooed across both fists, looked like he gave the orders.

"Mr Harris?" Byron said.

Trev's foreboding demeanour grew more menacing. "The old man's not here. Who the fuck are you and what do you want?" The background conversation, which had resumed, stopped again.

"My name's Mason and I wanted to ask you—" Byron looked about him. "Is there somewhere private we can talk?"

Tom held up his empty glass. "Get us a drink and we'll think about it." He summoned the barman who scurried to him. "Our friend here is getting the drinks in. What you having?"

Byron eyed the fingerprint-stained glasses on the shelf above the bar. "What you got in bottles?" If the worst happened, he'd have some sort of weapon.

"We ain't got any of that Red Stripe shit," the barman said.

"Becks will be fine." He nodded at the chiller cabinet.

The drinks arrived, and Byron gripped the warm bottle. The two brothers drained half their pints, staring at him the whole time. He saluted them and sipped a mouthful of lukewarm lager.

"About that private word..."

The two brothers exchanged a look and Tom beckoned the barman. "Toilets out of order again?"

"No, Tom they're fine — oh, yeah sure. I forgot to put the sign out." He produced a handwritten sign on a piece of card, attached to an old wire coat-hanger.

"Don't worry, we'll put it out for you." Tom got up, handed the sign to his brother and gestured to Byron to follow him.

Trev fell in behind him making Byron's neck itch and they processed to the toilets. The stench of stale urine and bleach made his eyes water. Tom checked both cubicles while his brother wedged the outer door shut. Byron gripped his bottle tighter and edged to a corner so he could see both brothers.

"In case someone out there can't read. We don't want anyone interrupting us, do we?" Tom showed his teeth. "Right, what do you want to know?"

This felt like a misjudgement, but now Byron was here, he might as well ask the question. "I need to get hold of McLaughlin and I was told—"

"You taking the piss?" A red-faced Trev stepped towards him, breathing beery fumes into his face.

"I heard you'd be able to put me in touch, but there's obviously been a mistake. Sorry to have wasted your time."

"You come here, to our pub, and taunt us." Tom produced an automatic and pointed it at Byron's head. "Well you've made a big mistake, boy."

CHAPTER 20

His captors slung The Boy on a pole like an animal and carried him to the vehicle where he rode to camp under the feet of his captors. Back at the camp they dragged him out and threw him into an enclosure. Miserable and defeated, he lay shivering in the night air, awaiting the dawn and his punishment. The pain of his injuries fused with the despair accompanying his failure. He sought solace in the fact he'd not brought the girl to suffer the same fate.

Morning brought great excitement to the camp; the other recruits gathered to witness his punishment. Despite his injuries, The Boy stood straight and stared back, but none would meet his gaze. Soldiers arrived and dragged him to the large open field they used for a parade ground. The recruits stood in a semi-circle around the edge, facing a long table. His custodians hauled him in front of it and made him stand, flanked by two armed guards.

He faced the empty table, and the officer appeared, followed by four colleagues. They took their seats and regarded him. One of them read the charge and, determined not to falter, The Boy came to attention. The girl arrived and limped towards them.

The Boy saw her injuries and for the first time, his resolve weakened. He received a further blow when, in a low voice, she denounced him. He realised then how they had discovered his escape. Devastated by this betrayal, he didn't even hear the sentence.

Siobhan greeted the college welfare officer and led her into the main office. She'd arranged for her to come in as Anthony's mother was in no state to offer him support. She remembered something from her visit to the Walcott home.

"Can you tell me if you have another welfare officer working with you?"

The woman's puzzled frown gave her the answer. Siobhan thanked her and returned to her desk. Unsure of the significance of this development, she put it to the back of her mind and reviewed the paperwork she'd prepared while they waited. She was sure Anthony would implicate the others and wanted to arrest them and search their homes once he did.

The solicitor told them his client was ready to make a statement. Siobhan and Eddy followed the welfare officer into the interview room, eager to finish. Anthony had become almost cheerful. Siobhan recognised it as a sign he'd be making a full confession.

"Anthony, you are aware you're still under caution?" Eddy asked.

"Yeah, sure," Anthony said in a strong voice.

Siobhan took over. "I want you to tell me what happened on Sunday night."

Anthony licked his lips before he started. "Liam was ripping us off, so we decided to punish him. Mugisa told Philip to get Liam to the old mill."

"The old mill?"

"Yeah, the place we met up sometimes." He gave them the address. "Mugisa said it was a good place for a trial."

"So it was Mugisa's idea?" Siobhan asked.

"Yeah." He looked at her as if she was stupid. "Like I said, Philip and Liam were close, so he had to get him there. The rest of us waited in the dark. The place gave me the creeps. When Liam got there, we grabbed him and Asif and Philip held him down. We wanted to tie him up but Asif forgot the ropes." He took a sip of water. "I read out the charge."

"The charge?"

"Yeah, like they do in court. You know, 'You, Liam McLaughlin are…'" he intoned in a sonorous voice before he seemed to choke and fell silent. He squeezed his eyes shut and took another sip of water. "Anyway, Liam wasn't playing. He was swearing and threatening to tell his uncle."

"Ritchie McLaughlin?" Eddy said.

Anthony nodded. "Yeah. So Mugisa and us—"

"Who else was there, Anthony?"

"Ryan."

Siobhan controlled her urge to rush out and initiate searches of the Asif and Ryan's homes.

"Anyway we pretended to think about it," Anthony continued. "But we'd already decided the verdict and then Mugisa told it to Liam."

"Which was?"

"Death."

"So what happened then?" The other three kept their attention on Anthony, rapt.

"Mugisa got his machete out and went to Liam, but the idiots let him escape. It was Philip's fault."

"So Liam escaped when Mugisa tried to kill him."

Anthony snorted. "He wasn't going to kill him. Just scare him. Liam got cut on the head because Philip let him go."

"So you're saying it was an accident?" Eddy sounded incredulous.

"Yeah." Anthony shook his head as if amazed at the stupidity of the question.

"So you accidentally killed him in the mill?"

Anthony glared at Eddy. "No, that happened later. He ran off, threatening to tell Ritchie. We were all scared; we couldn't let it happen."

"So what did you do then?" Siobhan took over again.

"We chased him on our bikes."

"What did Philip do?"

"He came with us." Anthony's gaze slid away.

"On his bike?"

"Yes. No. He didn't have one, but he followed us."

"What happened next?"

"Mugisa caught Liam. He lay on the floor, blood all over his head…"

"Are you saying he was already dead when you caught up with him?"

"I don't know." Anthony's voice reverted to a whisper.

"What happened then?"

"We each hit him with the machete." Anthony stared at the table for a few seconds.

"So you're saying all of you cut him?"

"Yeah, we had to stick together. That's what makes us strong."

"So, all of you — you, Matthew, Philip, Asif and Ryan — hit him with the machete."

"Yeah."

"Who kicked him?"

Anthony gave her another scornful look. "Nobody kicked him!"

"Really? Liam died from a severe kicking. The cut on his neck might have eventually killed him, but it didn't."

"But we all cut him."

"He was already dead."

Anthony closed his eyes, taking in the new information.

"Do you remember what shoes Mugisa was wearing?" They hadn't found any footwear at Mugisa's house which could have been used to kill Liam.

"No."

"And it was Mugisa's idea to set the fire?"

"My glove fell off when I helped to carry the bin and I thought I'd left fingerprints. I couldn't sleep, so I came back later…"

"Did you know there were two people in the neighbouring house?"

"No there wasn't. The whole street's derelict."

"A young couple, squatters. They both died of smoke inhalation."

Anthony shook his head and swallowed. Tears filled his eyes and he whispered, "I didn't know."

Siobhan spent an hour clarifying his story before she and Eddy were satisfied. Anthony's demeanour became more subdued as the interview progressed and the enormity of what he'd done sank in. He stuck to the line that none of them had kicked Liam. If the others stuck to the same story, it looked like Mugisa had killed him on his own. She was sure he was capable of it. The least they'd charge Anthony with was Manslaughter and as an Accessory to Murder. Siobhan's job now was to make sure she caught the others.

Siobhan's teams collected Asif Malik and Ryan Collins and brought them to the station. They kept them in separate interview rooms while officers searched their homes. Labelled bags of clothing and footwear arrived before going for forensic analysis. Both sets of parents, initially indignant at the boys' treatment, grew distressed as they learned of their sons' involvement in Liam's death.

Both youths stuck to their original version of events until confronted with Anthony's confession. Then they changed their stories and gave confessions corroborating his.

After charging them, Siobhan noticed the three sets of parents in the reception. Although together, each group formed a separate island, isolated from each other by a bubble of misery. She should say something to ease their pain but for the life of her she couldn't think what. She caught sight of Eddy with Mrs Lees and steeled herself to join him, but the chief superintendent's secretary appeared.

"The Chief Super wants you. Now," she announced to Siobhan before striding away without waiting for a reply.

The chief superintendent greeted Siobhan enthusiastically. "Chief Inspector," he said. "Well done. Great result." He shook her hand and ushered her into a chair.

"Thank you, sir. But we still need to find the other two lads, including the ringleader we suspect did the actual killing."

"Don't worry. That will just be a matter of time. You've arranged an appeal? You know we have a superb relationship with the local press."

Siobhan hesitated before telling him of her concerns.

"Chief Inspector, we don't let gangsters like McLaughlin dictate how we run our investigations. I'll get our press officer to come and see you."

She returned to her desk bracing herself for her next task when Eddy trudged into the outer office. Unlike his smiling colleagues, he looked like a man shouldering a heavy burden. She reached for the phone and made her call.

"Ritchie? Where the fuck…?"

"Mrs McLaughlin?" Siobhan said.

"Yes. Who's that?" Maria McLaughlin sounded drunk.

"It's Detective Chief Inspector Quinn. I've got good news for you."

"What? You've bought Liam back to life?"

Siobhan felt like she'd been slapped. "I'm sorry, Mrs McLaughlin, but I can't do that."

Maria paused, sniffed and mumbled, "No, I'm sorry."

"We've charged three youths with involvement in Liam's murder. They've all confessed."

Liam's mother didn't reply at once and Siobhan pictured her trying to come to terms with the news.

"Does that include the black lad?" she finally asked.

"No—"

"I thought not."

"We haven't located him yet." The line echoed in Siobhan's ear. "Mrs McLaughlin?" She rang back but got the engaged tone.

Siobhan exhaled and slumped into her seat. It had been a long day and the adrenaline, which had coursed through her system since the DNA results came back, evaporated, leaving her drained.

"Boss, a few of us are going for a drink — to celebrate." Debbie stood in the doorway.

Siobhan wanted to refuse but realised she should go. It presented a good opportunity to bond with her new colleagues. Debbie noted her hesitation.

"Don't worry, it's just a quickie. We're all knackered. I've not had ten hours sleep since Sunday."

"Yeah, why not?" Siobhan got up and collected her coat. Nothing else would happen tonight.

Adam measured out the rice and poured it into the boiling water. The strong smell of chilli and garlic filled his kitchen. The front door opened and Byron called out, "Sorry I'm late."

"Through here, mate." The lump of anxiety in Adam's gut loosened.

Byron walked into the kitchen and inhaled. "I thought your lot were Chinese not Mexican."

"Don't show your ignorance, Byron. My grandfather was a famous Hunan chef. So how did you get on?"

He snorted. "I owe that bloody Lynton a good kicking. The guys he put me onto hate McLaughlin with a passion. Thought I'd come to gloat about something he did."

"So, what happened?" Adam placed the wooden spoon on a saucer.

"I persuaded them I hate McLaughlin as much as they do. One of them said something which suggests they know about Liam's death. They also gave me his brother's number. Apparently, he's the business brains and tries to keep his big brother in check."

"That's good — he sounds like the one to speak to."

"Yep." Byron picked up the wooden spoon and prodded at the bubbling dish.

Adam took it off him. "Oi, non-players off the green. Go and make the call."

Byron left the room, but returned ten minutes later, looking troubled.

"You took your time." Adam lifted the spoon out of the pan. "Bad news?"

"Yes, but not what you think. The police have arrested three lads for the killing."

"That's good news, isn't it?"

"They've admitted what they did but claim they all did it, including Philip."

"Seriously? Who told you?"

"Kieran, Ritchie's brother."

Adam made a dismissive gesture. "He's bound to say that."

"I rang Samuel, and the police told him the same thing."

Adam didn't know what to say. "I'm so sorry, Byron. Samuel and Rebecca must be devastated."

"They're not the only ones." Byron rubbed his temples. "Kieran also said there will be an appeal in the papers tomorrow, for Philip and Mugisa. McLaughlin must have a man inside the investigation."

They both fell silent, lost in their thoughts until Adam said, "What did Kieran say about the trailer?"

"He said he'd talk to Ritchie, try to get him to back off. Kieran's all business; he's only interested in getting it back."

"Who's keen to get what back?" Philip walked in through the doorway.

"You hungry?" Adam gestured with the spoon.

"Bloody starving."

"Five minutes."

"Great. Can I use the phone, Adam?"

"As long as it's not to call the girl in New Zealand."

Philip smiled and left the room. The two men exchanged a look, wondering how much he'd heard. Once the police made an appeal Adam wasn't sure he could continue to hide Philip. It was one thing keeping him out of McLaughlin's clutches but this changed things.

Adam walked into the bar where he'd arranged to meet the rest of his Watch and found them in a noisy scrum.

"Adam! What time do you call this?" Mal tapped his wrist.

"It's your round," someone suggested.

"No, it's my shout. What you having?" Reed's voice rose above the clamour.

"No, Boss—"

"There's no boss here tonight, Adam."

"Sorry, Geoff. It's your birthday, so let me get this."

Geoff insisted, took his order and wandered off to the bar.

"It's bloody posh in here," someone observed.

"Yeah, but look at the totty."

"Over there." Mike pointed. "Bloody hell, that's the copper from Sunday night. She fancied you, didn't she, Adam?"

He glanced over and noticed the dark-haired beauty studying him. He smiled at her but couldn't see her companion.

"Not sure, Mike."

"Not sure she fancied you or not sure she's the same one?" Mike grinned at him.

"Both."

"Come on then, mate. Let's ask her."

He'd gone before Adam could object, so he followed in his wake. As they got nearer, Adam saw Siobhan and guessed from her smile she remembered him. Mike introduced them and proceeded to ignore them both, homing in on her companion.

"Sorry," Adam said. "He's like a force of nature."

"Don't worry; I'm with one of those." They shared a conspiratorial smile.

Byron finished his call to Louisa and sat for a few moments with a hollowness in his chest. It was the longest they'd been apart since Lilly's birth and thoughts of his nephew's predicament added to his suffering. Not wanting to upset her, he hadn't told Louisa the latest news. Although convinced Philip wasn't guilty, he needed to talk to him about the other boys' claims and what the Harris brothers had said. He walked into the hallway and called his nephew. The TV sounded from the living room, so he stuck his head in but Philip wasn't in there. Byron frowned and headed upstairs towards Philip's room.

"Philip?" he called again.

A gnawing sensation gripped his guts when he found the bedroom empty, his unease increasing as he checked the other rooms. On his way to check the garden, he discovered the back door unbolted. After searching the garden without success, he rushed back in and checked the cloakroom. Philip's jacket wasn't there. *Bugger!*

He realised he didn't know enough about his nephew to make even a wild guess where he could have gone. Picking up the phone, he dialled, hoping his brother would answer.

"Hello." Rebecca sounded like she was scarcely keeping herself under control.

He hesitated, unsure how to start. "Rebecca," he said.

"Byron?" She sounded surprised and then asked, "Philip's okay, isn't he?"

"He's gone."

"Gone? What do you mean?" An edge of hysteria entered her voice.

"I mean, he's gone." Realising how it might sound he added, "He's sneaked out."

The silence stretched for several seconds until she said, "So where were you when this happened?" Her tone glacial.

"I…" He hesitated. "I was on the phone."

"You're supposed to be taking care of him."

Byron's shoulders tightened. "I was in the next room."

She snorted. "Right, I'll ring round his friends. I suggest you search the local area." Her tone became brisk and business-like.

"Right, but can Samuel make the calls? I haven't got wheels. I'll start searching on foot, but can you come and collect me?" He gave her Adam's address.

Philip approached the bowling pavilion and slowed to allow his breathing to settle down. The walk had taken longer than he'd anticipated and he'd run the last few hundred metres, hoping Jenna wouldn't be too annoyed at having to wait. He reached the opening and hesitated, listening and letting his vision became accustomed to the inky darkness. A shoe scraped across the floor and he made out a darker shape.

His pulse jumped. "Jenna?"

"Philip."

He rushed towards her. They embraced and stayed locked together. The cares of his last few days melted away. Philip could face anything with Jenna at his side.

The blow across his neck sent a tremor down his spine. He gasped and his eyes snapped open. Strong hands grabbed him from behind. Jenna's scream sent a jolt through his heart and he wrestled out of his attacker's grip. Once he freed his arms, he lashed out, trying to do serious damage to their assailants. His fist hit a head and his target grunted.

Shadows wrestled in the darkness where he'd left Jenna and a man with a high voice exclaimed, "Bitch!"

A blow hit Philip on the cheek and he swung an elbow, catching a ribcage. A high-pitched yelp from Jenna filled him with rage. Bellowing her name, he aimed a punch at the nearest figure, catching the man on the jaw and knocking him to the ground. Philip ignored the pain in his hand and went for the next one. He wouldn't let these men hurt Jenna. Hot blood trickled down his neck.

A fist caught him on the cheek and he blinked and staggered. Someone grabbed his leg. He struck out with his other foot and grunted with satisfaction when it connected with something solid and fleshy. A yell told him he'd aimed well. He pulled his leg free, determined to get another one down and rescue Jenna.

The bulky shape of a man filled the opening to the pavilion and Philip charged at him. A cosh caught him behind the ear, scrambling his senses. His legs gave way. A second blow landed as he tried to regain control of his limbs. He crashed to the floor and, despite messages to break his fall, his arms failed him. His head bounced and blackness enveloped him.

CHAPTER 21

The punishment for escape was death, but, not wanting to upset the Big Man, the officer decided on a lesser sentence. They beat The Boy with bull-hide whips and left him bleeding in the enclosure. The officer gave the girl to the men who had captured him as their reward.

The Boy eventually recovered from his injuries and, in time, thick, wormlike scars grew across his back. As further punishment, they returned him to the indoctrination classes with the newcomers. Almost broken by the betrayal, he stayed at the back of the class, taking little part in the lessons.

His will to survive endured and he grew strong again. He trusted no one but gradually learned how to get people to do what he wanted. The girl avoided him, ashamed of her treachery.

Byron watched Rebecca change gear, forcing the lever into position like she wanted to snap the hardened steel. Since she picked him up, she'd spoken three words: "Close the door." Barely contained anger radiated from her. Although he understood her distress, it would be a long night if she didn't ease up.

"Where are we going?" he asked.

"The park."

He waited in vain for her to continue. "Why?"

Rebecca's lips formed a thin line. "The girls said he comes here with Jenna. She's also missing; Samuel rang Philip's friends."

"Which park?" That's what Philip must be up to, meeting his girlfriend, the sly fox. Byron's concern eased and he smiled.

"This one." The headlights picked out a set of wrought iron gates ahead of them. Despite the hour, the gates lay open. "And I see nothing amusing."

"Rebecca, I know you're angry with me, but—" He saw the blue lights before she did. "Over there."

Rebecca accelerated into the park, ignoring the speed limit posted at the entrance. Once in the park, they could see an ambulance and two police cars clustered around the pavilion. The hollowness in Byron's chest deepened and Rebecca slowed as they neared the emergency vehicles. A figure detached itself from the tableau and came towards them, waving its arms. Rebecca stopped the car and got out.

"Sorry, lady. You can't come in here. The park's closed."

She ignored him and brushed past, heading for the ambulance. The bewildered park keeper followed, but Byron grabbed him.

"Sorry, mate. She's looking for her son. He came here with his girlfriend."

The man pointed to the further of the police cars. "They're over there."

"Rebecca!" Byron shouted. "He's in the car."

He pointed to the vehicle and she jogged to it, opening the passenger door. A surprised constable looked up from her notebook.

"I'm looking for Philip, my son," Rebecca said.

The officer gestured to the rear seat where a couple in their thirties sat. "These folk found a young girl. They were just giving me a statement—"

"What about my son?"

"Sorry," the woman said.

"The girl's in the ambulance." The constable started to describe Jenna, but Rebecca rushed towards the vehicle.

"Philip?" she called, peering past the paramedic stowing the back step.

"Mrs Mason!" Jenna cried out.

Rebecca clambered into the ambulance and put her arms around the pale and frightened girl. Byron attempted to follow her but one of the policemen intercepted him.

"Officer, we're looking for her son. He's tall, about this height." Byron held a hand out at the level of his hairline.

The officer's expression changed. "The girl said they took her boyfriend. It sounds like your lad. I'm sorry, sir."

Byron's stomach did a somersault. Rebecca must have received the same news from Jenna and she stumbled out of the vehicle, her eyes unfocussed.

She looked at Byron. "You bastard. If you hadn't…"

He waited, at a loss for words. For a second he thought Rebecca would break down, but she took a deep breath and recovered herself.

"We must find him."

Byron nodded and addressed the constable. "How many were there?"

"Sorry, sir?"

"You said 'they' took him."

"Right. The girl said three—" The constable bit his lip seeming to regret giving Byron this information. "Detectives are on the way," he continued. "They'll want a word with you, sir." The constable spoke to Rebecca in a more sympathetic voice. "We'll find your son, madam. Don't worry."

Rebecca ignored this attempt at reassurance and jogged to her car.

Byron followed and opened the passenger door. "Shouldn't we stay and speak to the police?"

"You've changed your tune." The engine roared into life. "Are you coming, or do I have to do this on my own?"

Siobhan gave directions and Adam drove. She'd fancied him from seeing him at the fire and she'd enjoyed his company, but she wasn't sure she wanted a relationship yet. He pulled up outside her flat and they sat in the car for an awkward moment before both spoke.

They laughed and Adam said, "You first."

"I was going to say — do you want a coffee?"

He nodded and she led the way, heart tripping. At the door she hesitated, key in the lock, before opening it. *What are you playing at Siobhan Quinn? You hardly know him!*

She slammed the door and took his jacket. "Do you take milk and sugar?" she asked, eager to fill the awkward silence.

"Just milk."

She showed him into the lounge, putting on a low lamp and apologising for the odour of paint which still lingered. While the kettle boiled, she stepped into the bathroom and brushed her teeth before returning with the drinks.

"Did you want biscuits?" she asked, passing him a mug of coffee.

He smiled and shook his head. Their fingers brushed and he put his mug down, reaching for her hand. Her skin tingled and she let him take it, stroking the smooth callouses on his palm as he leant towards her.

He kissed her. They separated, smiling, and she knelt between his knees and he took her chin in his other hand. They kissed again and she moved her hand onto his chest and unbuttoned his shirt. Laughing, he copied her, struggling with the small buttons on her blouse. The shrill ringing of the phone cut through the sounds of their breathing.

"Feck." She eased his head away. "Sorry, Adam. I need to take this."

She scrambled to her feet and rushed out to the living room, reaching the phone before it stopped ringing.

"Chief Inspector Quinn," she said, trying to control her breathing.

"Sorry to disturb you, Chief Inspector. We've a reported kidnapping of a suspect in your case. Philip Mason, aged seventeen. Jenna Young, his girlfriend, reported the attack."

She concentrated on the call and her earlier mood evaporated. "What happened?" she asked, perching on the edge of the sofa.

"The lad was with his girlfriend and she says three or four men jumped them." He gave her a précis of Jenna's statement.

"Have we informed the parents?"

"Detectives are at his parents' house now."

"Okay, I'll meet them there." Siobhan hesitated before making her request, aware of Eddy's exhausted state. "Can you ask Sergeant Arkwright to join me?"

She ended the call and sat for a moment, her mind churning until she shivered. She grabbed a jacket from the hall stand and returned in to the bedroom to find Adam buttoning up.

"Duty calls?" he asked, not hiding his disappointment.

"I'll have to go. I'm sorry." Despite her frustration her mind had already focussed on the incident.

"So am I." He grinned. "Nice jacket."

She'd picked his up and embarrassed, she slipped out of it, becoming suddenly self-conscious. Once she'd grabbed her own, they walked to the car together.

"I'm really sorry, Adam." She leant forward to peck him on the cheek, but he moved so their lips met in a prolonged kiss before she broke away.

Breathless, she searched for her car then remembered she'd left it at work.

"Adam, can you give me a lift?" she asked, annoyed at herself for not getting Eddy to pick her up.

"No problem, where to?"

She told him. "You okay, Adam? You've gone very pale."

"Come on, let's go." He rushed to his car.

Mugisa studied the low building and shivered. Despite the many layers of clothing he wore, the cold seeped into his muscles. He'd watched Jenna's house for two hours when the men turned up in their big car. They'd not seen him and he waited until Jenna left the house and they followed her. He quickly realised from their behaviour they were not very disciplined. This wasn't a trained fighting force, and he felt better about his chances against them.

At the park, he'd followed them. The men were clumsy as a herd of cattle, but the girl didn't hear them tracking her. They hid in the bushes until Philip ran past them and Mugisa stayed in the shadows, waiting to discover what they intended to do.

When he saw them come out with the unconscious figure, he rushed back to his car and waited. He'd followed them and watched from a distance as they delivered their prisoner.

He waited for the second car to leave before approaching the building, knowing there were now only two men guarding Philip. The single-storey structure looked like an old factory. Avoiding the front, where he'd noticed security lights, he walked round it, checking the openings. The only useable doorway was at the front, and heavy metal bars protected all the windows. He peered into these but years of grime meant he could see nothing through them.

Mugisa knew he must act soon, before the others came back. He returned to his car and retrieved his spare machete.

Philip regained consciousness in the boot of a car. Whoever put him here had tied his feet together and his arms behind his back. Sticky tape covered his eyes and mouth. He breathed in through his nose, inhaling the odour of damp carpet and exhaust fumes.

The memory of Jenna's cry made him forget his own pain. He vowed to take retribution on the man who'd hit her. The car stopped and the engine died. Doors slammed and men spoke. Then a rush of cold air and the voices became louder.

"So what are we supposed to do with him?"

"Ritchie said to stick him in the storeroom and he'll deal with him later."

At the mention of Liam's uncle, Philip stomach lurched.

"Why the fuck can't he do it now?"

"Do you want to ask him?"

"Come on, lads. Let's get him inside. Then some of us can enjoy the rest of the night."

Rough hands grabbed Philip's legs and another pair lifted his torso. He had to find out what had happened to Jenna, and he struggled to free himself. Someone swore and the tip of a boot plunged into his back, crushing his right kidney. Unbearable pain spread through his torso, sending his muscles into spasm. Tears filled his eyes and, unable to open his mouth, he struggled to breathe. Then he expelled a mixture of tears and snot. His lungs fought to refill and he inhaled a mixture air and liquid through his nostrils. A voice broke through his agony. The man who'd hit Jenna.

"I said, keep doing that and I'll give you another one. Did you hear me?"

The pain spread round his torso, a girdle of lava, but receded and he concentrated on breathing.

"Did you fucking hear me?" The voice spat into his ear.

Fearful of another blow Philip nodded and struggled to say yes. The sound came out a moan and the man laughed. A rushing filled Philip's ears, almost making him forget the pain.

His captors picked him up and carried him, each jarring step bringing more agony. He tried to think of anything other than his body. The nature of the sounds changed and he realised they'd carried him into a building. One of the men slipped and dropped him on the floor. A surge of pain made him black out.

When he regained consciousness, the pain from his headache hit him followed by the agony from his kidney. Light attacked his eyes and he shut them. The tape covering his mouth had also gone and he moved his arms, surprised to find they were no longer bound.

Moving gingerly, he attempted to sit up. Agony spread from his lower back and with a gasp, he froze. The pain receded, he tried again and, by degrees, he sat up and studied the room. Square, with bare brick walls it had just one opening. Under him lay a stained foam mattress placed on a wooden platform taking up the whole of the wall opposite the door. Reddish-brown stains covered the original pale finish of the concrete floor. Philip didn't want to imagine what had caused these.

Beside the door, a portable gas heater spluttered. The flames produced a faint orange glow but no heat. The bare bulb illuminating the room wasn't much brighter. He shivered and noticed a blanket on the floor beside him. It must have fallen off and he reached for it. A piercing pain shot through his body and he became rigid, gasping and blinking away tears. The pain subsided and he took a few shallow breaths, careful to avoid sudden movement. Eventually, he began again and using his foot to reach for it, he recovered the blanket and covered himself.

The effort exhausted him and he closed his eyes. If he stayed still, the pain became bearable, but he knew any movement would aggravate it. He ignored the pressure on his bladder and tried to empty his mind, desperate to get to sleep. The pain and growing fear he wouldn't be rescued wouldn't let him rest. Byron and Adam had no way of finding him.

CHAPTER 22

Many months later, they forgave The Boy and allowed him to re-join the trainee soldiers. He progressed rapidly and the day came for him to go on a raid. Excited and eager, the new recruits collected their weapons and climbed onto the vehicles. The Boy was as enthusiastic as they were, but he looked around the vehicle and realised many of them came from his own village. Was this significant or a coincidence?

The Big Man led the raid and they travelled for several hours, before arriving at their destination at midday. The landmarks looked familiar and, as the village came into sight, he recognised the outcrop behind which the schoolhouse lay. None of his former school-friends noticed and all wore the expressions he had seen when others left the camp to go on raids.

Around him, the others laid waste to the rebuilt village, attacking anyone they found. But, for The Boy, the raid brought back the memories of his own capture and he moved as if in a dream.

Byron wasn't sure going to McLaughlin's flat was such a good idea. If he had snatched Philip, he wouldn't take him there, but he couldn't dissuade Rebecca.

The car approached the roundabout onto the Mancunian Way and Rebecca braked. "How did you find him last time?"

Surprised to be spoken to Byron said, "I had a description of where they'd taken Liam, so we looked for it, knowing Mugisa would probably take Philip there."

"How did you know where they took Liam?"

Byron didn't want to tell her but it would come out. "Philip took him there."

"No!" Rebecca gasped and blinked away tears. "So, what the police said…"

"Philip didn't kill Liam. He just got him there. The others did the killing."

"Yes, but the police said they all did it."

"These other lads are protecting their own skins. If they all say Philip helped kill Liam, it destroys his credibility as a witness."

"But they've already confessed."

Byron's thoughts had followed the same path. "They're probably punishing him. That's how Mugisa works, and he's their leader."

Rebecca looked stricken and Byron searched in vain for words to comfort her. She slowed as they reached the block containing McLaughlin's flat and Byron focussed on what they could expect. Five minutes later, they stood at the concierge's desk, frustrated by the uniformed functionary behind it. He insisted McLaughlin wasn't home and wouldn't let them pass.

"Can we just check?" Rebecca said, but the man shook his head.

Byron realised they'd not get anywhere and made his way to the exit. Rebecca snorted and pushed past him. As she snatched the door open, the man said, "You might find him at his club, on Mosley Street."

Byron thanked him. Apart from asking him if he knew the place, Rebecca didn't speak until they arrived at their destination. The premises hosted a nightclub and casino and the pavement outside thronged with revellers waiting to go in. Rebecca pulled up on the pavement and he opened the door.

"I'll go in. You'd better wait in the car."

He slammed the door before she could object. They were dealing with dangerous men and he didn't want her getting in the way. His pulse raced as he approached the entrance, bypassing the queue. People muttered, but he ignored them and none dared object. Three heavies scrutinised him as he approached and their body language told him they recognised him as a threat.

He approached the leader, a fat-necked man with a shaved head. "I'm looking for Ritchie."

"Who shall I say you are?" The man's elocution didn't match his appearance.

"Byron Mason. I've got a message for him."

The man's eyes widened when he heard the name and he disappeared into the club. The other bouncers studied Byron with a mixture of wariness and aggression. Footsteps sounded behind him and Rebecca arrived. He considered telling her to go back but her expression told him she wouldn't listen. He thought she was going to storm the last place, but that wasn't the way to deal with these people, not unless you possessed superior forces.

The man returned, accompanied by another, equally large, and with the pumped-up upper body of a steroid user. Someone had clouted him on the nose and a large graze disfigured his forehead. He wasn't one of the men who'd tried to invade his brother's home, but Byron already knew McLaughlin had a big crew. Was he one of the men Adam flattened at the warehouse?

"Yeah — you got a message for Mr McLaughlin?" the newcomer asked in a nasal, high-pitched voice.

"I have to deliver it in person." Byron stared at him.

The man's jaw muscles bunched and he stood for a few seconds before gesturing to the doorman to let them pass.

The smell of tobacco and alcohol enveloped them. He led them through a smart bar area with shiny black flooring and plenty of chrome and mirrors. The place heaved with a young and smartly-dressed crowd, exuberant but well-behaved. Byron guessed troublemakers weren't tolerated.

Steroid-man led them to a booth in an alcove where McLaughlin held court. Several champagne bottles littered the table and the man sipped from a martini glass. The crowd around him fell silent and studied Byron and Rebecca. McLaughlin dismissed most of them with a gesture, and the two visitors faced him and three heavies. Steroid-man and one other flanked them but Byron ignored them and focussed on their boss.

"Well, well, if it isn't the family of Liam's killer. Come to give me your condolences?" McLaughlin drawled.

In the ensuing silence, Byron stared until McLaughlin looked uncomfortable.

"Okay, give me your message and fuck off. We're trying to have a good time."

"Where's my son?" Rebecca demanded.

"How should I know? I'm not your son's keeper." McLaughlin smirked and one of the men beside him giggled. Rebecca glared at the man who reddened and shuffled his feet. "Maybe he's out shagging his girlfriend."

Rebecca lunged at McLaughlin, but Byron checked her. "You're scum," she spat and shook off Byron's hand.

Byron leant into McLaughlin. "We know you've got Philip," he said, in a quiet voice. "Let him go unharmed and I'll return your trailer."

At the mention of the trailer, the faces of McLaughlin's men changed. The impassive masks they'd worn so far showed naked anger for the first time. Rebecca recoiled from the two men who flanked them but Byron gave her a reassuring smile. McLaughlin grew bright red and he clenched his fists.

Byron realised Kieran hadn't relayed his earlier message to his brother. McLaughlin glared, barely in control of his anger. Byron waited for what seemed like minutes, waiting for McLaughlin's next move. He could hear himself breathing and the blood rushing round his head.

Raucous laughter from a nearby table broke the spell. McLaughlin must have realised there were too many witnesses. Byron recognised his opportunity and gripping Rebecca's arm, strode for the exit. The two men flanking them moved aside to let them pass and the other guests parted, making way for them. He'd expected her to at least resist but she let him lead her out. Outside on the pavement, she pushed his hand away and stopped.

Byron, aware the danger was far from over, grabbed her elbow. "Keep walking," he said, speeding up until they reached the car. "Let's go."

He pushed her towards the driver's door and walked around the car as Rebecca fumbled for the keys. As he scanned his surroundings she started the engine, and he leapt in, checking behind as they drove away. Byron considered his options. McLaughlin's reaction suggested he wouldn't listen to reason but if he calmed down…

Once away from the bustle of Moseley Street Rebecca said, "What was that about a trailer?"

"You don't need to know."

"We're talking about my son's life here."

Byron looked away. "I borrowed a lorry full of his gear."

She didn't respond for a few seconds. "You're seriously telling me that, while you should have been taking care of my son, you went out stealing?"

"I wasn't stealing."

"Oh yeah? What do you call it then?"

Byron shifted in his seat. "I thought if we could make McLaughlin back off…"

"That worked, didn't it?"

Byron opened his mouth to respond but said nothing.

"And who's the 'we'? Your friend Adam? *And* Philip?" Her voice rose.

"No, Philip was safe at Adam's."

"Thank, God! At least you didn't make him an accessory." She paused and a lightbulb seemed to illuminate. "That's where you were when I rang. You left Philip alone."

"No, we left one of Adam's friends guarding him. He was probably safer than if he'd been with us."

"That's not saying much."

Byron accepted the rebuke and they drove on in silence, her hands gripping the steering wheel like she wanted to crush it.

"Did McLaughlin take my son to get revenge?" she demanded.

"Don't be stupid."

"The man who steals from a mad psychopath calls me stupid."

"McLaughlin obviously planned the kidnapping a while back. He tried before, if you remember."

Rebecca didn't say anything and they sat in uncomfortable silence. Despite his retort Byron feared she might be right, and he'd run out of ideas of where they could find Philip.

Byron considered his options as Rebecca drove them to her house. McLaughlin must have another hideaway but how would he find it? Several police cars and two unmarked vehicles lined the road outside the house. Rebecca manoeuvred round them and approached her drive. The officer guarding the house recognised her but saw Byron and stopped her.

Rebecca wound down her window. "This is my brother-in-law, officer."

"Have you got any ID, sir?" he spoke across her.

"Are you serious?" she demanded.

"It's not a problem." Byron retrieved his driving licence and handed it to the officer. "At least he's doing his job."

The man noted the details before returning the licence and Rebecca parked on the drive. The downstairs lights blazed and Byron followed her to the front door. Her daughters besieged her, emitting shrill cries. She hugged them, uttering reassuring words. Byron edged past her and Samuel gave him an interrogative glance, but he shook his head.

A petite woman with strawberry blond hair and fine features stood behind Samuel, alongside a big bulky man a couple of inches shorter than Byron. His cropped hair and broken nose gave him the appearance of a thug, but Byron noted an alert intelligence. Coppers.

"Good morning, Mrs Mason," the woman said. "As I've just said to your husband, we'll do everything we can to find Philip."

Rebecca broke free of her daughters' embrace. "Thank you, Chief Inspector."

The policewoman regarded him with green eyes. "You must be Byron Mason."

Byron couldn't remember ever meeting her. "Sorry, do I know you?"

"Your brother told me you were with his wife. I'm Chief Inspector Quinn and this is Sergeant Arkwright." Her gaze bored into him.

Byron shook hands with both officers.

"Mr Mason," she addressed Samuel, glancing at his daughters. "Can we go somewhere to talk?"

Rebecca took the hint. "You two better get off to bed, it's way past bedtime. Go on, I'll be right up."

Samuel led them into his study and Byron brought up the rear, closing the door behind him.

Quinn addressed Rebecca, her tone brisk. "Can you tell me what you were doing at the park?"

"Searching for Philip."

"Why?"

"Because he went missing." Rebecca's voice rose.

Byron understood the policewoman. "*I* told them he was missing, Chief Inspector. Philip was staying with me and I noticed he'd gone, so I told his parents."

"And how come your nephew stayed with you but his parents didn't know about it?"

"Because I didn't tell them."

The Chief Inspector's expression belied her delicate appearance. "I'll need a statement from you Mr Mason. Where did you and Philip stay? Your brother says you're up from London."

Byron wouldn't drop Adam in it. "With a friend, but he knows nothing about what happened."

"I'll overlook the fact you shielded a suspect in a murder case for now, but I *will* deal with it later. Right now, finding Philip is the priority. Can you tell me where you've been since you spoke to my colleagues in the park?"

"We went to speak to Ritchie McLaughlin."

"That's brave, Mr Mason. Mr McLaughlin has a reputation. Can you tell me why you went to see him and to what effect?"

"I think he took Philip, but he denies it."

"Why would he take Philip?"

Both Rebecca and Samuel looked uncomfortable at the direction of the questioning, but Byron detected sympathy in

Arkwright's demeanour. "He believes Philip had something to do with his nephew Liam's death. He came here on Monday night to snatch Philip but failed, and he tried again tonight."

Siobhan studied Philip's parents. "When you reported this incident to my colleagues in Didsbury, you didn't mention he'd attempted to take your son."

Rebecca looked sheepish but didn't reply.

"I'll need a statement from you, this time the truth." She transferred her attention to Byron. "And anyone else who was here."

"Chief Inspector, shouldn't you concentrate on finding Philip, not what happened a few nights ago?" Rebecca said, returning to her normal spikiness.

"I agree, Mrs Mason. But I need evidence if I'm to investigate Mr McLaughlin. The fact he tried before is a good reason to suspect him."

Rebecca seemed to accept this.

Siobhan continued, "Now, when you saw him tonight, did he look like he'd just taken part in a kidnapping?"

"Point made, Chief Inspector," Byron conceded. "But he'll have sent his minions. In fact, he looked like he'd been working on an alibi."

"I'll send someone to take your statements," Siobhan said to Rebecca. "Mr Mason, I need to know where you hid Philip and the names of anyone else involved."

Byron considered refusing, but suspected she'd give him a hard time, and he couldn't afford to be out of action until they found Philip.

CHAPTER 23

Since the first raid, some of the men from the village remained close by and they soon arrived. The warning shout from the drivers alerted the raiders. Seizing the few children they had so far subdued, they made for their vehicles, but the villagers saw this and intercepted them.

The Boy recognised their adversaries, including his father and one of his brothers. Believing him dead, neither recognised him and, in the ensuing battle, his father suffered severe wounds. The Boy, cornered by a former neighbour, attacked the man whose son he'd grown up with. The man recognised his son's playmate and called his name as he fell. Shocked at hearing his name, The Boy paused but the man's expression of contempt shamed him and he turned away.

Siobhan's anger at the Mason family faded as Eddy drove her to McLaughlin's club and her thoughts drifted to the upcoming confrontation. They had discovered McLaughlin's whereabouts and a squad from the Tactical Aid Unit would meet them at the club. A senior detective from the local station organised the search warrants for McLaughlin's premises. He owned too many to search all of them simultaneously and although recognising the risk he might move the boy — or worse — if they didn't find him straight away, she hoped they might get lucky. At least she would show McLaughlin how serious she was.

During the drive, a troubled-looking Eddy voiced his concerns. "Don't you think we're jumping the gun here, Boss?"

Part of her agreed with him but she couldn't risk leaving Philip in McLaughlin's hands. "I appreciate your concerns Eddy, but I don't want to waste any time."

"Yes, but we haven't any hard evidence from the kidnapping yet, and the Masons haven't even made statements about Monday night."

"We already have Mrs Mason's assertion he 'invaded' their home and I'm confident we'll soon have the statements from the two men. There's also the forensic evidence at the pavilion where they snatched Philip."

"What did you think of Byron Mason?"

"What do you mean?"

"I wondered if you thought he had anything to do with what happened to Ritchie's man? The one someone almost killed."

"I thought you said we suspected members of another crime family?"

"He strikes me as the type who isn't scared of getting his hands dirty. He visited Ritchie tonight and accused him of taking his nephew. I wouldn't do that, not on my own and without the uniform behind me. And I wonder about Monday. His brother's a big guy, but he's in a wheelchair and Mrs Mason's not big. I don't see them giving Ritchie and his men a lot of trouble."

"You could be right. We'll bear it in mind, but for now let's find Philip."

An unmarked police minibus sat behind McLaughlin's club. They parked behind it and a uniformed inspector got out of the front passenger seat.

"All right, Eddy?" he said in a gruff but friendly voice, then offered Siobhan his hand. "Mike Wilson, good to meet you, Chief Inspector."

"Thank you, Mike. Call me Siobhan."

The inspector's giant paw enveloped her hand. Built on a similarly heroic scale to her sergeant, he presented a reassuring presence. "Here's the warrant but I've not been inside." He indicated the club. "They started chucking out just after we arrived and my lads are watching the entrances, just in case, but we've not seen anyone who fits the description of your lad."

"Thanks, Mike." She produced the photo Mrs Mason had given her. "Here's the lad we're looking for."

The inspector studied the photograph and showed it to his men.

Siobhan checked the warrant. "The crowds should have dispersed now — let's go in." Despite the presence of several burly colleagues the memory of her last confrontation with McLaughlin made the skin on her neck crinkle.

"Sorry, love, we're closed," the lead bouncer said.

She showed him the warrant. "I want you to take me to McLaughlin."

The man lifted a radio to his mouth. "I'll see if he's—"

"You'll do what the Chief Inspector says." Mike grabbed his wrist.

With bad grace he led them into the club. The smell of alcohol and tobacco hit Siobhan like a wall, reminding her why she hated nightclubs. Her hair and clothes would stink. The bouncer led them through the body of the club while Mike and his men spread through the premises. McLaughlin slouched in front of a booth in a back room, a phone clamped to his ear. He scowled as he noticed them and ended the call. Siobhan studied him as she approached.

By the time she reached him, he'd pasted a big grin on his face. "Chief Inspector, to what do I owe this pleasure?" He sounded drunk.

"Mr McLaughlin—"

"No need to be so formal, Siobhan. It's not as if we're strangers." The bouncer leant towards his ear and spoke. McLaughlin's grin died. "The fuck you doing searching my—"

Siobhan thrust the warrant at him and he snatched it from her. As he read it the colour drained from his cheeks. He *was* hiding something. Around them bouncers escorted a few stragglers to the door while bar staff collected glasses. Siobhan had learned the hard way the dangers of being overheard.

"Can we go somewhere quiet to discuss this?"

McLaughlin spun on his heel, stumbling before recovering and striding to a door in the far corner of the room. Siobhan and Eddy followed.

The occupant of the office he led them to, a balding man with a pencil moustache and dandruff on the shoulders of his jacket, scurried away as his boss barged in, leaving it to McLaughlin and the police officers. A smallish room, it contained a large dark-wood desk which cut the space in two. Behind this sat an office chair, covered in black leather. In front of it, stood two steel framed chairs, upholstered in stained and worn grey tweed. A calendar from a drinks company, featuring a scantily clad blonde in a suggestive pose, provided the only adornment on the walls. McLaughlin had recovered some of his composure and sat in the leather clad chair before leaning back and making an expansive gesture towards the two seats.

Siobhan ignored the invitation. "Mr McLaughlin, I'm here on a very serious matter. A group of men kidnapped a young man and we have evidence you're involved in his disappearance."

"I've been here all evening. Ask anybody."

"Don't worry, we will. In the meantime I'd like you to come to the station and answer a few questions—"

"I'd rather not."

"You can either come willingly or my colleagues can drag you through the club in front of your staff."

McLaughlin gave a half-hearted laugh. "You're serious, aren't you?"

"Oh yes, Mr McLaughlin. I am very serious. It's your choice."

McLaughlin got to his feet. Despite his attempt to disguise it, she recognised that he was hiding something. She hoped they found Philip before it was too late.

Adam waited for Siobhan to leave before approaching the house. The officer guarding the house wouldn't let him in until Rebecca identified him.

"Adam, did Byron ring you?"

"Where is he?"

"In Samuel's study, giving a statement."

"What happened?"

"Do you want to come through?" She led him into the kitchen, slumped into a chair and brought him up to date.

"All right, mate." Byron returned from giving his statement. He looked shattered and Adam checked the time: ten to four.

Rebecca got up to make him coffee. "Do you want something to eat?" she asked.

"Yes please, Rebecca." Byron gave her a tired smile. "Anything."

"What about you, Adam?"

"Yes please." He addressed Byron. "Everything okay?"

"I dropped you in it, mate. I told them Philip was staying with me at your place, but I said you knew nothing about him being on the run."

Adam gave a short laugh. "We'll see if they believe that." A flutter passed through his insides as he considered Siobhan's reaction when she found out. "Do you want to see if we can find him again?"

"Look, mate, I don't want to get you in any more shit."

Adam punched Byron on the shoulder and got a nod of thanks in return.

"Any ideas?" Adam asked.

"It won't be anywhere in McLaughlin's name. We have to assume the police will search those."

"Somewhere like the mill where we found him last time?" Adam thought of the disused buildings in the city. "That will be a nightmare."

"It will be somewhere McLaughlin owns, but not in his own name. Like the place we er…" He glanced at Rebecca.

"I'm guessing you have an idea how we're going to find these places?"

"I know a man," Byron replied.

"Is he the guy who sent you to see the psycho brothers?"

"Yup."

"How do you want to play it?"

"I'd like to spread him and Lynton round the walls of his house, but I need his help so I'll pretend he'd done me a favour. We got Kieran's number out of it."

Much good that did. "You're the boss."

Half an hour later Adam pulled up outside Cyrus's house. The shrill ringing of the bell reverberated as Byron kept his thumb on the switch. Muttered curses reached them and someone clumped down the stairs. Byron eased the pressure on the white button and stepped back. An athletic man of about twenty-five wearing boxers snatched the door open and regarded them, his bare chest thrust forward. The faint stink of marijuana smoke accompanied him.

"What the fuck you want?"

The hairs on Adam's neck rose and he prepared to defend himself. The man glanced at him before returning his attention to Byron.

"I need to speak to Cyrus again," Byron said conversationally. Lynton didn't move, so he added, "It's urgent."

Conflicting emotions played across Lynton's face before he made a decision. "Sorry, he's not available. Now fuck off and don't come back."

He pushed the door but Adam reacted quicker and kicked it. The force of the blow knocked Lynton into the wall and snatched the door out of his hands. He struggled upright and reached for something above the door but Byron grabbed his wrist and forced him backwards into the house.

"Like I said, this is urgent."

Lynton fought to free himself, hate in his eyes. More angry voices came from upstairs and two men descended. Both carried wooden bats, but didn't look in the mood for games. Adam studied them, his pulse racing but ready to deal with anything.

"Hi, Cyrus," Byron said. "I apologise for bursting in but it's a real emergency. McLaughlin's got my nephew."

Cyrus paused for a few seconds before nodding. Byron released Lynton's wrist and offered an apology but Lynton stormed into the living room, leaving the four men by the front door. Adam remained tense and kept his attention on the two men.

"Thanks, Cyrus. This is Adam, a good friend of mine. He's helping me."

Adam stepped forward and offered his hand.

Cyrus frowned at him and ignored the gesture, but he relaxed and lowered his bat. "You'd better come in."

He led Byron into the living room and Adam followed. The smell of ganja Adam noticed on the doorstep grew stronger. The other man brought up the rear, his bat held by his side. Adam's scalp crawled and he slowed, making sure the man stayed too close to take a swing at him.

The small sitting room had been the scene of partying which looked to have just finished. Empty cans and bottles lay scattered everywhere. The stink of spilt alcohol and smoke mingled with the odour from several takeaway containers. A few of these had been used as ashtrays and smoke still rose from one. The thought of how they'd react if he gave them a fire safety talk made Adam smile.

Lynton wasn't in the room, but a beaded curtain in front of a door at the far end of the room swung side to side. Cyrus pushed a fried chicken container onto the floor and picked empty cans off a sofa then sat on it. He offered the other sofa to his two guests.

"No thanks, mate," Byron said. "We're in a hurry. I need to find my nephew. McLaughlin grabbed him last night."

"Did you get the number for Ritchie?"

"Great, thanks. Trev was very helpful, gave me Kieron's number. Nice lads, we had a couple of drinks."

Cyrus exchanged a surprised glance with his sidekick and thought for some time, all the while studying his two visitors. Coming to a decision, he nodded and addressed Adam.

"You the other one Byron talked about? You in the army with him?"

"Close enough."

"You any good?"

Adam held his gaze.

Cyrus chuckled. "I bet you are. Lynton!" he shouted at the door. "Lynton, don't be a pussy."

The door opened and the young man stuck his head through the beaded curtain. He glared at the two visitors but didn't speak.

"Our friends here are looking for somewhere McLaughlin might keep a prisoner."

Lynton shrugged. "There's a few places. I need to make some calls." He disappeared into the kitchen.

The four men in the lounge waited in silence, not feeling much like making small talk. The murmur of Lynton's voice reached them through the kitchen doorway and a shriek of girlish laughter came from above their heads. Lynton returned after a few minutes, clutching a stained envelope which he thrust at Cyrus, who took it and read it before handing it to Byron.

"Thanks, Cyrus. I owe you one," Byron said. "Thanks, Lynton."

Lynton sucked his teeth noisily and retreated into the kitchen.

"That's two you owe me now," Cyrus observed. "Get that bastard off the scene and we'll call it quits." His face broke into a big grin.

Byron nodded and, without another word, strode to the car. Adam recognised his expression and steeled himself for what lay over the horizon.

CHAPTER 24

As the remaining village men returned, the raiders escaped, leaving behind dead and injured villagers and a few of their colleagues. The Boy's companions whooped and yelled, celebrating their survival. He looked across at the truck; it contained half a dozen miserable prisoners.

The sight of his father and brother awakened the desire to return home. But the memory of his former neighbour's expression as he struck him down, told him this would be a forlorn dream. For many weeks afterwards, he mourned his lost life but, over time, the shell protecting the memories of his younger self grew thicker and harder. Its core shrank until it disappeared inside the growing body of a young fighting machine.

The Boy thrived and he grew bigger and stronger. Careless of his own safety and ruthless, he became a respected warrior. By eleven, he'd become a veteran of more than a dozen raids. His intelligence and ability to get people to do what he wanted marked him out for leadership. Success in this role led to him being given a new name, Mugisa, or 'lucky'.

Eddy drove Siobhan back to the station and the idea Adam got close to her because of the investigation wouldn't leave her. Since Adam had told her he knew the Masons she'd replayed the events of the evening, but couldn't detect any hint of insincerity from the firefighter. Had lust blinded her? She'd seen it often enough. *But no, he'd meant it, unless he's a bloody good actor.* She dismissed her concerns and concentrated on her forthcoming interview with McLaughlin. A young man's life might depend on it.

McLaughlin had sobered up by the time they arrived at the station and he insisted on having his solicitor present. While they waited for him to arrive from the suburbs, Siobhan drank a second strong coffee at her desk while studying Rebecca Mason's revised statement. Siobhan read the account of her cutting McLaughlin's ear. No wonder he'd been embarrassed about the injury. She made a call to the local station to request they collect samples but forgot to ask if they'd faxed Byron Mason's statement. She wanted to see where he'd hidden his nephew.

Before she could call them back, Eddy knocked on the doorframe. "They've just finished searching the club."

"Nothing?" She hadn't expected McLaughlin to take Philip anywhere near his club.

"Like you said, Boss. Although we found shedloads of contraband, especially fags."

"Have we contacted customs?"

"Oh yes." He smiled. "We're now concentrating on the industrial and commercial stuff, but Ritchie has a lot of properties which aren't in his name."

"Those are the ones we should look at."

"You're right, but we can't prove he owns them so can't get warrants."

Siobhan frowned. "Make a list of those you know of and get them checked. If they see anything suspicious, report back. They can always break in to make sure it isn't being burgled." She winked at her sergeant.

Eddy grinned and left to compile the list, returning to tell her McLaughlin's solicitor had arrived. Siobhan stilled her nerves on the walk to the interview suite and strode into the room. McLaughlin's solicitor, Martin Farmer, resembled an overfed budgie with thinning hair swept over his skull and oiled so it glistened in the harsh light. She assumed he was also the source of the overpowering aftershave. He shared McLaughlin's taste in tailoring; his suit looked to have cost more than most people spent on a family holiday.

After cautioning McLaughlin, Siobhan started. "Mr McLaughlin, I must remind you how serious kidnapping is. You deny knowing the men who attacked the young couple."

"I told you, I was in my club and I've no idea what you're talking about."

Siobhan questioned him for several minutes but he stuck to the same story. She changed tack. "So you don't know the young man who disappeared — Philip Mason?"

"Never heard of him."

"Do you know Ms Maria McLaughlin?"

"Of course, she's my sister-in-law."

"So why did she say you'd gone to have a word with Philip Mason?"

McLaughlin folded his arms. "No comment."

"Three witnesses have identified you at his address on Monday evening."

"No comment."

"We've taken a butcher's knife and forensic samples from the house. We believe we'll find your blood. Can you explain how it got there?"

A flash of anger distorted McLaughlin's features, and he stroked the grubby bandage covering his ear.

"Inspector, I need to speak to my client in private."

Siobhan and Eddy waited outside. "What do you reckon, Boss?"

"McLaughlin's far too wily to make the mistake Anthony Lees made. They'll concoct a story about why he went there on Monday."

"What about the guns?"

"They didn't use them so unless we find them, we might struggle." They were still no nearer finding Philip but if McLaughlin had him, Siobhan doubted his men would do anything to the lad without his say-so. The longer she detained him here the better their chances of finding Philip alive. Unless he'd already given the order… No, she couldn't think that.

They returned to the interview and as she'd predicted, Farmer read a statement explaining that McLaughlin had called on the house to speak to Philip about his nephew's disappearance but the occupants attacked him.

"Which one of them? Mrs Mason, who's a foot shorter and half your client's weight, or her husband, who's in a wheelchair?"

McLaughlin reddened but didn't speak.

"Do you want to press charges against the Masons?" she asked, barely controlling her anger.

"Considering the distress the family is suffering, my client doesn't want to press charges. Furthermore, he doesn't understand why you're not linking the disappearance of Philip to the savage murder of his nephew. It's obvious someone is targeting these young men—"

"Thank you Mr Farmer. I don't need advice on how to do my job." She poured water into a plastic cup and sipped it. "Mr McLaughlin, now your memory has improved, do you want to reconsider your earlier answer?"

"No comment."

Siobhan continued questioning him, hoping to receive the message saying they'd found Philip, until Farmer stepped in again. "Inspector, my client has answered your questions. In the meantime you have no reason to hold him."

"Mr Farmer, I appreciate it's early." She smiled at him. "My rank is *Chief* Inspector and we're not holding Mr McLaughlin. He's here of his own volition."

Farmer flushed. "You threatened him with violence."

"Me?" She gestured at her slim frame before regarding McLaughlin's hulking figure. "He's free to make an official complaint."

McLaughlin shook his head before standing. "If you're not holding me, then why the fuck am I still sat here?"

"I'll make a note you're refusing to cooperate. Sergeant Arkwright will show you out. Don't leave the city without informing us." She waited until they reached the door. "By the way, Customs and Excise will want to speak to you about the contraband we discovered in your storeroom." McLaughlin's expression almost made up for the frustration of not having enough to arrest him with.

Eddy showed them out and returned. "What do you reckon?"

"I'm sure we can persuade the Masons to bring charges for Monday night's incident. I don't think he'll intimidate them. But I get the feeling that if he's got Philip, he has no intention of giving him up."

Byron gripped the door handle as Adam drove away from the building at speed. Yet another of the addresses they'd got from Lynton had been a waste of time. The first, a betting shop in a small shopping parade was empty, and much too small. This, the second, was a derelict pub, and he suspected Lynton had been having another joke at his expense.

He checked the list and gave directions as he read the map. He needed to think about what would happen when they found Philip. McLaughlin's men would be armed and would, most likely, outnumber them.

Adam shared the same thoughts. "Can Cyrus supply weapons?"

"Yeah, but I don't want to risk it. We'd be in enough shit if we got caught with firearms but there's also a chance they might be dirty…"

"Do you know anyone else?"

"Not anyone nearby."

"So it's the crowbars then."

Byron hoped they'd get close enough to be able to use them. "Crowbars, and the element of surprise."

They checked out three more of the addresses Lynton had provided and as Byron ticked them off the list, a sense of déjà vu overcame him. They arrived at the last place on the list, an industrial estate with a site map at the front entrance. McLaughlin's unit sat at the end of one of the arms of the Y-shaped estate. Although they'd started before five in the morning, time had moved on and streetlights flickered off. Most of the units had lights on. Not holding out much hope, he directed Adam.

The two-storey office block, tucked out of sight of the rest of the units, sat in darkness and had roller-shutters over each ground floor opening. Although it the most promising of the places they'd seen, doubt tempered Byron's excitement. They split up and circled the building on foot, meeting each other along the back wall.

"Anything?" Byron said.

"Someone's left a window open on the other side."

Byron followed Adam, who pointed to a narrow opening above a larger one on the first floor. A sliver of a gap showed at the bottom of the frame.

"Good spot. You reckon you can get through it?"

"No chance, but if I can reach down and open the main window…"

Byron checked round the front. Someone had parked a car half on the pavement but they'd gone. Paint peeled off the alarm box on the front of the building and a stencilled sign warned intruders to keep away. Byron hadn't heard of the company providing the security and assumed it was a small local outfit.

A wheeled dumpster and a stack of wooden pallets leant against the back wall. By piling them on the lid, they made a platform for Adam to work from. Byron boosted him up and stood back, keeping a lookout.

Adam got his fingers into the gap and prised the window open. He reached his arm inside but his head wouldn't fit. After a minute of struggling, he pulled his arm out. "I can't quite reach it, but I haven't got your gibbon-like arms..." He flexed his knees making the platform sway. "Mind you, this might not take your weight."

"Cheeky pup — come on then." Byron made a stirrup with his hands.

"Hey! Come down off there!" An older man wearing shapeless blue overalls stood at the corner of the building brandishing a radio.

Byron helped Adam to the ground and offered his most professional smile. "I'm glad you've turned up."

The man had the handset to his mouth but surprise made him stop.

"We're looking for my nephew. He's a bit wayward and likes to hide in empty buildings. We thought he might be in there."

"He shouldn't be breaking into places."

"That's what I keep telling him, but you know what kids are like these days." Byron held his hands out in a gesture of helplessness.

"So is he in there?" The man lifted his radio.

"I couldn't see — it opens onto a landing," Adam said. "Can we have a look?"

"Right, oh, bloody hell… I don't have any keys — we don't normally do this building. They've got their own people. Bloody cowboys." He made a face. "We're just doing it for a few days." He walked up to the bin and studied the window. "Did you open that?"

"It was already open — that's why we thought my nephew was in there," Byron said.

The man ran a hand through thinning hair, dislodging flakes of dandruff. "I'll have to get someone out to lock it. You can see if your lad's in there when they get here."

Forty minutes later a hard-faced woman drove a Mercedes saloon up to the front door and got out with a bunch of keys. Byron opened the car door, making Adam jerk awake.

"Key holder here?" he asked, his voice slurred.

"Stay here, mate. I'll go in."

Adam shook himself awake and opened his door. "Let's get this done."

Byron followed, his legs heavy. He related his story to the woman.

The woman shielded the alarm panel with her body as she punched in the numbers. "You two go upstairs and we'll do the ground floor." She indicated the security guard.

A flight of stairs he'd normally take without thinking left Byron exhausted and they split up at the top. Apart from a bin with a hole in it and a broken telephone, Byron found nothing. Then, a piercing scream from downstairs filled his body with energy. He arrived at the head of the stairs ahead of Adam and they raced down. The sobbing woman stood in the corridor, the security guard comforting her. She pointed to a half-open door.

Byron reached inside and flicked the light switch. Nothing. Then, his heart racing, he stepped into the room. The stench of sewage and unwashed body pervaded the air. Light from the corridor illuminated a bundle by the far corner.

"You got a torch?" he shouted, not taking his gaze from the bundle. Was it big enough to be Philip?

The security guard's lamp lit up a pile of filthy bedding. On the wall someone had written 'EAT THE RICH' using excrement.

The adrenaline energising Byron drained away and weariness made him dizzy. Had McLaughlin already killed Philip?

The disappointment of having to release McLaughlin and their failure to find Philip weighed on Siobhan.

"All right, Boss?" Eddy called from the doorway.

"Sorry, Eddy. Miles away." She checked the time, eight already. "You need to get off home to your kiddies."

He made a face. "They'll be in bed. I just thought I'd give you this." He placed a folder on her desk. "These are places we think McLaughlin owns, but we don't have any proof."

Could Philip be in one of these? "Thanks, I'll look at it later."

"Have you heard the latest?"

Eddy seemed to have a line to every piece of gossip in the force. "Grab a seat."

"You know someone's attacked two of McLaughlin's men—"

“Don’t tell me we’ve got evidence linking him to either of them?”

“No such luck, but Stockport found a body in the boot of Steve Harris’s burnt-out car. They reckon it’s him — he’s in competition with McLaughlin and he’s been talking about taking him out over some dog he killed. Harris has two sons, real nasty pieces of work. McLaughlin will have his hands full if they suspect he’s killed their dad.”

CHAPTER 25

The army got bigger as they captured more recruits and their influence grew. In reaction, the government, supported by international forces, set up a special task force to hunt them.

The force struck hard. Mugisa and his band retreated across the border, an invisible, but effective barrier. They set up base in the new country where the government left them in peace, provided they confined their attacks to their homeland.

Mugisa led the remnants of the raiding party back from the latest attack. Encountering unexpected resistance, they left behind many dead and wounded, including the most senior officers. He gave the order to abandon their vehicles when the enemy helicopters located them and they crossed the border, exhausted. Their camp was still a day's march away and they rested, hiding in the undergrowth.

Woken by the noise of combat, he opened his eyes and heard the confusion of sounds, shouts of rage, the clash of weapons and the screams of the wounded. He leapt up and reached for his Kalashnikov. A shout came from behind him and a figure charged out of the darkness.

After a good six hours' sleep, Adam came downstairs to find Byron on the phone in the living room.

"…sure, Samuel. How are the girls coping?"

Adam made a pot of coffee, feeling guilty that he'd wanted Philip out of the house, and wishing the lad would walk in. Byron finished his call and came through to the kitchen.

"How you doing, mate?" Adam filled two mugs.

"Not great. Police won't tell me anything — even Samuel's not getting much information. Kieron's not answering his phone and nobody seems to know anywhere else we could look for Philip."

Adam sipped his coffee, distressed at seeing his friend so helpless. "I'll ask Siobhan what they've found out."

"Oh yeah? Siobhan, is it? And why would she tell you?"

"We met up last night."

"Met up, as in 'met up'?" Byron sounded incredulous.

Adam's cheeks grew hot.

Byron's laugh rumbled round the kitchen. He shook his head. "Bugger me. She's one scary lady — nice looking, but scary." Byron became serious. "You realise, if she's seen my statement, she'll know Philip stayed at your place, and I don't think she'll be too impressed. Sorry, mate. It was my idea to take him there."

"Don't worry about it. I knew what I was doing." Rather than ring her, Adam decided he should go to see her and put things straight. She was as likely to put the phone down as speak to him. He finished his drink and, telling Byron he wouldn't be long, he set off. Someone had left the main door to her block of flats open and, closing it behind him, he started making his way to her flat. Before he reached it, he heard a scream. Adrenaline surged through his blood and he leapt up the stairs.

The thud of a heavy blow and wood splintering spurred him on. As he rounded the top landing, he froze for an instant. Philip stood outside Siobhan's door, attacking it with a machete but as the young man spun to face him he realised it was not Philip, but Mugisa, eyes fierce.

Adam advanced and Mugisa yanked the knife out of the door. He swung it at Adam, who leapt back. The blade missed him by centimetres, then crunched into the bannister, burying itself into the timber.

Adam charged as Mugisa pulled at it. Instead of focussing on the stuck weapon, the youth kicked Adam, knocking him onto the landing. By the time he recovered, Mugisa had extracted the blade and disappeared down the corridor. Adam followed, seeing him leap through a fire exit.

Once sure he'd gone, Adam ran back to the flat. The machete had splintered the top right door panel, but he'd not got through.

"Siobhan, it's Adam." He listened — the thought she might be injured was making him nauseous.

Locks clicked, and she stood in the door, ashen. "Has he gone?"

"Yes, you okay?"

She held herself together. "I'll be fine. Thank you."

Relief flooded through him and he wanted to hold her but wasn't sure how she'd react.

"Do you want to come in? I've called my lot."

He entered and she locked the door. Bits of splintered timber lay in the hall, white paint clinging to them. In the lounge she poured two glasses of brandy and picked one up. Her hand shook, spilling some, then she began sobbing.

Adam put his arms round her, and she clung to him. After a while, her trembling ceased, and she eased away from him. "Thank you." She gestured at her face. "I'd better do something before the troops turn up." She disappeared into the bathroom.

Adam sipped his brandy which burnt his throat. He placed the glass on the table next to a folder. It contained Polaroid's of buildings clipped to sheets of paper. One looked familiar, a close-up showed a roller-shutter with a stencilled sign on it. He tried to remember when he'd seen it.

"Please put those down." Siobhan stood in the doorway, make-up repaired.

"Are these McLaughlin's?"

"Sorry, Adam. It's nothing to do with you." Restored and apparently annoyed with him, she scooped the papers into the folder before he could read the address.

After his failed attempt to get rid of the policewoman, a shaken Mugisa returned to the disused factory where he'd seen the men take Philip. His first attempt to get in failed when the second car returned and he'd spent the last day watching it, waiting for an opportunity to attack, but his enemies always had at least four men on guard. Now, instead of two cars, one sat outside. This was his chance to overpower the guards and finish Philip. He approached the front of the building, the machete tucked into the scabbard in his jacket, and waited for the security lights to come on. Nothing happened. He'd hoped to trigger the lights and get them to investigate. He waited, considering his options then drew the knife, strolled to their car and smashed the side window. A shriek rent the air as the alarm sounded and the hazard lights flashed.

He strode to the entrance and, flattening himself against the wall, waited. As he listened, he gripped the handle of the machete. His hands tingled, the skin hyper-sensitive. The car alarm finished, and he listened for sounds of movement inside. Nothing. Had they fallen asleep? Having seen how unprofessional they'd been when capturing Philip, it didn't surprise him.

He'd have to reactivate the alarm. Before he'd gone two steps, bolts scraped and the heavy front door crashed open. A figure ran out. Mugisa, caught by surprise, froze but the man rushed past him and faltered.

"Gary, put the lights on," the man shouted, adding, "Oi, you little bastard, fuck off before I give you a good hiding."

Mugisa lifted the machete and stepped forward. The man whirled round and, using the light spilling out of the open doorway, Mugisa slashed at his throat. The blade struck the junction between the man's neck and collarbone. He didn't even cry out before collapsing. He fell to his knees and toppled forward, a fountain of blood spraying the ground beneath him.

Mugisa stepped aside, breathing hard, and twisted the blade, freeing it from the wound. A shape moved across the light. A figure stood in the doorway and Mugisa ran at him, machete raised.

As he reached the opening, a row of bright lights came on, shining straight into his face. He screwed up his eyes and took a swing at the blurred shape in the doorway. The blade bit into the doorframe. The man cried out in alarm and the door slammed. Mugisa pulled the machete out of the wood and hurled himself at the door which shook but resisted his efforts.

Bright light bathed the car park and Mugisa ended his attack to contemplate his options. Frustration made his muscles quiver as he realised he couldn't get at his quarry. And if he waited, reinforcements would arrive.

Philip woke in his cell, suddenly alert. Excited chatter came from upstairs and he guessed more people had arrived. Had something happened? The noise died down. They must have changed guards. How long had he been here? It felt like days but he had no idea. The pain from his kidneys had faded but flared up when he moved and he still passed blood. The stench from the bucket in the corner wafted towards him and he gagged. After a few moments he closed his eyes and dozed.

The voice of the man who'd hit Jenna cut through his torpor and he shuddered. He took a few seconds to realise he wasn't dreaming. Why the hell had he returned? A key turned in the door, and it slammed open. He jumped. Three figures crowded in the opening. Their leader possessed sharp features and the physique of one of those morons who spend all day in the gym. He gave Philip a nasty grin but his beady eyes didn't smile.

"If it isn't Sir Galahad. How's the kidneys?" He laughed.

Philip wanted to tell him where to go but couldn't speak. Did he just want to torment him or were they taking him away? The men dragged him to his feet and he tried to control his fear. The pain made him gasp and his legs gave way but the men held him up and secured his arms. Someone wound a strip of tape round his mouth, cutting off his protests.

"Shall I blindfold him, Lenny?" the man with the tape asked.

"Not yet, I want him to see everything." Lenny thrust his grinning face into Philip's, giving him a blast of his stale breath. "Struggle and I'll do your other kidney." He prodded Philip in the chest.

Fear paralysed Philip. He remembered the noise Jenna made when the man hit her and his anger returned. He wouldn't show him how terrified he was.

"Right, boys," Lenny said. "Bring him out, it's time we ended this."

He left the room and the others dragged Philip out. Their leader waited by the door and Philip saw the pistol in his hand. Despite his resolve, his legs weakened. The men holding him stopped. His knees shook and he sensed movement behind him. A large hand gripped the back of his neck and cold steel touched his ear. The barrel of the pistol dug into the side of his head.

"On your knees, fucker." The hand pushed him down and the hammer clicked. Philip's bladder loosened.

Once the police arrived at Siobhan's flat and she assured him she'd be fine, Adam left her, returning home to find an agitated Byron waiting for him.

"I thought something had happened to you?"

"Sorry." Adam explained what had occurred. "I found a folder at her flat and recognised one of the buildings." He described the stencilled warning on the shutter.

"There was one in the office we searched."

"Was there? I didn't notice but I've seen it somewhere else in the last few days." Adam produced a notepad and listed where he'd been in the past week. Had he seen it at the chemical incident? The memory of the car fire and the two thugs who arrived hit him like a blow. He told Byron, and making sure they took the crowbars, they set off.

As they rounded the bend leading to the disused rope works, Adam recognised it but instead of finding it empty, security lights blazed from the eaves. An SUV stood on the gravel car park outside the main entrance. Adam drove past — they would be seen if they approached. Once out of sight, he parked.

"Mal's a twitcher," he said. "See if there's anything in the glove compartment."

Byron rummaged under a couple of bird books and produced a pair of compact binoculars. "Mal comes up trumps again."

They trotted to a group of trees from where they could see the factory. Byron studied the building through the field glasses. The first rays of the morning sun attacked the twilight.

"Could it be this one?" Adam peered at the building six hundred metres away, unable to make out much detail.

"It looks promising," Byron said. "Apart from the lights, they've got security cameras on the front and all the openings look secure."

Adam couldn't remember security lights. They hadn't come on when they'd dealt with the car fire. "What do you want to do? I could ring the doorbell and say I'm lost. If it's someone innocent we move on?"

"Hmmm. Risky. Let's keep watch."

Adam wanted to see for himself but let Byron continue with his narrative and peered into the darkness. The front door opened and a man came out carrying a television. He walked to the car and placed it on the rear seat. Another man came out holding a box.

"Looks like they're moving out," Byron said, passing the glasses to Adam.

They continued watching as the men carried on loading the back seat with items. Adam scanned the building for signs of weakness but they'd not found any when they'd been called out for the fire. The cameras didn't cover the sides, but even there, they'd struggle to get in.

Adam lowered the glasses. "What do you want to do if they leave?"

"I don't think they'd leave unless it's empty, so we have to follow them." Byron made a gesture of helplessness. "We haven't got the resources to split up."

Adam agreed then he noticed the two men reappear at the door. He raised the glasses. The men struggled to carry a large item wrapped in plastic sheeting, its shape unmistakeable. A body. His insides grew icy.

"Byron." He returned the binoculars.

Byron peered through the eyepieces and focussed on the two men. "We're going in now."

CHAPTER 26

Mugisa refused to capitulate and, although wounded, overpowered his bigger opponent. Breathing hard over the body of his fallen foe, he listened. The sounds of fighting had ceased and his soldiers were defeated. Shouts from his enemies told him they'd seen him.

He slipped into the forest and ran, pursued by the sounds of his enemies. Many hours later, the hunters, following the trail of blood he left, caught up with him, and too weak to fight, they captured him.

His desire to live remained undiminished and after many days on the edge of death, he awoke. The found himself in a large and well-organised prison camp. His fellow inmates were, like him, former child soldiers, snatched back from their abductors. Fed well and treated with unexpected kindness, he recovered.

One night, new people came, Europeans amongst them, and questioned him. When they asked if he wanted to go home, he didn't know the answer. It was a question he'd avoided for many years. That night he dreamt of his childhood and took it as a sign. They took him home in the back of a white Land Cruiser.

Byron ran towards the car, imagining having to tell Philip's parents and sisters he was dead. As he opened the door, he heard a familiar whine followed by a thud. A bullet hit the inside of the door.

"Incoming!" he shouted and leapt into the passenger seat. His adrenaline levels, already elevated, rose further.

Crouched low in the driver's seat, Adam started the engine and the car leapt forward, moving erratically to disrupt the aim of the shooter. "He's down."

"What the hell happened?"

Adam studied the rear-view mirror. "He must have slipped."

Byron checked through the rear windscreen and could make out a shape on the ground, now well out pistol of range. The euphoria of surviving the close escape made his blood fizz. "They must have a perimeter guard."

"I don't think he's with McLaughlin's lot — he's black," Adam said. "Do you think your old friend employs ethnic minorities?"

Byron couldn't remember McLaughlin having any friends who weren't white but he couldn't worry about who'd shot at him now. He reached into the back of the car and retrieved the two crowbars, gripping one and placing the second in the foot well. It seemed to take an age to reach the car park. The two men carrying the body had almost reached their car. Struggling with their heavy load, they didn't react to the approaching vehicle until it was less than eighty metres away.

The one holding the legs acted first. He dropped his end of the load and ran for the front door. The other one seemed too intent on berating his companion to notice them. Ten paces from him, Byron threw his door open and leapt out. He needed to make sure he didn't lose his balance on the gravel when he landed. The shock as he hit the ground travelled up to his skull, jarring his teeth. His legs moved too fast as he ran to stop himself falling.

The man dropped the body and faced him. His hand flew into his jacket. Byron took another two steps, over-striding as he fought to control his balance. The dark metal of an automatic appeared in the man's hand. Byron hit him with the crowbar, snapping both bones in his forearm. With a cry of pain, he dropped the pistol. Byron snatched it up and checked on Adam.

Adam had left the car and stood over a man's body. From the man's screams it didn't sound as if he would give them trouble. Byron checked him over, making sure he wasn't carrying another weapon.

Adam left his victim moaning on the ground and charged into the building. Byron followed, pistol to the fore. He took a few seconds to adjust to the bright fluorescent lights. He'd entered a large room which would have once been the reception area. Adam slipped through a door on the left. Byron checked the next one. The body odour and smell of fast food told him the men had spent time here.

Byron returned to the reception as Adam reappeared, cradling a shotgun pistol. "There's a cell through there where they must have kept him."

Byron didn't want to think about what had happened to Philip. They finished the search and met at the entrance. He stepped out and scanned the darkness for the man who'd taken a shot at them before walking over to the two men who lay groaning on the gravel.

The one Adam had dealt with looked in a bad way. He'd broken his femur but luckily for him his thigh hadn't swollen up, meaning he hadn't damaged his femoral artery. Byron saw his other leg and winced. The remains of his kneecap shone white through his shredded jeans. The black plastic-covered body lay near the back of the men's vehicle.

Byron walked to it on stiff legs and stared.

Adam took a deep breath before walking over to the bundle. "Come on, mate, let me do it."

Byron's expression made Adam fear what he'd do to the two men. He handed Byron the shotgun and crouched beside the bundle. Byron stared into the distance. Adam's stomach flipped over as he peeled the sheets of black polythene away from the head. He'd recognised the marks of dried blood on the floor of the cell he'd discovered, glad he'd found it and not Byron. His hands trembled as he peeled off another layer. He saw the hair first. *Thank God.* He continued until the face of a dead stranger lay exposed. He released a breath he didn't realise he'd held.

"It's not him," he said.

Byron grunted like someone had punched him in the gut, but you couldn't mistake his relief. Adam studied the corpse, a blond-haired white man of about thirty. A gash in his neck showed how he'd died. Caused by a wide blade, like a machete, the edges of the wound gaped. The identity of the man who'd shot at them became clear and Adam scanned the edge of the pool of brightness created by the security lighting.

"What time did this happen?" Byron demanded.

The one with the smashed knee winced. "Last night, about ten."

"Did you see who did it?"

"I saw a big black lad out here, messing with the car."

Adam folded the sheeting over the dead man's face and straightened as Byron continued his questioning. "That why you moved Philip?"

Neither man spoke.

"Where did they take him?"

Again neither man responded. Byron walked towards the nearest and reached for the man's knee. Long before he made contact, he let out a terrified shriek.

"Okay. I'll tell you," he said, panting with fear. "They've taken him to a flat in Kersal."

"You'll have to do better than that. What's the address?"

"I don't know it."

Byron prodded the knee with the toe of his boot.

The man screamed.

Adam felt sick.

The man gasped for breath. "Please, Lenny didn't tell me." Fear made his voice rise. "You have to believe me."

The second man found his voice. "They hadn't decided," he said. "Lenny said he'd choose when they got there. Ritchie's got loads of flats over there."

"Lenny? The soprano steroid user?"

"That's him."

"What's his address?"

"You what?" The man looked puzzled.

"Lenny's address. We want it," Byron said.

"I don't know it."

Byron swung his toe. The man with the ruined knee screamed before passing out. Byron walked over to the other one, standing over him as the man licked his lips and looked at Adam imploringly. Adam ignored the hollowness in his chest and stared back.

The man looked around in panic. "We don't know, you have to believe me."

Byron reached for his shattered forearm.

"Okay, okay. I'll tell you."

Ten minutes later, they possessed a list of addresses, including Lenny's home and those of the two men with him. The one with the ruined knee regained consciousness and screamed when they attempted to pick him up, so they left him in the car park. They locked the other in the cell which Philip had once occupied, before taking the men's mobiles and smashing the phone in the building.

As they drove towards Lenny's home, Adam cleared his throat. "We should tell the police what we've found. This is too big for two of us, especially if we have to search all the blocks of flats."

Byron stared out of the windscreen. "Yeah, you're right." He took out his phone.

Adam retrieved Siobhan's card from his jacket and handed it to Byron.

"She gave you a business card then?"

Byron dialled the number, putting the phone on speaker.

"DCI Quinn," Siobhan answered on the second ring, sounding tired.

"Hello, DCI Quinn, Byron Mason here."

"How did you get my number?" she snapped.

"It's on the card you gave my brother."

"Oh, sorry." She paused. "I'm in the middle of something. How can I help you?"

"We've found the place where they were holding Philip—"

"What do you mean 'were holding'? Have you released him?"

"Unfortunately not. They've moved him and we're not sure where to. Apparently, Ritchie's got some flats in a block in Kersal where they've taken him. They kept him in an old factory and if you go there, you might find clues we missed. There's also a dead man and couple of McLaughlin's men there."

"Who's the dead man?"

"I think it's one of McLaughlin's men. Two of them were removing the body when we arrived and it looks like Mugisa's work. The two men have minor injuries, so you'll need an ambulance for both of them." Byron gave her the address and ended the call before she could press him further.

He put the phone away and Adam started the car. They left the main road and he noticed a car keeping track with them.

"We've got company," he announced.

"McLaughlin?"

"I don't think so. This looks like a banger, so it could be a coincidence, but best not take chances." Adam changed down two gears and the engine growled. After four rapid changes of direction along the side-streets, he lost the tail. "False alarm," he announced and returned to the main road, to continue on their way.

"Adam." Byron sounded uncomfortable. "What if these guys aren't home?"

"You've got an idea?" Adam dismissed the growing feeling of dread.

"If we don't know the address of the right flat, we'd have to search all of them and when we do, they'll realise what we're up to. They'll do something to Philip unless we hit the right one first time."

"We won't have to check all the blocks," Adam protested. "They'll have their cars and I'm betting they'll stand out."

"So we get the right block but we still have to find the right flat."

"What do you suggest?" Adam didn't want to hear the answer.

"We make them tell us, or better still, release Philip in an exchange."

Adam saw Byron's determination. Taking the families of these men to make them release Philip was a legitimate tactic, but he wasn't sure he had the stomach for it, or for the consequences. Not anymore.

"If it's the only way..." He felt numb, making those men in the car park talk was bad enough. What Byron planned was another step.

"I'll do it alone." Byron held up his hand to cut off Adam's protest. "No discussion, he's my nephew."

They were almost there. Adam left the main road and drove down a side street. He parked and pointed to a house across the road. "That's it." His heart shrank. The small hatchback with child seats in the rear wasn't the type of car one of McLaughlin's men would drive.

Byron took off his seatbelt and opened the door.

"Hang on," Adam said.

The door opened and a young woman came out, backing out of the door and dragging a pushchair behind her. Two small boys followed on foot and she straightened the pushchair before strapping the smaller of the boys into it. Byron watched for a few seconds, his expression unreadable.

Siobhan and her team arrived in convoy and she recognised the building from the folder Eddy had given her — the one she'd stopped Adam looking at. A surge of anger at him made her clench her fists but she pushed it away and focussed on the two bodies laid out in the car park.

"Bloody hell!" Eddy said.

"Pull up, we don't want to contaminate the scene." Siobhan reviewed the procedures. She got out and signalled to the others to do the same. As they approached the bodies, she considered Eddy's comments about Byron.

One of the prone figures moved and sat up. "Fucking hell, I thought you were never coming, you bastards."

"Hello, Gary. Lovely to see you," Eddy replied. "Shall I check the other one, Boss?"

"Yes please." She briefed the rest of the team. "Search the building for any more casualties. There should be one more, and don't take any chances while you're doing it." She crouched beside him. "Gary, what happened?" She examined his injuries. The sight of his knee made her nauseous.

"They ran me over. There were two of them, but the Chinky drove. Me fucking leg's broken and look what he did." He gestured at his ruined knee and winced.

Siobhan's ears pricked up. "One of the men was Chinese?"

"Yeah. The other one was that big black fucker Ritchie's after."

"Oh, yeah. Byron Mason." Although her emotions churned, Siobhan kept her voice casual at the confirmation of Adam's involvement — it couldn't be anyone else. She'd given him the benefit of the doubt when she'd discovered he'd sheltered Philip but he must be close to the family for him to be involved in something like this.

"Yeah, that's him."

"Boss, this is one of Ritchie's," Eddy called out. "Wayne something." He stood up and walked towards her. "It looks like someone's thrust a blade into his throat."

"Yeah, that one almost got me." Gary confirmed and pointed towards the door. "He hit the doorframe, took a big chunk out of it. He *was* a big black bastard."

"The same one?" Siobhan's mind raced.

"I'm not sure." Gary paused for a second. "No, it couldn't have been. The one in the car didn't know who was dead." He nodded towards Wayne's body and winced as his knee moved. "That's why it's open, they wanted to look at the body."

"Boss!" The shout came from the building.

Siobhan ignored it and signalled to Eddy to deal with it. A siren wailed in the distance — the ambulance would be here soon.

"We'll soon have you in a nice warm hospital bed." Siobhan smiled. "Do you know where the two men went?"

After a brief internal struggle she saw he would tell her. The ambulance crunched across the car park. She didn't have much time. Once he'd reconsidered, he'd clam up.

"Okay, I'll tell you what I told them, but only so you can catch them. I'll deny it if it comes to court."

"Of course." By the time the paramedics strapped him to a stretcher, she'd written the addresses down, hoping Eddy could make sense of them.

Mugisa drove around for a few minutes after the men had lost him, a fog of disappointment weighing him down. He didn't have the car or the driving skills to keep up with them. He decided to return to the factory. It represented his only link to Philip and he could get the guards to give him the information they'd given to the two men. He drove back in a hurry, worried they'd have gone before he returned.

Half a mile from the factory flashing blue lights approached. Mugisa slowed. An ambulance, with a police car following in its wake. Uneasy, he drove on, saw the cars outside the factory and continued.

A car sat in the spot where he'd shot at the big man. As he drew level, he recognised the two men standing by the car and watching the factory. He'd seen them at Philip's house on Monday night and guessed they knew where he'd been taken. Without slowing, he passed their car and turned round before parking in a spot where he could see them. He didn't have to wait long before they returned to the car and drove off.

He had no problem following them, and after a few miles, they entered a part of the city he didn't recognise. The road dipped, and as they rounded a bend, the land opened out below them. In the field below, several blocks of flats sprouted, towering above their surroundings. The early morning autumn sun glinted off their windows and, from a distance, they looked like the turrets of a fabulous palace but when they came closer, he saw a less romantic reality. What looked from afar like tinted glass, turned out to be plywood covering broken windows.

The car ahead slowed and pulled into the small car park at the bottom of one of the tower blocks, pulling into a space between an old Ford Escort and a Vauxhall, their large SUV looking out of place. They got out, locked their vehicle and walked towards the front doors.

Mugisa drove on and parked in a bus stop with a graffiti-covered concrete shelter alongside it. He checked on the men he'd followed. They'd reached the doors of the building. Mugisa got out of the car, his pulse racing. This must be where they kept Philip. He checked his pistol, left the car and set off at a run. The front doors were still swinging when he reached them.

With his hand on the butt of his automatic, he entered the foyer. It was empty. The room stank of stale smoke and urine, with walls a shade of institutional magnolia and the stained floor covering pitted with small burns.

A wooden door to his left opened onto the staircase and a pair of steel-clad lift doors faced him. Each served alternate floors and one of them emitted groans and squeaks as it wheezed upwards. The illuminated numbers above it advanced before stopping at fourteen. Mugisa smiled and started up the stairs.

The icy floor leached heat from Philip's battered body and a spasm made his teeth chatter. His headache and the pain in his back now seemed to have suffused through his whole body, making thinking of anything else impossible. Waves of nausea engulfed him and he fought to control his gut. Faint sounds reached him from outside but he didn't know where he was. He remembered being shoved into a lift stinking of piss but that didn't narrow it down much.

After the mock execution, which Lenny found hilarious, they'd dragged him to the front entrance, blindfolded him and dumped him into the boot of a car before driving him here. The idea of getting his revenge on Lenny kept him going. He pushed the pain away and listened for clues. They must have a reason for moving him. Although he wanted to believe it was because Byron had found their last place, he knew he should dismiss the idea. Voices reached him from outside the door and it flew open, making him jump.

"Right, get up." Lenny's voice filled him with fear, but he braced himself and struggled to his feet.

Lenny removed the blindfold, taking half his eyelashes, and led him to the lift. To his surprise it went up and, following a long slow ascent, they stopped.

"Lenny, should we untie the lad?" one of the men asked. "He won't try anything, will you?" He prodded Philip in the chest.

Philip whispered, "No."

Lenny grumbled but agreed, making the consequences of misbehaving clear. Philip worked to regain the circulation in his arms. Lenny herded him into a flat. A short corridor led to four internal doors and he waited outside one of these. The faint odour of damp mingled with cooking smells. Lenny opened one of the doors and gave Philip a shove, propelling him into a dark cavern. His foot caught on something soft, a darker rectangle on the floor, and he stumbled. The door slammed shut, plunging him into darkness. A thin strip of light at the bottom of the door provided the only illumination. The stink of stale body odour and unwashed clothing pervaded the room.

Arms outstretched, he shuffled across the floor, exploring his new home. He reached the windows and discovered why the room was so dark. Someone had nailed a sheet of plywood to the inside of the window frame. The room contained the thin mattress he'd tripped over and a plastic bucket. He found the door but it didn't have a handle on his side.

He lowered himself onto the mattress. A small lumpy pillow and blanket lay scrunched up against one end and he pushed them away, suspecting the odour originated from them. Tired, hungry and in pain, he leant against the wall, fighting a sense of despair.

Mugisa's loping strides ate up the distance to the fourteenth floor. One floor below, he slowed and took the last two flights at a walk, allowing his breathing to recover. He took out the Makarov and slid a round into the chamber, relishing the reassuring weight of the spare magazine in his pocket. Fifteen shots remained.

At the door onto the landing, he paused and took two deep breaths before he opened it. Arms extended, he swept an arc with the pistol, checking the landing was clear. Four doors led off it but which one concealed Philip and his captors? He began at the nearest, bending to peer through the letterbox.

The lift groaned and his heart lurched. He stared at the lift doors waiting for them to open but realised the men he'd followed had arrived at this floor before he started up the stairs. Whoever was using the lift, it wasn't them. He lifted the flap of the letterbox again but couldn't see or hear anything from the pitch-black interior. He moved to the next door, ensuring he made no noise. An obstruction blocked the letterbox and he pushed against it.

Behind him, the lift doors slid open. By the time he turned, one occupant had got out. The man shouted something, and pointed towards Mugisa, a long dark object in his hands. Mugisa raised the Makarov feeling he was moving in slow motion. He saw the flash and the blast filled his ears.

CHAPTER 27

The whole village waited to greet their prodigal son. Mugisa's father had become a stooped greybeard with a withered leg. The injuries he suffered in the second raid had allied with tragedy and time to diminish this once-strong man. His brothers, now young adults with their own families, looked upon this stranger as another mouth to feed.

Before long, he became the target of the bitter hatred directed against the raiders. On the second night back in the village, a group of young men, the sons of the man he'd injured, waylaid him. He fought ferociously and the injuries he inflicted on these men ensured they left him in peace.

Nothing remained of the remembered happiness of his childhood and his father, now a peripheral figure in the family, blamed him for his diminished status. The brothers resented having to support this stranger, who knew nothing of work.

When the white Land Cruiser returned three weeks later, he climbed on board and left without a backwards glance.

Byron released the door handle and refastened his seatbelt. "Let's go."

Adam started the engine and pulled away, his relief palpable.

The woman and two boys grew smaller in the mirror and the weight on Byron's shoulders lifted. "Let's go to the flats — someone might have seen something when they delivered him."

"You made the right decision, Byron."

"Yeah, I know." He exhaled. "I hope it doesn't mean we don't find Philip in time."

They drove on in silence until Byron's mobile rang. He checked the caller. Not recognising the number, he hesitated but took the call.

"Byron?" Kieran McLaughlin said.

"I've been trying to get hold of you. You were supposed to call him off—"

"Sorry, Byron, I've been trying to talk sense into him but he won't listen. We've had enough of him, it's bad for business."

"Where's Philip?"

"Safe for now, but Ritchie's talking about doing to him what he did to Liam."

"Philip didn't touch Liam."

"I believe you, but Ritchie…"

"What do you want?"

"You can have him back, as long as I get the trailer, but you need to come before Ritchie gets back."

"What's going to happen when he sees Philip gone?"

"Let me worry about that. And come on your own — I don't fancy getting done for kidnapping."

Byron used an old biro from the glove compartment to scribble the address Kieron gave him on the cover of the road map.

"Make sure you come alone. I'll be watching, and if you're with anyone the boy disappears." Kieron ended the call.

"That was Ritchie's brother and it sounds as if they're planning a coup." Byron relayed his message.

"That where he's waiting?" Adam indicated the writing on the map.

"Yup." Byron read out the address. "Do you know it?"

Adam nodded. "The whole area's awaiting redevelopment."

"It should be nice and quiet on a Saturday morning."

Adam looked thoughtful. "Can you trust him?"

"Maybe." Byron wasn't convinced. "But it could be a hoax, to keep us away from the real place."

"Do you want to ignore it?"

Byron couldn't decide. If they'd put Philip here, going to the flats would be a waste of time. But if Philip was at the flats…

"Siobhan and the police should be at the flats by now."

"You're right, we'll have to check it." If Byron had made the wrong decision, he prayed the police would keep Philip safe.

Siobhan waited by the entrance to the Community Centre behind the flats where Gary had directed them. Beside her stood Eddy and Ian Meehan, the inspector in charge of the armed response team. They watched impatiently as the scruffy, unmarked police car returned. The couple in it, undercover drug squad officers, had driven round the blocks of flats to check for any vehicles that looked out of place. The car stopped and the driver wound down his window.

He addressed Meehan, pointing at a map with a red circle marked on it. "This one, Boss." He handed him the map.

The circle surrounded the third block in the series.

"What did you find?" Siobhan asked him.

"There's two big SUVs in the car park and a third arrived as we passed."

"Yeah, we saw it. I'm sure they were Ritchie's men, Boss," Eddy said.

"Thanks, guys, well done." Siobhan dismissed them and spoke to her sergeant. "Eddy, have you got the list of tenants for that block?"

Already searching for the list in a folder, he handed it to her before she finished speaking. She smiled her thanks and took it.

"Quite a few empties," he observed.

Siobhan scanned the list. "Third, fourteenth and top floor are the emptiest, ninth has also got one empty." She addressed the inspector. "Ian, I think the third is the most likely, it's near enough to ground level to give them an emergency escape."

"Sorry, Boss. I disagree," Eddy said. "They'll probably use the top floor — all the flats are empty and the floor below has only two occupied. If they keep the lift at the top and block the stairs nobody can reach them."

She thought for a few seconds and decided it made sense. "Okay, Eddy. We'll go with your call. Ian, have we got enough bods to cover both floors?"

Meehan shook his head. "We'd need another team." He checked his watch. "And they'll be at least twenty minutes."

Siobhan chewed her bottom lip and considered the significance of the build-up of McLaughlin's troops. "Okay. We'll go in now." She hoped she'd made the right call.

The teams gathered for a final briefing then used the community minibus to approach the building. Someone on the first floor buzzed them in. Both lifts were at the top of their travel so Eddy pulled the fireman's switch. The lifts should have returned to ground, but the lights didn't move.

Siobhan made the decision. "Okay. We'll take the stairs."

A collective groan escaped from the detectives.

"Take it steady, lads," said Meehan, leading the way.

He set off and his team trotted after him. Siobhan waited for them to pass and studied her officers. One or two looked like they'd struggle.

"Like he said, let's take it steady," she said. "We've still got to do our jobs after we get there."

As she passed through the door, the first shot rang out. Siobhan heart jerked against her ribcage and everyone froze, immobilised by the sudden noise. Three more shots followed producing the same effect on the officers as a starter's gun. The instruction to take things steady forgotten, they made their long ascent at maximum speed. Siobhan concentrated on her breathing, hoping they weren't already too late.

Mugisa fired three times and the men fell. The echoes of the shots died away and he gulped in air. Every sense heightened, he welcomed the familiar feeling of invincibility.

He looked at the fallen men. Dead, or they soon would be. Pools of thick blood grew under each body and flowed together, to create a large red slick. One of the bodies lay in the lift. The one who'd shot him had fallen across the door, keeping it from closing.

Blood ran down his face and he examined the wound in his forehead. The man had used a sawn-off shotgun. The pockmarks on the wall behind him showed the shot pattern concentrated at head height, well above his crouching position, he'd been lucky. There wasn't much time, the shooting would alert the others. The desire to get Philip conflicted with his need to escape. Before he could decide, a figure appeared in doorway to the stairs.

A man he recognised from the night before stood in the doorway. A muzzle-flashed and something punched his left shoulder. He swung his pistol up in an arc, pulling the trigger. The first shot hit the man in the thigh, the second in the midriff. The man cried out and fell.

A second gunman crouched behind him and Mugisa fired twice more. A red bloom appeared at the man's throat before he fell with a gurgle, landing on top of his wounded colleague and pinning him to the floor. Mugisa stepped forward, swung his pistol towards the wounded man's head and ignoring his plea for mercy, shot him.

He didn't realise he'd run out of bullets until he pulled the trigger three times without effect. When he tried to retrieve the spare magazine from his pocket, his shoulder didn't respond. He examined the rebellious limb with irritation. Blood soaked through his shirt and jacket and dripped onto the floor. His breaths became shallow and his heart raced. As his body went into shock, he slowed his breathing. He must calm down and think.

The realisation more of Philip's captors would investigate cut through the fog enveloping him. He checked the doors on the landing. They remained closed. What did this mean? The two men he'd just killed came down the stairs. Reinforcements would come up, and fighting off waves of nausea and dizziness, he understood.

Philip must be upstairs, and these two were his guards. There couldn't be many left upstairs — he'd already killed four and they were not men of high calibre. Even one-armed, he could overpower them and kill his quarry. He gritted his teeth and discarded his useless weapon, picking up one dropped by the men he'd killed.

Meehan led his team up the stairs. More shots came from above, each report acting as a spur. He checked behind him as he negotiated yet another flight, the thirteenth, and saw his men just behind him. The new DCI brought up the rear with the rest of her team several floors below. He rounded the final flight to the fourteenth floor and stopped, trying to take in the sight before him.

Two bodies lay across the stairs, one keeping the door onto the landing open. Meehan signalled for his men to wait and studied the scene over the sights of his weapon. The sounds from the detectives several floors below carried over the noise of his breathing. He recognised the men in the doorway were both dead and signalled to one of his men to recover their weapons. Moving silently, he led his team past the bodies. The stench of death filled his nostrils.

He stepped onto the landing. Two more bodies lay in the lift. Already at a high pitch, the sight made his pulse rate spike. The four doors facing them remained closed, but he knew the gunman could be behind any of them. From the floor above came a thud followed by a cry as something large fell. He ignored it — his job was to clear this floor.

Siobhan, waiting on the half landing below, heard the same sounds. She hesitated for a split second before passing the dead bodies and heading for the next flight of steps. The armed officer guarding his team's back signalled her to wait. She shook her head and indicated she intended to pass him. His demeanour changed and he rolled his eyes before charging up the stairs ahead of her, his gun held ready.

"That's it." Adam indicated the long building up ahead.

A memory from a school trip to the Museum of Science and Industry flooded back to Byron, a photo of the same mill taken at the end of the nineteenth century. He recalled it as one of the biggest cotton mills in Lancashire. The five floors now looked in a sorry state, with windows broken and boarded up. A high fence surrounded the mill, the only gap protected by two mismatched gates. The larger secured by a padlock but the smaller, too narrow for their car, swung on its hinges.

Byron reconsidered his plans. He'd assumed the caller would keep a watch and intended to drive up to the building, with Adam hidden in the back.

"You'd better get out here," Byron said. "I'll drive up to the gate and leave the car."

"I don't like it, Byron. It smells of setup."

Byron shared his friend's concerns, but he remembered Rebecca's accusation of not looking after Philip. "I'll take the pistol — the shotgun's too big."

Byron checked the pistol and stuffed it into his jacket. Adam retrieved the shotgun and climbed out. Byron waited for him to disappear behind the vehicle before driving up to the gates. He left the car and examined the front of the building, looking for signs of life. A faded blue door in the far corner stood open. Feeling exposed and vulnerable, he headed for it, scanning the windows on his approach.

He stopped beside the door and took out the automatic. After a few deep breaths, his anxiety eased and a familiar calmness came over him. Light leaked in through grimy windows and the place smelt of musty decay. A doorway on his right led into the ground floor, nailed shut, and a wide stone staircase in front of him lead upward. Taking care not to make a sound, he climbed to the next level. A massive, sliding steel-clad door blocked his way off the stairs. A rusty padlock secured it, and he found the same on every level until he reached the top floor.

This door slid open. The uneasy sensation he'd experienced since arriving intensified and he checked the automatic again, releasing the safety catch. He edged his head through the opening. A long, empty corridor lined with doors bisected what had once consisted of a large open space full of looms.

Byron eased through the opening and began a search of the corridor. What the hell was Kieron playing at? The first door he came to gaped open into an empty room. He moved to the next one and found the same.

A scraping and rustling came from behind the fourth door. Nerves taut, he pushed at the closed door but it wouldn't budge. After taking a slow breath, he kicked it. The flimsy lock gave way and he burst in, pistol at the ready. A pair of pigeons took flight in a cloud of feathers. He smiled in relief.

Cold metal touched the back of his neck. He froze. The skin tightened making the hairs rise and he lifted his hands.

"Sensible lad."

With a sinking sensation, he recognised the voice.

McLaughlin took the weapon from him and pushed him into the room. Byron attempted to turn but McLaughlin pressed the barrel into the side of his head. Two men drew alongside, flanking him. One had a sharp ferrety face and a wiry build and he exuded a restless energy. The other had a large head with a creased forehead and a jowly, round face. Where the hell was Kieron?

Round-face slid a thick noose over Byron's head. He stiffened.

"Easy," the man said in a London accent.

The cargo sling passed over his shoulders and Byron forced his muscles to relax. It slid to his elbows before tightening and he flexed his muscles against it.

"It's got a breaking strain of three tonnes. Too much even for you, I'm guessing?" McLaughlin walked round in front of him.

Byron studied him, noting the tension in his posture. The automatic in McLaughlin's left hand pointed at the centre of his chest. Byron glanced round the room. Light streamed in through three broken and dirty windows set into the far wall. The lino covering the floor looked like it had been down for decades. Pigeon excrement covered the faded pattern. A selection of tatty old desks and assorted broken office furniture stood under the windows. Attached to the wall behind him lay a workbench, covered in debris, and a chair sat in front of it.

McLaughlin nodded to his men and heavy hands grabbed Byron, forcing him backwards towards the chair. He resisted, but a flick of the barrel from McLaughlin made him change his mind.

"Nothing to say to an old school friend?" McLaughlin asked.

"I think I said it last time we met." Byron stared at the bandage on McLaughlin's ear.

McLaughlin flushed and raised his hand before grinning and letting it drop. "I'm sure you'll agree, my riposte is appropriate." He nodded to his men.

The sling loosened and ferret-face grabbed Byron's left bicep. He let the man pull his arm out of the sling and it tightened again, trapping his right arm against his body. Ferret-face pulled at his arm but Byron resisted. Red hot pain shot through his shoulder and he gasped. Round-face held a blade above his shoulder, ready to plunge it in again. Byron relaxed his arm. Ferret-face pulled it straight, forcing it onto the top of the bench. Blood soaked through Byron's shirt and the pain spread across his shoulders.

Round-face came round to his left side and wiped the bloody knife on Byron's top. He put it away and produced a hammer. Byron's insides fluttered and he struggled against the grip on his arm but McLaughlin pointed the barrel towards his groin.

"Your choice." He smiled.

Byron stopped struggling. "I'm guessing you want the trailer."

"That? Oh yeah, but it can wait."

Round-face raised the hammer and paused. He grinned before slamming it down. The debris on the bench top jumped and the vibration went through Byron's arm. The hammer ripped a dent in the wood, less than three inches from his hand, and the three men laughed.

The laughter died and round-face lifted the hammer again. They looked at Byron hungrily; this time it was for real. Byron braced himself. Round-face focussed on Byron's hand and he grinned. The hammer descended. Byron looked away and twisted his arm. His hand moved. At first it felt numb, then intense pain shot up his arm.

Bile rose in his throat and he hyperventilated. He swallowed and forced himself to examine his hand. The blow had landed on the outside edge, splitting the skin where the impact had crushed it against the worktop. Blood oozed round the hammerhead as it lifted for a second blow.

CHAPTER 28

Mugisa endured a difficult few weeks back in the transit camp. Following the build-up to his homecoming, the realisation that a return to his old life was impossible and he was now alone in the world hit him hard. He withdrew into himself and the people who ran the transit camp worried. His will to live weakened and his physical condition deteriorated.

One morning, he woke and decided he would survive. He ate breakfast, ravenous after weeks of neglecting himself. He realised he needed no one else, but he wanted to get out of this country and escape his painful memories.

Other children had gone to far-off countries, making new lives, so he studied English, a language with which he was already familiar, and took active part in the rehabilitation classes. The decision not to make friends sometimes hurt, but he knew it was the best way.

The people who ran the camp seemed happy and eager to help him and, before long, he understood what they wanted. When they quizzed him, he observed their reaction to his answers. In a few short months, he gave the desired answer to every question. More people came and, this time, one of them asked him if he wanted to go to England.

It was far from here and so he agreed. A man with kind eyes collected him but nobody came to see him off. Mugisa didn't mind, he was on his way to start his life again, and this time it would be better.

The first shots rang out and Philip struggled to his feet, fear helping him ignore the pain. He held his breath, hoping it was his rescuers. When nobody came, he worried, thinking they'd been shot. Different scenarios played in his mind and he imagined his uncle lying in a pool of blood. Or maybe he *had* killed the kidnappers and would soon be here.

The door flew open and he jumped. Lenny's silhouette in the doorway destroyed his hope. Lenny carried his pistol and Philip knew, this time, it wouldn't be for a mock execution.

"Come on, we're going." Lenny gestured with the automatic.

Philip didn't move.

Lenny stepped into the room and grabbed his arm, twisting it behind his back. Philip tried to resist, but the man was too powerful. Lenny pulled him close and screwed the barrel of the pistol into Philip's ear.

"Just give me an excuse to use this."

Paralysed with fear, Philip didn't respond. Lenny shoved him towards the door. He gasped in pain, but his captor ignored him, opening the door and pushing Philip out into the corridor. The lights made him squint after the darkness of his cell. He stumbled and Lenny kicked him.

More shots rang out, making him jump. The fact Lenny's body also jerked made him feel better. The front door loomed as a rectangle of brightness and he stumbled towards it. Pushed out onto the landing, he looked around frantically. A cardboard box on the floor prevented the lift doors from closing.

Lenny pushed him towards it, then the door at the top of the stairs eased open. Lenny ducked back into the flat, dragging Philip with him. A tall dark figure appeared at the top of the stairs before the door to the flat slammed shut. Philip cried out in pain as the grip on his arm tightened.

"Shut up, you soft bastard." Lenny released him and pushed him down the corridor.

Lenny used his free hand to bolt the door. His eyes darted from side to side, his breathing fast and shallow. Once he'd secured it, he returned his attention to Philip who, grimacing in pain, showed Lenny his teeth.

"I don't know what you think's funny, you little shit," Lenny hissed. "Anyone comes through that door and you're the first one to get it." He levelled the gun at Philip with an unpleasant grin.

The door behind him shook as someone hit it. The impact made Lenny jump and seeing his enemy's obvious terror gave Philip courage. Philip stared at the door but instead of a second blow, someone crashed to the floor outside with a groan. Was that Byron he'd glimpsed at the top of the stairs? What had happened to him?

Lenny took out his phone and made a panicky call. Philip realised he wasn't paying him any attention. He looked around for a weapon. A long piece of timber lay against the skirting board in the kitchen. He slid towards it, careful not to make a noise.

Philip crouched down and grabbed it, lifting one end. The end other scraped against the floor. He froze and checked on Lenny. He'd ended the call but didn't seem to have heard him. Philip gripped the timber in both hands and stepped towards the door. Remembering Jenna's cry and the terror and pain this man had inflicted on him, he swung it. Lenny turned, but too late.

The impact caught him across the side of his head, the force of it almost ripping the timber out of Philip's hands. Without checking, he knew Lenny wouldn't get up again. He threw the piece of timber away and examined his hands, surprised they weren't bleeding. He retrieved Lenny's pistol, then as if in a trance, he drew the bolts on the front door. It swung open and, desperate to meet his rescuers, he stepped out onto the landing.

"Hello Philip."

His insides froze when he recognised the voice. He looked down. Mugisa sat against the wall, his legs splayed out in front of him. A bloody stain tracked down the wall above his left shoulder and more blood ran from a wound in his forehead. In his right hand he cradled a pistol, pointing at the centre of Philip's torso.

Philip swallowed. The pistol he carried pointed at the floor. He wasn't even sure if the safety catch was on or, if it was, how to take it off.

The door to the stairs flew open and Philip's pulse jerked, until he realised it was a policeman. He carried a gun, and breathing hard, he stepped onto the landing.

"Armed police!" he shouted. "Drop your weapon."

Philip glanced down at Mugisa but realised with a start that the policeman's weapon pointed at him. Still stunned from finding Mugisa here, he didn't respond.

"Armed police! Drop your weapon." The man raised his voice.

Sweat poured into Philip's eyes and he opened his mouth to explain, but it was too dry and no words came out. Mugisa moved. The barrel of his pistol swung towards the officer and Philip realised what he planned to do. He must stop him.

The officer spoke a third time. "Drop your weapon, or I will fire."

Philip swung the pistol at Mugisa's head. A shot rang out.

Byron's arm trembled and he resisted the urge to cry out as round-face raised the hammer. The phone drowned out his laboured breathing and the three men froze. McLaughlin frowned but checked the screen and took the call.

"Lenny, what the fuck do you want?"

"He's shot Ian and…" Lenny's voice carried to Byron before McLaughlin covered the speaker. He strode to the window and muttered into the microphone. Byron swallowed the acid and examined his injured hand. Already it had swollen like an inflated rubber glove. Then he saw something which made his pulse race. The shock wave from the hammer blow had exposed a rusty screwdriver from under the detritus on the bench.

The two men waited for their boss and the grip on his arm relaxed. Byron flexed his hand — the ring and pinkie fingers didn't move but the thumb and other two fingers responded. Ignoring the pain, he tore his arm out of ferret-face's grip and swept up the screwdriver in a clumsy grip between thumb and index finger. Before the others could react, he plunged it into round-face's neck, puncturing his carotid artery.

The man dropped the hammer and collapsed. Byron held on to the screwdriver which pulled free with a sucking sound and blood sprayed from the wound. He struggled to his feet and attacked ferret-face before he assimilated what was happening. Sweeping his arm round the man's neck, he pushed the blood-stained screwdriver into the soft flesh under the corner of his jaw. Byron stepped behind his prisoner and faced McLaughlin.

McLaughlin looked at him, surprise changing to rage. He dropped the phone and raised the automatic, pulling the trigger twice. Byron saw the flash and closed his eyes.

Adam worked his way round to the rear of the mill complex and tried to climb the fence, but he struggled to find purchase on the smooth boards. It was too high for him to reach the top. With the shotgun tucked into his waistband under his jacket, he couldn't jump up without dislodging it. He searched for something to help him. Someone had dumped five barrels near the edge of the road. With unaccustomed thanks to the fly-tippers, he examined them.

Four were full and too heavy to move but he shifted one. The liquid in it sloshed around as he wrestled it towards the fence and climbed onto it. The top bowed and he reached up, grabbing the top of the fence and boosting himself over. Heart still pounding, he lowered himself on the other side and checked his surroundings while retrieving and reloading the shotgun. Piles of old rubbish and overgrown weeds filled the ground behind the mill. Coarse brickwork sealed the lower windows' openings. He headed for the nearest corner and peered round it.

Two large cars waited at the side of the building and someone moved in the front of one. He swore and ducked back. There could be six or seven men here and he had five cartridges. He returned to the rear of the building and fought his way through the debris. By the time he reached the far corner, he was sweating and filthy. His heart shrank when he saw the far side harboured as much refuse as he'd already traversed. Byron was on his own until he could join him so he pressed on.

He'd covered a few yards when the shots rang out. His stomach flipped and he tightened his grip on Gary's shotgun. He hesitated for an instant before deciding which way would be quicker. He ran forward, careless of the obstacles in his way.

Warm liquid splashed Byron's cheeks and ferret-face stiffened. The weight on his arm told him the man was dead or unconscious. The roar of the shots echoed in his ears.

McLaughlin laughed. "I see your hostage, and raise you," he said, his accent, a poor imitation of Sean Connery playing Bond. "Your call, Mr Mason."

Byron dropped the screwdriver and released his prisoner. The man fell and a red pool spread from his head to join the one from round-face. The stench of blood and death filled the air. McLaughlin gestured towards the chair and Byron sat down again. McLaughlin walked round behind him and shoved the still warm barrel into his ear. Byron waited, believing his end had arrived.

McLaughlin picked up a metal object. The hammer? The pistol barrel was no longer there. Before Byron could react a bar swung at him. He raised his free hand and something hard slammed it against his neck, trapping it. The pain as McLaughlin crushed the already mashed flesh against his neck almost made him pass out.

McLaughlin forced his head back, using the handle of the hammer to crush Byron's windpipe. The force increased and the metal bar bit into his throat. The chair slid backwards until McLaughlin slammed his knee into Byron's back. He stopped, but the bar continued. Byron pushed his chin down, tensing the tendons in his neck.

He tried to twist free but his feet couldn't get purchase on the blood-slicked floor. His trapped fingers screamed in agony and the tendons in his neck felt on fire. As consciousness slipped away, a recently recalled memory returned. The vision of his thirteen-year-old self with the broom handle round McLaughlin's neck felt so real he could smell the bleach in the janitor's room.

The image faded and light flashed in front of Byron. He knew he wouldn't last much longer and hoped Adam would survive to free Philip. Regret he'd never see Lilly grow up, or even know if she had a brother or sister filled his mind. He heard a rattling gurgle and realised it came from him.

"Pheeesse," he whispered.

"Speak up." McLaughlin lowered his head and spoke into Byron's ear.

Byron pushed forward, into the bar. Surprised, McLaughlin relaxed his hold. Knowing he had just one chance, Byron hurled his head back with as much force as he could muster. It smashed into McLaughlin's face. He grunted and cried out. The hammer fell into Byron's lap and, ignoring the dizziness, he struggled to his feet.

McLaughlin reeled away, blood pouring from his ruined nose. Byron swung his left foot round and caught McLaughlin with a roundhouse kick to his temple. Dizzy and unable to use his arms for balance, he couldn't help himself when his right foot slipped and he landed on his back.

Gasping for breath, he struggled to get up but his left arm wouldn't work. McLaughlin got to his hands and knees, barely conscious, but he crawled towards his pistol, which lay a metre away. Byron gave a desperate lunge and hooked his foot round McLaughlin's neck. He pulled and McLaughlin fell to the floor. Byron used his other foot to encircle the man's neck before linking his feet together and applying the power of his thighs.

McLaughlin hands tugged at Byron's calves, fingers digging into the unyielding muscle. Byron ignored the pain and pulled harder. McLaughlin's complexion reddened, but still he glared at Byron. The anger Byron first saw in them when he was eleven, undiminished.

He steeled himself and kept the pressure on as the light dimmed in McLaughlin's eyes. At first Byron thought he'd imagined the figure stepping into his field of vision. Then he saw the pistol pointed at his head.

Siobhan found herself once again in disposable coveralls with Eddy next to her. They finished checking the flat where the gangsters held Philip. The body of a man Eddy identified as Lenny, one of McLaughlin's heavies, lay by the front door. The armed response team was on their way home, their work done. She examined the room where the stinking mattress lay.

"What do they use these rooms for?" she asked.

"Trafficked girls, usually. Most spend about a week here before they get moved on to the brothels."

She shuddered and backed out of the room. "Let's see how they're getting on downstairs."

They came out of the flat and waited for the forensics team to load the rest of their equipment out of the lift. Siobhan felt disconnected from her body; the sight of so much butchery was hard to take in and she thought of what she still had to do; difficult tasks to perform.

Careful to avoid the many bloodstains on the landing, they got into the lift and, as the doors closed, the wail of an ambulance reached them.

The safety catch clicked and Byron froze.

"You can let go now, Byron. He's dead." Kieran gestured to his brother.

Byron relaxed his scissor grip, his leg muscles burnt and his ankles ached. McLaughlin slumped to the floor, unseeing eyes staring out of his mottled face. Byron untangled his legs from the corpse and pushed himself away. Kieran kept his attention on him. Byron couldn't read his expression but expected a bullet in retribution.

Kieran raised his eyebrows. "I don't hold grudges, Byron. The king is dead, long live the king." He pointed at his chest.

Byron realised Kieran had been watching for some time. "You set this up."

Kieron didn't deny it. "If you'd failed, these two," he waved at the two dead men, "would have made sure Ritchie joined you. This way, I don't have to worry about word getting back to the other lads. Some were touchingly loyal to my brother."

Byron sat up and Kieran waved the automatic.

"Don't get any ideas."

"What now?"

"I still want our…" He smiled. "My trailer back."

"I told you; you agree to leave Philip alone—"

"And I told you, I've no interest in the boy. He was his obsession." He pointed at his brother. "Or more accurately, you were."

"Okay." The agony from Byron's left arm made him dizzy and consciousness threatened to slip away. He closed his eyes and took a deep breath. Then he sat up, intending to stand and daring to hope this would soon be over. "I'll get the trailer. Just make sure your men don't harm Philip."

"No." Kieran lunged forward shoving the barrel towards Byron's right eye. So close he couldn't focus on it. "You're going nowhere until I have the trailer." The barrel swung until it pointed at Byron's left knee. "Sorry about this, but I can't have you wandering off."

CHAPTER 29

Adam arrived at the blue door out of breath and his pulse racing. He rushed in, saw the locked doorway and hurtled up the stairs. The dread he'd be too late filled him with a sense of panic but, gripping the shotgun, he pushed himself onwards.

At the top, he hesitated. The sliding door across the stairs stood open, the gap wide enough for him to slip through. Sweat ran down his forehead and he wiped it away with his forearm. The musty smell of damp masonry and pigeon droppings filled his nostrils. He held his breath and listened. Indistinct voices carried above the thrum of the pulse in his ears. Although he couldn't hear the words, the speakers sounded calm. He poked his head into the corridor. It was empty, so he stepped into it.

The voices came from a room off the corridor. Taking care where he put his feet, he shuffled towards the door. Byron's bass rumble carried through the timber and relief surged through him. Adam paused outside the closed door, listening, trying to judge the positions of the people talking. Unable to tell, he hesitated, then, levelling the shotgun, he slammed his heel into the door. It crashed open, and he charged in, the barrel of the shotgun held ahead of him. The stench of blood filled the air and behind it the familiar odour of gunshots. Light streamed in through grimy windows, illuminating a large open room. Three bodies lay on the bare boards, two covered in blood and the third clearly dead. Adam focussed on the two still alive and swung the barrel towards them.

Byron sat on the floor. A man stood behind him, an automatic in his hands levelled at Byron's legs. If Adam fired, most of the shot would hit Byron. He dropped the shotgun and ran at the gunman. By the time Kieran realised what was happening, Adam had halved the distance between them. Kieran swung the pistol towards Adam and pulled the trigger. Byron slapped the gun arm upwards as Adam launched himself. He screwed his eyes up against the flash but the heat from the expanding gases scorched his cheek. His shoulder hit Kieran's sternum and, legs pumping, he drove him backwards, towards the window.

With a crash of glass, Kieran flew out. Adam blinked, shook himself and scanned the room. After establishing he'd eliminated all threats, he regarded Byron. Blood leaked from his shoulder and his left hand, which had swollen to three times its normal size. His friend grimaced, obviously in pain. Adam bent towards him and examined his injuries. Byron kept guard on the door while Adam released him from the cargo sling.

"Did he shoot you?" Adam asked, puzzled.

"Knife from matey there." Byron pointed at the nearest body.

"What about the hand?" He studied the discoloured flesh.

"Hammer. Same guy."

Adam helped him to his feet, feeling queasy. "There's a first aid kit in the car. Where's your pistol?"

Byron nodded at McLaughlin. "In his pocket."

Adam retrieved it and recovered the shotgun. Byron, now steadier, followed him, getting stronger with each step. Wary of running into more of McLaughlin's men, but mindful of the need to hurry, they rushed down the staircase.

When they reached the exit, they ran across the yard to the main gates. At the car, Adam patched the knife wound in Byron's shoulder. It needed stitches but the dressing would do for now. The hand had stopped bleeding but he could do nothing else for it. Byron struggled into his jacket, forcing the swollen hand through the sleeve and grimacing.

Adam drove and, as they raced through the streets, he checked the time. They'd wasted two hours, and he hoped nothing had happened to Philip.

Byron leaned forward and peered through the windscreen as they approached the blocks of flats. Abandoned police and support vehicles surrounded the base of the tower, like a flock of vultures around a carcass. Byron, soaked in sweat, consigned the pain suffusing his whole arm into the background and studied the scene with a growing sense of helplessness. They were too late.

He recognised the futility of revisiting decisions already made, but couldn't help himself. Adam, his face etched with concern, drove past. Neither spoke. A few minutes later they returned, having hidden the firearms and ammunition in a storm drain. Adam slowed the car to a stop just outside the unmarked cordon created by the abandoned emergency vehicles. They got out and walked towards the entrance but two constables intercepted them before they reached it.

"Sorry, gentlemen," the older of the two said, "the building's off limits to all but residents."

Byron stilled his trepidation and smiled at the officer. "It looks like you've had a busy morning."

The man studied Byron's injuries with interest, then his young colleague blurted out, "Too right we have."

"What happened?"

"Some psycho shot a load of people. It's bloody carnage up there—"

"Are you reporters?" the older policeman interrupted.

"No, we're not, officer," Byron said, his alarm intensified by the other constable's account. "Do you know who's hurt?"

"Just some scrotes." The young constable dismissed the victims.

"I'm looking for my nephew."

The older officer gave his colleague a stern look. "Can you describe him, sir?"

"Seventeen, about six four, athletic build, short black hair."

The two constables exchanged a glance.

His apprehension increasing, Byron demanded, "What's happened to him?"

"Which flat was he in?"

"No idea. We just know he's in this block."

The constable took out his radio. "Do you mind waiting here, sir?" He walked towards the building and spoke into the microphone.

Byron spoke to his young colleague. "What's happened to my nephew?"

The officer started to speak but thought better of it, and his colleague returned before he changed his mind. "Someone will be down shortly."

"Can't you tell me what's happened?" The certainty something had happened to Philip filled him with panic.

"I'm sorry, we don't really know. Someone's on the way down. You won't have to wait long now."

The three minutes they waited crawled by. Byron ignored the pain from his wounds and imagined a variety of scenarios, all of which involved Philip being maimed, or worse. He paced as he waited and Adam watched him, wearing a stricken expression.

"Byron!" Adam's call alerted him.

Siobhan and Eddy made their way towards them. Adam smiled in greeting but Siobhan ignored him and focussed on Byron, her expression grim.

Byron started towards them. "Chief Inspector—"

"Mr Mason."

"What's happened to Philip? These two won't tell me."

"They don't know who the hell you are." She looked into his eyes. "I'm sorry to have to tell you, Philip's been shot."

Eddy drove Siobhan to the hospital, Adam and Byron in the back. Seeing Adam, Siobhan's feelings veered between gratitude for saving her last night and fury that he'd used her.

Byron interrupted her train of thought. "Will you charge him with involvement in Liam's death?"

"That's not my decision."

"He had nothing to do with it."

"Like I said, it's—" Eddy put the siren on as they approached a roundabout.

"How did Liam die?" Byron said when the sound died.

"Someone cut him in the neck with a machete, a potentially fatal wound, but he died from internal injuries." The thought of what the boy had suffered still upset Siobhan. "The killers kicked him to death."

Byron expelled a loud breath. "I met Tom and Trev Harris. I presume you know them."

She recognised the surname and glanced at Eddy who nodded.

"They told me they'd given him a good kicking."

"And why would they tell you that?"

Byron hesitated. "It was what you could call an intense moment. I had to convince them I wasn't a friend of

McLaughlin's, so I told them I'd been responsible for his twin brother's death."

"He died in an RTA," Eddy said.

"Yeah, chasing me after I beat up his brother. Anyway, Tom laughed and said they'd given his nephew a hiding and told me what happened until his brother shut him up."

"What did they say happened?" Siobhan said.

"They'd been following him in the car, and when he escaped from the others, they tracked him to an alleyway. Tom said he fell and they laid into him."

Anger made her muscles quiver. "Did they say why?"

"I got the impression they didn't need much of an excuse."

"The families hated each other," Eddy said, "But there were rumours one of McLaughlin's men killed old man Harris's favourite guard dog. They run a scrapyard."

"That explains the old motor oil in Liam's wounds. We assumed it came from the alleyway." Siobhan's mind whirred. "Do you know where they live, Eddy?"

"Oh yeah."

"Get someone to pick them up as soon as we park up." Their inability to trace the car they'd seen on the CCTV still bothered her. But the owners of a scrapyard wouldn't have any problem getting hold of old number plates.

The confirmation Philip's actions hadn't led to Liam's death lifted a huge weight off Byron's shoulders. Signs for the Infirmary appeared, and the car slowed. They pulled off the road and followed signposts to the main car park. Byron struggled to undo his seatbelt until Adam did it for him. He headed for the entrance, followed by Adam and Siobhan while Eddy made a call.

Samuel's car sat in a disabled space. Rebecca strode towards the entrance, leaving the two girls waiting for their father to get into his chair.

"Rebecca!" His shout stopped her in her tracks.

Surprise changed to fury, and she advanced towards him. "How dare you come here? You promised me you'd bring him back safely."

Feeling a measure of responsibility, Byron didn't respond.

Adam stepped forward. "If it wasn't for Byron, we wouldn't have found Philip." He glared at Rebecca. "And he almost got killed..."

Rebecca studied Byron, taking in his injuries, before turning away and marching up to Samuel and the girls. She stroked his hand before putting her arms across the girls' shoulders.

"Shall we see our son?" Samuel said, wheeling his chair towards the entrance. Byron watched them troop in behind his brother.

Eddy arrived. "They're picking them up now, Boss."

Adam put his hand on Byron's good shoulder. "Come on, mate. Let's see Philip, unless you want to go straight to casualty."

"This can wait. Let's go."

He followed them into the bright interior. The smell of disinfectant mingled with a gentler, flowery bouquet. The doors to a large lift facing them slid open and Samuel led his family into it. Byron and his entourage followed, and they rode up to the third floor. Lost in their thoughts, nobody spoke. Rebecca gave Byron a half-hearted glare, before staring at her reflection in the door. The lift stopped, and the doors opened with a soft swish. They paused for a few seconds, unsure of which direction to take, until Samuel led the way.

At the doors to the ward, a nurse intercepted them. "I'm sorry, you can't all go in. It's only two visitors per patient."

Eddy smiled at her. "Hello Bridie." The two of them held a whispered conversation and, after a few moments, she addressed the waiting delegation.

"Okay, you four can go first." She gestured at Philip's parents and sisters. "The rest of you will have to wait."

Adam studied Byron, looking stricken and lost, and wishing he could say something to make him feel better. He jumped when Siobhan gripped his elbow.

"A word please, Adam." She guided him to one side. "What the hell were you playing at Thursday night?" Her eyes flashed. "I don't like being used. You'll regret this."

Her vehemence stunned him but he found his voice. "I realise how this looks, but I had no ulterior motives. What happened Thursday night was genuine on my part." He wasn't sure if she believed him.

"You have a lot of explaining to do. How did you find out where McLaughlin was holding Philip? Did you steal one of my documents? And what's happened to him?" She jerked a thumb at Byron.

Adam avoided answering. "How did Philip get shot?"

Her expression softened. "We got to Philip just as Mugisa was about to shoot him, but Philip had a gun and one of our men thought he was attacking Mugisa, so he shot him."

"Is he okay?" Adam ran his hands through his hair.

"He'll live. I knocked the gun aside, and he got shot through the trapezius muscle."

"What about Mugisa?"

"Philip hit him with a gun and he's also in there." She pointed towards the ward. "Some of McLaughlin's men shot him, but he'll live."

Byron joined them and Adam saw his friend's relief. "You heard?"

"Yeah." Byron sounded exhausted. "The nurse says Philip will be out in a few days and should make a full recovery." He paused. "Physically at least."

Byron's body seemed to weigh far more than he could support. The pain from his shoulder had settled to a fiery ache but his hand sent shards of pain with every movement. He wondered how much damage it had sustained. At least he didn't rely on it for his living. And the fact Philip would recover made the pain bearable. The sound of happy laughter announced the return of the others. The girls, relieved to see their brother alive, if not entirely unharmed, chattered. Their parents smiled and came to a stop in front of Byron.

Rebecca had trouble meeting his gaze. "I'm sorry, Byron," she whispered. "I heard what happened. Thank you for what you did." She kissed him on the cheek.

Byron, embarrassed, smiled and Samuel clasped his good hand mouthing, "See you later", before he joined his wife and daughters.

He watched them make their way towards the lifts.

Siobhan addressed him and Adam. "You two will have to wait to see Philip. We need to speak to him." She glared at Adam. "You have a lot of questions to answer. Don't even think of going anywhere."

Byron mouthed, "Scary lady." Did she wink at Adam as she left? Adam's grin as he watched her walk away told him the answer.

Mugisa couldn't remember what had happened. Voices came from a distance and he tried to make out the words.

A woman spoke in an urgent undertone. "I don't think you realise the risk to your staff. This is a very dangerous young man."

A man replied, irritated. "If you say so, Chief Inspector. But I'm not letting you handcuff one of my patients to his bed. He's very weak; he's lost a lot of blood. I don't believe he's going to get out of bed and cut our throats."

"I wouldn't bet on it. He's killed at least five people, two *after* he had the bullet in his shoulder."

"Surely that's for the courts to decide?"

The woman sighed. "Okay, we'll do it your way, but I'm posting two armed men in here." Her footsteps faded and Mugisa drifted into unconsciousness.

The sun rose high above the grassland and the men and older boys were away, guarding the cattle. The boy had spent the morning in school. The small whitewashed hut stood behind him, empty now the teacher had gone off in her battered white Fiat. A cloud of black smoke pursued her, as she made her way to the next village school, where a group of excited children awaited her arrival.

He played football in the shade of the acacia trees with a few friends, their meagre schoolbooks stacked in four small piles as substitute goalposts. The ball was a bundle of rags, tied together into a small, solid sphere and the game was close, the two sides well matched. One side claimed a disputed goal and the boys stood arguing in high voices.

A shrill call cut across their argument and reluctantly they ended the game, picked up their slight bundles and ran homeward. The boys rounded the small outcrop which lay between their homes and the school. He saw the familiar figures of his beloved mother and sister waiting for him to come for his meal. Both smiled as he ran towards them.

A NOTE TO THE READER

Hello and thank you for taking the time to read my novel. I hope you enjoyed reading it and spending time with the different characters. Although I focus on Byron and Adam, I'm interested in all the characters that go to make this story work, even Ritchie.

I've been an avid reader since I was six or seven and I've always entertained the idea I'd write someday. I worked as a firefighter in Wiltshire for a while then moved to Manchester – a real culture shock. But wherever I worked, I found the job full of characters and often found myself at the centre of dramatic and sometimes tragic events. When I finally decided to start writing, ten years after I left the Fire Service, it was a natural subject to revisit. I decided to write about two male friends of equal status because it's not a subject that's often explored in thrillers and crime novels. Even in Sherlock Holmes, although Watson is a friend, he's not Holmes's equal. The same goes for Morse and Lewis.

The idea of Mugisa came to me when I was holidaying in Ethiopia. I came across a group of boys and girls playing football, using a bundle of rags as the ball. I joined in for a short while – we were at altitude and I'm not as fit as I once was – enjoying the fun and laughter. A few weeks later, I read a report of instability in the area and I began to think what those kids' lives would be like if conflict broke out. Fortunately it didn't there, but for countless children that's not the case.

Although I'm writing a series of books featuring Adam and Byron, I'm planning to explore the lives of some of the other characters. I'd be happy to hear your thoughts on this.

I would really appreciate it if you could leave a review on **Amazon** or **Goodreads**, apart from letting authors know what we're getting right – or wrong – reviews help other readers when they're making decisions on what to read.

I'm keen to hear from you and please feel free to contact me through my **Facebook** page, via **Twitter** or through my **website.** If you join my mailing list you will be kept abreast of what's happening with my writing.

David Beckler

21324838R00194

Printed in Great Britain
by Amazon